AF147703

In The Track Of The Troops

by

R. M. Ballantyne

In The Track Of The Troops
by R. M. Ballantyne

Copyright © 2023

All Rights reserved.

No part of this publication may be reproduced, stored in a retrieval system, or transmitted in any form or by any means, electronic, mechanical, photocopying or Otherwise, without the written permission of the publisher.
The author/editor asserts the moral right to be identified as the author/editor of this work.

ISBN: 978-93-60467-17-3

Published by

DOUBLE 9 BOOKS

2/13-B, Ansari Road
Daryaganj, New Delhi – 110002
info@double9books.com
www.double9books.com
Tel. 011-40042856

This book is under public domain

ABOUT THE AUTHOR

R. M. Ballantyne was a Scottish writer of young adult literature who produced more than a hundred books between 24 April 1825 and 8 February 1894. He was also a skilled artist; some of his watercolors were on display at the Royal Scottish Academy. The ninth of ten children and youngest son of Alexander Thomson Ballantyne (1776-1847) and his wife Anne, Ballantyne was born in Edinburgh on April 24, 1825. (1786-1855). Robert's uncle James Ballantyne (1772-1833) was Sir Walter Scott's printer, and Alexander worked as a newspaper editor and printer in the family business "Ballantyne & Co" based at Paul's Works on the Canongate. The family is documented to have resided at 20 Fettes Row in Edinburgh's northern New Town in 1832-1833. The Ballantyne printing company collapsed the next year with debts of £130,000 as a result of a UK-wide banking crisis, which caused a decrease in the family's finances. Ballantyne moved to Canada at the age of 16 and worked for the Hudson's Bay Company for five years. He traveled by canoe and sleigh to the regions that are now the provinces of Manitoba, Ontario, and Quebec to trade with the local First Nations and Native Americans for furs; these experiences served as the inspiration for his book The Young Fur Traders.

CONTENTS

Chapter One
A Tale of Modern War 7

Chapter Two
Is Still More Explosive than the First.....................................16

Chapter Three
An Interview with Men in Power..22

Chapter Four
A Day with the Torpedoes 29

Chapter Five
Terrible Torpedo Tales, Followed By Overturned Plans 39

Chapter Six
Turk and Bulgarian—A Wrestling Match and a Dispute 48

Chapter Seven
The Black Clouds Gather..58

Chapter Eight
Treats of Torpedoes, Terrible Catastrophe,
Unexpected Meetings, and Such Like.....................................64

Chapter Nine
In which Lancey is Tried, Suspected, Blown Up,
Captured, Half-Hanged, Delivered, and Astonished.........................71

Chapter Ten
Involves Lancey in Great Perplexities, which
Culminate in a Vast Surprise 81

Chapter Eleven
Refers to two Important Letters, and a Secret Mission.........................92

Chapter Twelve
My First Experience of Actual War, and
my Thoughts Thereon...96

Chapter Thirteen
Shews what Sometimes Happens in
the Track of Troops 106

Chapter Fourteen
Tells More of what Occasionally Happens
in the Track of Troops...111

Chapter Fifteen
Simtova—New Views of War—Lancey Goes to
the Front, and Sees Service, and Gets a Scare......................118

Chapter Sixteen
Lancey gets Embroiled in Troubles, and Sees
some Peculiar Service..125

Chapter Seventeen
In which some Desperate Enterprises are Undertaken......................133

Chapter Eighteen
Treats of one of our Great Ironclads.....................................143

Chapter Nineteen
Describes a Stirring Fight 154

Chapter Twenty
Treats of War and some of its "Glorious" Results 160

Chapter Twenty One
More of the Results of War...171

Chapter Twenty Two
The Fall of Plevna 175

Chapter Twenty Three
Woe to the "Auburn Hair!" After the
Battle—Prowling Villains Punished 183

Chapter Twenty Four
Farewell to Sanda Pasha—A Scuffle, and
an Unexpected Meeting...189

Chapter Twenty Five
Describes a Wreck, and the Triumph of Love 197

Chapter Twenty Six
Some More of War's Consequences.......................................203

Chapter One
A Tale of Modern War

Reveals the Explosive Nature of my Early Career.

The remarkable—I might even say amazing—personal adventures which I am about to relate occurred quite recently.

They are so full of interest to myself and to my old mother, that I hasten to write them down while yet vivid and fresh in my memory, in the hope that they may prove interesting,—to say nothing of elevating and instructive—to the English-speaking portions of the human race throughout the world.

The dear old lady to whom I have just referred—my mother—is one of the gentlest, meekest, tenderest beings of my acquaintance. Her regard for me is almost idolatrous. My feelings towards her are tinged with adoration.

From my earliest years I have been addicted to analysis.

Some of my younger readers may not perhaps know that by analysis is meant the reduction of compound things to their elements—the turning of things, as it were, inside out and tearing them to pieces. All the complex toys of infancy I was wont to reduce to their elements; I turned them inside out to see what they were made of, and how they worked. A doll, not my own, but my sister Bella's, which had moveable eyelids and a musical stomach, was treated by me in this manner, the result being that I learned little, while my poor sister suffered much. Everything in my father's house suffered more or less from this inquiring tendency of my mind.

Time, however, while it did not abate my thirst for knowledge, developed my constructive powers. I became a mechanician and an inventor. Perpetual motion was my first hobby. Six times during the course of boyhood did I burst into my mother's presence with the astounding news that I had "discovered it at last!" The mild and trustful being believed me. Six times also was I compelled to acknowledge to her that I had been mistaken, and again she believed me, more thoroughly, perhaps, than at first. No one, I think, can form the least idea of the delight with which I pursued this mechanical will-o'-the-wisp.

Growing older, I took to chemistry, and here my love for research and analysis found ample scope, while the sufferings of my father's household were intensified. I am not naturally cruel—far from it. They little knew how much pain their sufferings caused me; how earnestly I endeavoured to lessen or neutralise the nuisances which the pursuit of science entailed. But I could not consume my own smoke, or prevent explosions, or convert bad and suffocating odours into sweet smells.

Settling down to this new pursuit with intense enthusiasm, I soon began to flow in my natural course, and sought to extend the bounds of chemical knowledge. I could not help it. The particular direction in which my interest ultimately became concentrated was that of explosives.

After becoming acquainted with gun-cotton, nitro-glycerine, dynamite, lithofracteur, and other combinations of powerfully-explosive agents, I took to searching for and inventing methods by which these might be utilised. To turn everything to good account, is a desire which I cannot resist.

Explosives naturally drew my attention to mines—tin-mines, coal-mines, and other commercial enterprises. They also suggested war and torpedoes.

At that time I had not reflected on the nature of war. I merely knew it to be a science, cultivated chiefly by the human race, and that in its practice explosives are largely used. To "blow-up" effectively, whether in a literal or figurative sense, is difficult. To improve this power in war, and in the literal sense, I set myself to work. I invented a torpedo, which seemed to me better than any that had yet been brought out. To test its powers, I made a miniature fortification, and blew it up. I also blew up our groom, Jacob Lancey. It happened thus:—

The miniature fortress, which was made of cardboard, earth, and bricks, was erected in a yard near our stables. Under its walls the torpedo was placed, and the match lighted.

It was night and very dark. I had selected the hour as being that most suitable to the destruction of an enemy's stronghold. The match was very slow in burning. Matches invariably are so in the circumstances. Suddenly I heard the sound of footsteps. Next moment, before I had time to give warning, Jacob Lancey came round the corner of the stables with a pitchfork on his shoulder, and walked right into the fortress. He set his foot on the principal gateway, tripped over the ramparts, and falling headlong into the citadel, laid its banner in the dust. At the same instant there came a terrific flash and crash, and from the midst of smoke and flames, the groom appeared to shoot into the air!

With feelings of horror I sprang to the rescue and dragged the poor fellow from the smoking débris. He was stunned at first, but soon recovered, and then it was found that one of the fingers of his left hand had been completely blown off. Words cannot describe my feelings. I felt as if I had become next thing to a murderer. Lancey was a tall powerful man of about thirty, and not easily killed. He had received no other injury worth mentioning. Although the most faithful of servants, he was irascible, and I anticipated an explosion of temper when he recovered sufficiently to understand the nature of his injury, but I was mistaken. The blowing-up seemed to have quite cured his temper—at least as regarded myself, for when I afterwards went to see him, with a very penitent face, he took my hand and said—

"Don't take on so, Master Jeffry. You didn't do it a purpus, you know, and, after all, it's on'y the little finger o' the left hand. It'll be rather hout o' the way than otherwise. Moreover, I was used to make a baccy stopper o' that finger, an' it strikes me that the stump'll fit the pipe better than the pint did, besides bein' less sensitive to fire, who knows? Any'ow, Master Jeffry, you've got no occasion to grieve over it so."

I felt a little comforted when the good fellow spoke thus, but I could not forgive myself. For some time after that I quite gave up my chemical and other experiments, and when I did ultimately resume them, I went to work with extreme caution.

Not long after this event I went to college, and studied medicine. My course was nearly completed when my dear father died. He had earnestly desired that I should enter the medical profession. I therefore resolved to finish my course, although, being left in possession of a small estate named Fagend, in Devonshire, and an ample income, it was not requisite that I should practise for a livelihood.

One morning, a considerable time after my studies were completed, I sat at breakfast with my mother.

"Jeff," she said (my name is Jeffry Childers); "Jeff, what do you think of doing now? Being twenty-four, you ought, you know, to have some fixed idea as to the future, for, of course, though independent, you don't intend to be idle."

"Right, mother, right," I replied, "I don't mean to be an idler, nevertheless I don't mean to be a doctor. I shall turn my mind to chemistry, and talking of that, I expect to test the powers of a particular compound today."

"And what," said my mother, with a peculiar smile, "is the nature of this compound?"

"Violently explosive," said I.

"Ah, of course, I might have guessed that, Jeff, for most of your compounds are either violently explosive or offensive—sometimes both; but what is the name of this one?"

"Before answering that," said I, pulling out my watch, "allow me to ask at what hour you expect Bella home to-day."

"She half promised to be over to breakfast, if cousin Kate would let her away. It is probable that she may arrive in less than an hour."

"Curious coincidence," said I, "that her lover is likely to arrive about the same time!"

"What! Nicholas Naranovitsch?"

"Yes. The ship in which he sailed from St. Petersburg arrived late last night, and I have just received a telegram, saying that he will be down by the first train this morning. Love, you know, is said to have wings. If the pair given to Naranovitsch are at all in keeping with his powerful frame, they will bear him swiftly to Fagend."

It may interest the reader at this point to know that my only sister, Bella, had been engaged the previous year to one of my dearest college friends, a young Russian, whose father had sent him to finish his education in England. My own father, having been a merchant, many of whose dealings were with Russia, had frequently visited St. Petersburg and twice my mother and sister and I accompanied him thither. While there we had met with the Naranovitsch family.

Young Nicholas was now in the army, and as fine-looking a fellow as one could wish to see. Not only was he strong and manly, but gentle in manner and tender of heart. My sister Bella being the sweetest—no, not quite that, for there *is* a pretty young—well, no matter—Bella being, as I may say, *one* of the sweetest girls in England, he fell in love with her, of course. So did she with him; no wonder! During a visit to our place in Devonshire at the end of his college career, he and Bella became engaged. Nicholas returned to St. Petersburg to obtain his parents' consent to the union, and to make arrangements. He was rich, and could afford to marry. At the time I write of, he was coming back, not to claim his bride, for his father thought him still too young, but to see her, and to pay us a visit.

"Now you know, mother," said I, "after the young people have seen each other for half-an-hour or so, they will naturally want to take a walk or a ride, and—"

"Only half-an-hour?" interrupted my mother, with one of her peculiar little smiles.

"Well, an hour if you like, or two if they prefer it," I returned; "at all events, they will want a walk before luncheon, and I shall take the opportunity to show them some experiments, which prove the power of the singular compound about which you questioned me just now."

"The explosive?"

"Yes. Its name is dynamite."

"And what may that be, Jeff? Something very awful, I daresay," remarked my mother, with a look of interest, as she sipped her tea.

"Very awful, indeed," said I; "at least its effects are sometimes tremendous."

"What! worse than gunpowder?"

"Ay, much worse, though I should prefer to say *better* than gunpowder."

"Dear me!" rejoined my mother, lifting her eyebrows a little, in surprise.

"Yes, much better," I continued; "gunpowder only bursts things—"

"Pretty well that, Jeff, in the way of violence, isn't it?"

"Yes, but nothing to dynamite, for while powder only bursts things, dynamite shatters them."

"How very dreadful! What *is* dynamite?"

"That is just what I am about to explain," said I. "You must know, then, that it is a compound."

"Dear, dear," sighed my mother; "how many compounds you have told me about, Jeff, since you took to chemistry! Are there no uncompounded things—no simple things in the world?"

"Why, yes, mother; *you* are a simple thing, and I only wish there were a good many more simple things like you in the world—"

"Don't be foolish, Jeff, but answer my question."

"Well, mother, there are indeed some simple elements in creation, but dynamite is not one of them. It is composed of an excessively explosive oil named nitro-glycerine (itself a compound), and an earth called kieselguhr. The earth is not explosive, and is only mixed with the nitro-glycerine to render that liquid less dangerous; but the compound is named dynamite, in which form it is made up and sold in immense quantities for mining purposes. Here is some of it," I added, pulling from my pocket a cartridge nearly two inches in length, and about an inch in diameter. "It is a soft, pasty substance, done up, as you see, in cartridge-paper, and this little thing, if properly fired, would blow a large boulder-stone to atoms."

"Bless me, boy, be careful!" exclaimed my mother, pushing back her chair in some alarm.

"There is no danger," I said, in reassuring tones, "for this cartridge, if opened out and set on fire by a spark or flame, would not, in the first place, light readily, and, in the second place, it would merely burn without exploding; but if I were to put a detonator inside and fire it by means of *that*, it would explode with a violence that far exceeds the force of gunpowder."

"And what is this wonderful detonator, Jeff, that so excites the latent fury of the dynamite?"

I was much amused by the pat way in which my mother questioned me, and became more interested as I continued my explanation.

"You must know," I said, "that many powders are violently explosive, and some more so than others. This violence of explosion is called detonation, by which is meant the almost instantaneous conversion of the ultimate molecules of an explosive compound (i.e. the whole concern) into gas."

"I see; you mean that it goes off quickly," said my mother, in a simple way that was eminently characteristic.

"Well, yes; but much more quickly than gunpowder does. It were better to say that a powder detonates when it *all* explodes at the *same* instant. Gunpowder appears to do so, but in reality it does not. One of the best detonators is fulminate of mercury. Detonating caps are therefore made of this, and one such cap put into the middle of that cartridge of dynamite and set fire to, by any means, would convert the cartridge itself into a detonator, and explode it with a *shattering* effect.

"A human being," I continued, "sometimes illustrates this principle figuratively—I mean the violent explosion of a large cartridge by means of a small detonator. Take, for example, a schoolmaster, and suppose him to be a dynamite cartridge. His heart is a detonating cap. The schoolroom and boys form a galvanic battery. His brain may be likened to a conducting-wire. He enters the schoolroom; the chemical elements are seething in riot, books are being torn and thrown, ink spilt, etcetera. Before opening the door, the good man is a quiet piece of plastic dynamite, but the instant his eye is touched, the electric circuit is, as it were, completed; the mysterious current flashes through the brain, and fires his detonating heart. Instantly the gleaming flame shoots with lightning-speed to temples and toes. The entire man becomes a detonator, and he explodes in a violent hurricane of kicks, cuffs, and invective! Now, without a detonator—a heart—the man might have burned with moderate wrath, but he could not have exploded."

"Don't try illustration, Jeff," said my plain-spoken mother, gently patting my arm; "it is not one of your strong points."

"Perhaps not; but do you understand me?"

"I think I do, in a hazy sort of way."

Dear mother! she always professes to comprehend things hazily, and indeed I sometimes fear that her conceptions on the rather abstruse matters which I bring before her are not always correct; but it is delightful to watch the profound interest with which she listens, and the patient efforts she makes to understand. I must in justice add that she sometimes, though not often, displays gleams of clear intelligence, and powers of close incisive reasoning, that quite surprise me.

"But now, to return to what we were speaking of—my future plans," said I; "it seems to me that it would be a good thing if I were to travel for a year or so and see the world."

"You might do worse, my boy," said my mother.

"With a view to that," I continued, "I have resolved to purchase a yacht, but before doing so I must complete the new torpedo that I have invented for the navy; that is, I hope it may be introduced into our navy. The working model in the outhouse is all but ready for exhibition. When finished, I shall show it to the Lords of the Admiralty, and after they have accepted it I will throw study overboard for a time and go on a cruise."

"Ah, Jeff, Jeff," sighed my mother, with a shake of her head, "you'll never leave off till you get blown up. But I suppose you must have your way. You always had, dear boy."

"But never in opposition to your wishes, had I? Now be just, mother."

"Quite true, Jeff, quite true. How comes it, I wonder, that you are so fond of fire, smoke, fumes, crash, clatter, and explosions?"

"Really," said I, somewhat amused by the question, "I cannot tell, unless it be owing to something in that law of compensation which appears to permeate the universe. You have such an abhorrence of fire, fumes, smoke, crash, clatter, and explosions, that your only son is bound, as it were, to take special delight in chemical analysis and combination, to say nothing of mechanical force and contrivance, in order that a balance of some sort may be adjusted which would otherwise be thrown out of order by your— pardon me—comparative ignorance of, and indifference to such matters."

"Nay, Jeff," replied my mother, gently, with a look of reproof on her kind face; "ignorance if you will, but not indifference. I cannot be indifferent to anything that interests you."

"True; forgive me; I should have said 'dislike.'"

"Yes, that would have been correct, Jeff, for I cannot pretend to like the bursting, smoking, and ill-smelling things you are so fond of; but you know I am interested in them. You cannot have forgotten how, when you were a boy, I used to run at your call to witness your pyrotechnic, hydraulic, mechanic, and chemic displays—you see how well I remember the names—and how the—"

"The acids," I interrupted, taking up the theme, "ruined your carpets and table-cloths, and the smoke stifled and blinded, while the noise and flames terrified you; no, mother, I have not forgotten it, nor the patient way you took the loss of your old silk dress, or—"

"Ah! yes," sighed the dear old lady, with quite a pitiful look, "if it had been any other than my wedding dress, which—but—well, it's of no use regretting now; and you know, Jeff, I would not have checked you for worlds, because I knew you were being led in the right way, though, in my folly, I sometimes wished that the way had been a little further removed from smoke and smells. But, after all, you were very careful, dear boy—wonderfully so, for your years, and your little accidents did not give me much pain beyond the day of their occurrence. The poisoning of the cat, to be sure, was sad, though unavoidable, and so was the destruction by fire of the cook's hair; but the flooding of the house, after the repairs you executed on the great cistern, and the blowing out of the laundry window at the time the clothes-boiler was cracked, with other trifles of that sort, were—"

The remainder of my mother's speech was cut short by a clattering of hoofs.

Next moment my sister Bella came round the corner of the house at full gallop, her fresh face beaming with the exercise, and her golden hair streaming in the breeze.

She pulled up, leaped off her pony, and ran into the room. As she did so, I observed a tall, soldierly man appear in the avenue, advancing with rapid strides. Well did I know his grave, handsome face.

"Here comes Nicholas!" said I, turning round; but Bella had fled.

I observed that my friend, instead of coming straight to the room from the window of which my mother and I had saluted him, turned sharp off to the library.

I was running to the door to welcome him, when my mother called me back. I turned and looked at her. She smiled. So did I. Without uttering a word we both sat down to finish our breakfast.

"Ah! Jeff," said my mother, with a little sigh, "how I wish you would fall in love with some one!"

"Fall in love, mother! What nonsense! How could I? No doubt there are plenty loveable girls, and there *is* one charming little—well, no matter—"

At that moment Nicholas entered the room, heartily saluted my mother, and cut short our conversation.

Chapter Two
Is Still More Explosive than the First

Much to my surprise, I found that neither Nicholas Naranovitsch nor Bella nor my mother would consent to witness my experiments with dynamite that day.

As my old chum approached to greet me on the lawn before breakfast the day following, I could not help admiring his fine, tall, athletic figure. I don't know how it is, but I have always felt, somehow, as if I looked up at him, although we were both exactly the same height—six feet one without our boots. I suppose it must have been owing to his standing so erect, while I slouched a little. Perhaps my looking up to him mentally had something to do with it.

"You'll come to-day, won't you?" I said, referring to the experiments.

"Of course I will, old boy; but," he added, with a smile, "only on one condition."

"What may that be?"

"That you don't bother Bella with minute details."

Of course I promised not to say a word unless asked for explanations, and after breakfast we all went to a part of the grounds which I wished to bring under cultivation. It was at that time encumbered with several large trees, old roots, and a number of boulders.

"Come along with us, Lancey," I said to the groom, who was also my laboratory assistant, and whom I met in the stable-yard, the scene of his memorable blowing-up. "I am about to try the effect of an explosive, and wish you to understand the details."

"Yes, sir," replied Lancey, with a respectful touch of his cap; "I must say, sir, if you'll allow me, I never knowed any one like you, sir, for goin' into details except one, and that one—"

"Ah, yes, I know, that was your friend the Scotch boy," said I, interrupting; but Lancey was a privileged servant, and would not be interrupted.

"Yes, sir," he resumed, "the Scotch boy Sandy. We was at school together in Edinburgh, where I got the most o' my edication, and I never did see such a boy, sir, for goin' into—"

"Yes, yes, Lancey, I know; but I haven't time to talk about him just now. We are going to the bit of waste ground in the hollow; follow us there."

I was obliged to cut him short, because this Scotch hero of his was a subject on which he could not resist dilating on the slightest encouragement.

Arrived at the waste ground, we met the manager of a neighbouring mine, who was deeply learned in everything connected with blasting.

"I have brought my mother and sister, you see, Mr Jones," said I, as we approached. "They don't quite believe in the giant-power which is under your control; they seem to think that it is only a little stronger than gunpowder."

"We can soon change their views on that point," said the manager, with a slight bow to the ladies, while I introduced Nicholas as an officer of the Russian army.

"This is one of the stones you wish to blast, is it not?" said Mr Jones, laying his hand on an enormous boulder that weighed probably several tons.

"It is," I answered.

The manager was a man of action—grave of countenance and of few words. He drew a flask from his pocket and emptied its contents, a large quantity of gunpowder, on the boulder. Asking us to stand a little back, he applied a slow match to the heap, and retired several paces.

In a few seconds the powder went off with a violent puff and a vast cloud of smoke. The result was a little shriek of alarm from my mother, and an exclamation from Bella.

"Not much effect from that, you see," said the manager, pointing to the blackened stone, yet it was a large quantity of powder, which, if fired in a cavity inside the stone, would have blown it to pieces. "Here, now, is a small quantity of dynamite." (He produced a cartridge about two inches in length, similar to that which I had shown to my mother at breakfast.) "Into this cartridge I shall insert a detonator cap, which is fastened to the end of a Pickford fuse—thus."

As he spoke, he inserted into the cartridge the end of the fuse, to which was attached a small cap filled with fulminate of mercury, and tied it tightly up. This done, he laid the cartridge on the top of the boulder, placed two or three similar cartridges beside it, and covered all with a small quantity of sand, leaving the other end of the fuse projecting.

"Why the sand?" asked Bella.

"Because a slight amount of confinement is advantageous," replied Mr Jones. "If I were to bore a short hole in the stone, and put the dynamite therein, the result would be still more effective; but the covering I have put on it will suffice, and will serve all the better to show the great difference between this explosive and gunpowder."

"But," said my mother, who had a tendency to become suddenly interested in things when she began to have a faint understanding of them; "but, Mr Jones, you did not give the powder fair play. If you had covered *it* with sand, would not its effect have been more powerful?"

"Not on the stone, madam; it would only have blown off its covering with violence, that would have been all. Now, ladies and gentlemen, if you will retire behind the shelter of that old beech-tree, I will light the fuse."

We did as we were desired. The manager lighted the fuse, and followed us. In a few moments there occurred an explosion so violent that the huge boulder was shattered into several pieces, which were quite small enough to be lifted and carted away.

"Most amazing!" exclaimed Bella, with enthusiasm.

It was quite obvious that she had no anticipation of such a thorough result. Nicholas, too, who I may mention had no natural turn of taste for such matters, was roused to a state of inquiry.

To a question put by him, Mr Jones explained that, taking its powers into consideration, dynamite was cheaper than gunpowder, and that it saved much labour, as it would have taken two men a considerable time to have bored an ordinary blasthole in the boulder he had just broken up.

I now led the way to another part of the ground on which grew a large beech-tree, whose giant roots took a firm grasp of the ground. It was a hundred years old at least; about twelve feet in circumference, and sixty feet high. One similar tree I had had cut down; but the labour had been very great, and the removal of the stump excessively troublesome as well as costly.

Mr Jones now went to work at the forest-giant. In the ground underneath the tree he ordered Lancey to make a hole with a crowbar. Into this he pressed some cartridges of dynamite with a wooden rammer. Then the cartridge, with the detonator inside of it; and the fuse, extending from its mouth, was placed in contact with the charge under the tree. The hole was next closed up with some earth, leaving about a foot of the fuse outside. The light was then applied, and we retired to a safe distance. In a few moments the charge exploded. The tree seemed to rise from its bed. All the earth under it was blown out, and the roots were torn up and broken, with the exception of four of the largest, which were fully ten inches in diameter. A small charge of dynamite inserted under each of these completed the work, and the old giant, slowly bowing forward, laid his venerable head upon the ground.

Another charge was next placed in the soil under some loose and decayed roots, which were easily broken to pieces, so as to permit of their removal. Thus, in a short time and at little cost, were trees and roots and boulders torn up and shattered.

"But is dynamite not very dangerous, Mr Jones?" asked my mother, as we walked slowly homeward.

"Not at all dangerous,—at least not worth speaking of," replied the manager; "nitro-glycerine by itself is indeed very dangerous, being easily exploded by concussion or mere vibration; but when mixed with infusorial earth and thus converted into dynamite, it is one of the safest explosives in existence—not quite so safe, indeed, as gun-cotton, but much more so than gunpowder. Any sort of fire will explode gunpowder, but any sort of fire will not explode dynamite; it will only cause it to burn. It requires a detonator to explode it with violence. Without its detonator, dynamite is a sleeping giant."

"Ay, mother," said I, taking up the subject, "the case stands thus: gunpowder is a big athlete, who slumbers lightly; any spark can wake him to violent action: but dynamite is a bigger athlete, who sleeps so soundly that a spark or flame can only rouse him to moderate rage; it requires a special shake to make him wide-awake, but when thus roused his fury is terrific, as you have just seen. And now," I added, as we drew near the house, "we will change the subject, because I have this morning received two letters, which demand the united consideration of our whole party. I will therefore call up Bella and Nicholas, who have fallen behind, as usual. Mr Jones will excuse my talking of family matters for a few minutes, as replies must be sent by return of post."

I then explained that one of the letters was an invitation to me and my mother and sister, with any friends who might chance to be visiting us, to go to Portsmouth to witness a variety of interesting experiments with torpedoes and such warlike things; while the other letter was an offer by a friend, of a schooner-built yacht for a moderate sum.

"Now, Nicholas," said I, apologetically, "I'm sorry to give you such an explosive reception, but it cannot be helped. If you don't care about torpedoes, you may remain here with my mother and Bella; but if you would like to go, I shall be happy to introduce you to one or two of my naval friends. For myself, I must go, because—"

"We will all go, Jeff," interrupted Bella; "nothing could be more appropriate as a sequel to this morning's experiments. A day among the torpedoes will be most interesting, won't it?"

She looked up at Nicholas, on whose arm she leaned. He looked down with that peculiar smile of his which seemed to lie more in his eyes than on his lips, and muttered something about a day anywhere being, etcetera, etcetera.

My mother remarked that she did not understand exactly what a torpedo was, and looked at me for an explanation. I confess that her remark surprised me, for during the course of my investigations and inventions, I had frequently mentioned the subject of torpedoes to her, and once or twice had given her a particular description of the destructive machine. However, as she had evidently forgotten all about it, and as I cannot resist the temptation to elucidate complex subjects when opportunity offers, I began:—

"It is a machine, mother, which—"

"Which bursts," interrupted Bella, with a little laugh.

"But that is no explanation, dear," returned my mother; "at least not a distinctive one, for guns burst sometimes, and soap-bubbles burst, and eggs burst occasionally."

"Bella," said Nicholas, who spoke English perfectly, though with a slightly foreign accent, "never interrupt a philosopher. Allow Jeff to proceed with his definition."

"Well, a torpedo," said I, "is an infernal machine—"

"Jeff," said my mother, seriously, "don't—"

"Mother, I use the word advisedly and dispassionately. It is a term frequently given to such engines, because of their horrible nature, which suggests the idea that they were originated in the region of Satanic influence. A torpedo, then, is a pretty large case, or box, or cask, or reservoir, of one form or another, filled with gunpowder, or gun-cotton, or dynamite, which is used chiefly under water, for blowing-up purposes. Sometimes men use torpedoes to blow up rocks, and sunken wrecks; and sometimes, I grieve to say it, they blow up ships and sailors."

"Dreadful! my dear," said my mother; "nevertheless I should like to go with you on this excursion, and see what devices men invent for the purpose of killing each other."

"Very well, that's settled," said I. "Now, as to the other letter about the yacht. I will buy it, mother, and go on a cruise to the Mediterranean, on one condition, namely, that you and Nicholas and Bella go with me."

"Impossible!" exclaimed my mother, firmly; "I never could bear the sea."

"But you've had little experience of it," said I.

"Well, not much—but I cannot bear it."

"Now, mother," said I, coaxingly, "here is Bella dying to go to sea, I know. Nicholas has loads of time, and cannot be left behind, and I wish very much to go; but all will fall to the ground if you refuse to accompany us. We cannot leave you in this house alone. The sea air will certainly do you good, and if it does not, we can land, you know, at Lisbon, Gibraltar, Nice,—anywhere, and return home overland."

"Well, then, I will go," returned my pliant mother.

"That's right," said I, sitting down to write. "Now, then, all of you get ready to go to London this afternoon. We shall spend a day or two there, because, before leaving, I must see the first Lord of the Admiralty on particular business. Afterwards we shall run down to Portsmouth by the afternoon express, spend the night there, and so be ready to face the torpedoes in the morning."

Chapter Three
An Interview with Men in Power

There is something peculiarly exhilarating in bright sunshine and calm weather. This is no doubt a truism; but there are some truths of which one never tires, and in regard to which one feels ever-recurring freshness. Who ever wearied of a balmy breeze, or a bright sunrise? Even a glorious noon cannot pall upon us unless it be too hot.

When bright sunshine is associated with good health, pleasant company, a successful courtship, and the prospect of light on a favourite study, the reader will understand how it was that my mother and I, with Nicholas and Bella, formed a peculiarly happy quartette as we perambulated the streets of London prior to my visit to the Admiralty.

It was a Friday forenoon, and there were many holiday-keepers hastening to trains. At the corner of one of the main thoroughfares a crowd partly blocked the road. The cause of it became apparent to us when the head and arched neck of a black charger appeared, and then the white plume and polished cuirass of a Life Guardsman. We stood on a door-step, so that Bella might see the troop.

As they passed before us, with that stately bearing of man and horse which has always seemed to me peculiar to the Life Guards, and the sun flashed in dazzling gleams from breasts and helmets, I glanced at my friend Naranovitsch. His soldierlike form was drawn up to its full height, while the flashing eye, flushed countenance, distended nostrils, and compressed but slightly smiling lips told, I thought, of a strong feeling of martial joy. Doubtless he was thinking at the moment of his own regiment, to which he had been but recently appointed, and of his comrades-in-arms.

"Fine-looking fellows!" I whispered.

"Splendid! glorious!" he said, in a deep, low voice.

Bella looked quickly up at him, displaying an anxious, sorrowing face, and bright eyes, dimmed with ill-suppressed tears.

"You are not ill, Bella?" he whispered, bending down with a look of tenderness, not unmixed with surprise.

"No; oh, no," she replied, in a low tone; "but the sight of the Guards has made me very sad."

I knew full well the cause of her emotion, but the crowded street was not a suitable place for explanation.

"Come, follow me," I said, and walked quickly along in the direction of the Strand, where I turned abruptly into one of those quiet courts which form, as it were, harbours of refuge from the rattle and turmoil of the great city. Here, sauntering slowly round the quiet precincts of the court, with the roar of the street subdued to a murmur like that of a distant cataract, Bella told Nicholas, in tones of the deepest pathos, how a German lady, Elsie Goeben, one of her dearest friends, had been married to the handsomest and best of men in one of the Prussian cavalry regiments. How, only six months after their union, the Franco-Prussian war broke out, and Elsie's husband Wilhelm was sent with his regiment to the frontier; how in many engagements he had distinguished himself; and how, at last, he was mortally wounded during one of the sorties at the siege of Metz.

"They did not find him till next day," continued my sister, "for he had fallen in a part of the field so far in advance of the ground on which his dead comrades lay, that he had been overlooked. He was riddled with bullets, they say, and his noble face, which I had so often seen beaming with affection on his young wife, was so torn and disfigured that his friends could scarcely recognise him. He was still alive when found, and they knew his voice. When they raised him, he merely exclaimed, '*At last*, thank God!' with a deep sigh, as if of relief. The words were few, but they had terrible significance, for they told of a long, long night of agony and dreadful solitude; but he was not quite alone," my sister added, in a low voice, "for he was a Christian. He died before reaching the tents of his division."

Bella's voice faltered as she said, after a moment's pause, "Dear Elsie never recovered the shock. She joined her husband in heaven two months afterwards."

"Truly," said I, "war is a terrible curse."

"I hate it! I detest it!" cried Bella, with a sudden tone and look of energy, that was all the more impressive because of her natural character being gentle and retiring.

I saw that Nicholas was surprised and pained. He would fain have comforted Bella, but knew not what to say, for he had been trained to talk of "martial glory," and to look on war through the medium of that halo of false glitter with which it has been surrounded by too many historians in all ages. The young Russian had hitherto dwelt chiefly on one aspect of war. He had thought of noble and heroic deeds in defence of hearth and home, and all that man holds sacred. To fight for his country was to Nicholas an idea that called up only the thoughts of devotion, self-sacrifice in a good cause, duty, fidelity, courage, romance; while, in regard to the minor things of a warrior's life, a hazy notion of dash, glitter, music, and gaiety floated through his brain. Of course he was not *ignorant* of some of the darker shades of war. History, which told him of many gallant deeds, also recorded numberless dreadful acts. But these latter he dismissed as being disagreeable and unavoidable accompaniments of war. He simply accepted things as he found them, and, not being addicted to very close reasoning, did not trouble himself much as to the rectitude or wisdom of war in the abstract. Neither did he distinguish between righteous and unrighteous war—war of self-defence and war of aggression. Sufficient for him that he served his country faithfully. This was a good general principle, no doubt, for a youthful officer; but as one who expected to rise to power and influence in his native land, something more definite would ultimately be required of him. As yet, he had neither experienced the excitement, beheld the miseries, nor bathed in the so-called "glory" of war; and now that a corner of the dark cloud was unexpectedly flung over him in Bella's sorrow, he felt deeply sympathetic but helpless. A sad look, however, and a gentle pressure of the hand that rested on his arm, was quite sufficient for Bella.

To relieve my friend from his embarrassment, I pulled out my watch and urged that we should walk in the direction of the Admiralty, as the hour for my interview had nearly arrived.

At Charing-Cross we parted, and I proceeded on my mission with the plan of my torpedo, which Nicholas styled the "infernal machine," in my pocket, and a rather anxious heart in my breast, for although I was quite certain that my invention was superior to all others, inasmuch as it fulfilled several conditions which were not fulfilled by other torpedoes, I did not feel sure that the Lords of the Admiralty would take the same view of it that I did. Besides, the machine had only been tried as a model, and might not act perfectly when tested in actual warfare. But, of course, I knew that my inventive powers would readily overcome each weak point as it cropped into view in practice.

I met with a very gracious reception from the first Lord. Beside him were seated two elderly gentlemen, whom I judged to be brother Lords.

It were needless to recount all that passed during that memorable interview. Suffice it to say, that after I had given a most careful and clear explanation of my invention, to which the three Lords listened with marked attention, the first Lord said, with a bland smile—

"But what, Mr Childers, is the peculiar point of superiority over other torpedoes which you claim for yours?"

I confess that the question damped me a little, for I had been remarkably explicit in my explanations, which lasted nearly an hour. However, with the utmost alacrity, I went again over the chief points.

"You observe, my Lord," said I, pointing to my drawing, which lay spread out on the table, "that this watch-work arrangement in the heart of the machine is so intimately connected with that lever and screw on its exterior, that in passing out of the case from which it is launched into the sea, the machinery is set in motion, and the first act of the torpedo is to set or regulate itself for the special purpose for which it is designed. Thus it may be styled an automatic torpedo. The celebrated Whitehead fish-torpedo, beautiful and cleverly contrived though it be, can only advance straight to its object at a certain depth below the surface; but mine, as you see, by this arrangement of the main pneumatic engine, which connects the watch-work regulator with an eccentric wheel or fin outside, causes the torpedo to describe a curve of any size, and in any direction, during its progress. Thus, if you wish to hit an enemy's vessel, but cannot venture to fire because of a friendly ship happening to lie between, you have only to set the eccentric indicator to the required curve, and send the torpedo on its mission of destruction right under the bottom of the friendly ship; or by laying the torpedo on its side, it will easily go round it, and afterwards hit the enemy."

"Ah! I see," said the first Lord, with a grave nod; "you have at last succeeded in making that which has so long been held impossible; an instrument which will shoot round the corner."

"Well, a—; yes, my Lord, although I confess it had not struck me in that light before. But," I continued, feeling my enthusiasm rise as the first Lord became more appreciative, "the weapon may be used even in attacking fortresses from the sea, for by making what I may call the inverted trajectory of the curve very high, the torpedo may be made to rush under the surface of the water, gradually curve upwards, then shoot right out of its native element, and go straight into a fort or town on a hill, at least a hundred feet above the level of the sea."

"Indeed!" exclaimed the first Lord.

I observed that the other two Lords were gazing at me, with looks from which were banished every expression except that of intense surprise. Regarding this as a sign that the merits of my invention were beginning to tell on them, I went on—

"Yes, my Lord, the action of the thing is absolutely certain, if the distance of the object aimed at be ascertained to a nicety, and the arrangements of the watch-work indicator adjusted to those of the eccentric wheel and the pneumatic engine with mathematical precision. This, of course, in these days of thorough education, can be easily done by even the youngest officer in a ship. I should have mentioned, however, that if it were required to send the torpedo into a citadel or fortress on a hill, it would be necessary to use a stronger explosive than any yet known, —gun-cotton and dynamite being too weak, and nitro-glycerine too dangerous, therefore inadmissible."

"Ha!" exclaimed the first Lord, "and where is such an explosive to be found?"

"In my laboratory down in Devonshire, my Lord," I answered, with a look of diffidence, feeling uncertain how he would take the announcement.

For a few moments he contemplated me in perfect silence, and I observed that the other two Lords smiled. I felt perplexed, but the awkwardness of the moment was quickly removed by the first Lord asking what my new compound was made of.

"That, my Lord," said I, "is a secret."

"Just so, and you wish to sell your secret to Government?"

"No, my Lord," I replied, with dignity; "I wish to let my Government possess any slight gift which it lies in my power to present to it, in addition to that of a loyal heart; but I cannot afford to let my secret be known, unless I have some assurance that it shall be held inviolable."

"That assurance you have," said the first Lord, "but I should have supposed that to so loyal a subject the character of the British Admiralty would have been sufficient guarantee, and that nothing further would have been required from me."

"I do *not* require further assurance, my Lord," said I, hastily; "I merely wish you to understand how important it is that secrecy should be observed. I will reveal it to you."

Here I rose and whispered in the first Lord's ear. He turned pale, as I sat down, and whispered to the other two Lords, who looked very grave, from which I augured good fortune to my invention. At the same time I was surprised, for my communication to him was in no way alarming, though connected with explosives.

Presently the first Lord touched a bell. A servant in uniform appeared, and after a few words, disappeared. I was puzzled, but silent.

"Mr Childers," said the first Lord, "I shall give your invention my best attention; but I must tell you that there are many others in this country, as well as yourself, who are exerting their minds to discover the most effectual method of spreading wholesale devastation among their fellow-creatures, and—"

"Forgive my interrupting you, my Lord," I exclaimed, with a look of horror, "but I repudiate entirely any intention to destroy my fellow-creatures. My motives in this matter have been purely scientific."

"I have no doubt of it," returned the first Lord, with a smile, "nevertheless the tendency of your labours is towards destruction; and my reference to the fact is merely for the purpose of informing you that there are many other inventors who have claimed my attention to their designs, and that you must not expect an immediate decision in regard to yours."

With this I was politely bowed out, and as I passed down the corridor, I could not help feeling disappointed at the rather faint success of my visit. The idea, too, that I was a would-be destroyer of my species had never before occurred to me, my whole soul and faculties having hitherto been engrossed in the simple idea of perfecting a chemical explosive and a mechanical contrivance. Thus, unintentionally, do we sometimes lend ourselves to that from which our hearts revolt.

I noticed, too, that the servant who had been summoned by the first Lord while we were discussing the torpedo, was particularly attentive to me, and very careful in seeing me off the premises; and then, for the first time, it flashed across my mind that I had been taken for a madman.

I was so tickled with the idea, that I burst into a sudden fit of hearty laughter, an act which induced a little boy, a policeman, and an old woman, who chanced to be passing, to imbibe the erroneous view of the first Lord.

However, although grievously disheartened, I was not subdued. Hope, which tells so many flattering tales, told me that after proper consideration the Admiralty would infallibly perceive the value of my invention; and in regard to the destruction of my fellow-creatures, I consoled myself with the reflection that torpedoes were much more calculated for defensive than offensive warfare.

Before quitting this subject, I may state that from that day to this, I have never heard from the Admiralty in reference to my invention. This fact gives me no pain now, although it did at first. I will explain why.

There is a friend of mine—a grave, kindly, young man, yet withal sarcastic and eccentric—who met me immediately after my visit to the Admiralty. He is a strange being this friend, who crops up at all sorts of unexpected times, and in divers places, when one least expects him. His name is U. Biquitous.

"My dear Childers," said he, when I had explained matters, "you are a victim;—you are the victim of self-delusion. You were victimised by self-delusion when I first met you, at the time you thought you had discovered perpetual motion. Your torpedo, as you have just described it to me, is an impossibility, and you yourself are—"

"An ass?" said I, looking up in his face.

"No, by no means," returned Biquitous, earnestly; "but you are an enthusiast without ballast. Enthusiasm is a fine, noble quality. The want of ballast is a grievous misfortune. Study mechanics, my boy, a little more than you have yet done, before venturing on further inventions, and don't theorise too much. You have been revelling of late in the regions of fancy. Take my advice, and don't do it."

"I wont," said I, fervently, "but I cannot give up my cherished pursuits."

"There is no reason that you should," returned my friend, grasping my hand, "and my earnest advice to you is to continue them; but lay in some ballast if possible."

With these cheery words ringing in my ears, I rejoined my mother and sister, and went off to Portsmouth.

It is well, however, to state here that my personal investigations in the matter of explosives had at this time received a death-blow. I went, indeed, with intense interest to see the display of our national destructive powers at Portsmouth, but I never again ventured to add my own little quota to the sum of human knowledge on such subjects; and the reader may henceforth depend upon it, that in all I shall hereafter write, there shall be drawn a distinct and unmistakable line between the region of fact and fancy.

Chapter Four
A Day with the Torpedoes

The sentence with which I finished the last chapter appears to me essential, because what I am now about to describe may seem to many readers more like the dreams of fancy than the details of sober fact.

When my mother and I, with Nicholas and Bella, arrived at Portsmouth, we were met by my naval friend, a young lieutenant, who seemed to me the *beau-idéal* of an embryo naval hero. He was about the middle height, broad, lithe, athletic, handsome, with a countenance beaming with good-will to, and belief in, everybody, including himself. He was self-possessed; impressively attentive to ladies, both young and old, and suave to gentlemen; healthy as a wild stag, and happy as a young cricket, with a budding moustache and a "fluff" on either cheek. Though gentle as a lamb in peace, he was said to be a very demon in war, and bore the not inappropriate name of Firebrand.

"Allow me to introduce my friend, Lieutenant Naranovitsch, Mr Firebrand, my mother and sister; not too late, I hope," said I, shaking hands.

"Not at all. In capital time," replied the young fellow, gaily, as he bowed to each. "Allow me, Mrs Childers—take my arm. The boat is not far off."

"Boat!" exclaimed my mother, "must we then go to sea?"

"Not exactly," replied Firebrand, with a light laugh, "unless you dignify Portchester Creek by that name. The *Nettle* target-ship lies there, and we must go on board of her, as it is around and in connection with her that the various experiments are to be tried, by means of gunboats, launches, steam-pinnaces, and various other kinds of small craft."

"How very fortunate that you have such a charming day," said my mother, whose interest was at once aroused by the youth's cheery manner. "Do you expect many people to witness the experiments, Mr Firebrand?"

"About five hundred invitations have been issued," answered the lieutenant, "and I daresay most of those invited will come. It is an occasion of some importance, being the termination of the senior course of instruction in our Naval Torpedo School here. I am happy to think," he added, with an arch smile, "that an officer of the Russian army will have such a good opportunity of witnessing what England is preparing for her enemies."

"It will afford me the greatest pleasure to witness your experiments," replied Nicholas, returning the smile with interest, "all the more that England and Russia are now the best of friends, and shall, I hope, never again be enemies."

In a few minutes we were conveyed on board the *Nettle*, on whose deck was a most animated assemblage. Not only were there present hundreds of gaily-dressed visitors, and officers, both naval and military, in bright and varied uniforms, but also a number of Chinese students, whose gaudy and peculiar garments added novelty as well as brilliancy to the scene.

"Delightful!" murmured Bella, as she listened to the sweet strains of the Commander-in-chief's band, and gazed dreamily at the sun-flashes that danced on the glassy water.

"Paradise!" replied Naranovitsch, looking down into her eyes.

"What are they going to do?" asked my mother of young Firebrand, who kept possession of her during the whole of the proceedings, and explained everything.

"They are going to illustrate the application of torpedo science to offensive and defensive warfare," said the lieutenant; and just now I see they are about to send off an outrigger launch to make an attack with two torpedoes, one on either bow, each being filled with 100 pounds of gunpowder. Sometimes gun-cotton is used, but this 100 pounds charge of powder is quite sufficient to send the vessel in which we stand to the bottom in five or ten minutes. Come this way—we shall see the operations better from this point. Now, don't be alarmed, there is not the slightest danger, I assure you.

He spoke in reassuring tones, and led my mother to the side of the ship, whither I followed them, and became at once absorbed in what was going on.

The outrigger launch referred to was a goodly-sized boat, fitted with a small engine and screw propeller. Its chief peculiarities were two long poles or spars, which lay along its sides, projecting beyond the bows. These were the outriggers. At the projecting end of each spar was fixed an iron case, bearing some resemblance in shape and size to an elongated kettle-drum. These were the torpedoes. I heard the lieutenant explain to my mother that if one of these torpedoes chanced to explode where it hung, it would blow the boat and men to atoms. To which my mother replied, "Horrible!" and asked how, in that case, the crew could fire it and escape. Whereupon he responded, "You shall see presently."

Another peculiarity in the launch was that it had a species of iron hood or shield, like a broad and low sentry-box, from behind which protection the few men who formed her crew could steer and work the outriggers and the galvanic battery, without being exposed.

This little boat seemed to me like a vicious wasp, as it left the side of the ship with a rapid throbbing of its engine and twirling of its miniature screw.

When at a sufficient distance from the ship, an order was given by the officer in charge. Immediately the outrigger on the right or starboard side was run out by invisible hands to its full extent—apparently fifteen feet beyond the bow of the launch; then the inner end of the outrigger was tilted violently into the air, so that the other end with its torpedo was thrust down ten feet below the surface of the water. This, I was told, is about the depth at which an enemy's ship ought to be struck. The launch, still going at full speed, was now supposed to have run so close to the enemy, that the submerged torpedo was about to strike her. Another order was given. The operator gave the needful touch to the galvanic battery, which, like the most faithful of servants, *instantly* sent a spark to fire the torpedo.

The result was tremendous. A column of seething mud and water, twenty feet in diameter, shot full thirty feet into the air, overwhelming the launch in such a shower that many of the unprofessional spectators imagined she was lost. Thus an imaginary ironclad was sent, with a tremendous hole in her, to the bottom of the sea.

That this is no *imaginary* result will be seen in the sequel of our tale.

"Why, the shock has made the *Nettle* herself tremble!" I exclaimed, in surprise.

"Oh, the poor boat!" cried my mother.

"No fear of the boat," said young Firebrand, "and as to the *Nettle*—why, my good fellow, I have felt our greatest ironclad, the mighty *Thunderer*, of which I have the honour to be an officer, quiver slightly from the explosion of a mere five-pounds torpedo discharged close alongside. Few people have an adequate conception of the power of explosives, and still fewer, I believe, understand the nature of the powers by which they are at all times surrounded. That 100-pounds torpedo, for instance, which has only caused us to quiver, would have blown a hole in our most powerful ship if fired in *contact* with it, and yet the *cushion of water* between it and the tiny launch that fired it is so tough as to be quite a sufficient protection to the boat, as you see."

We did indeed "see," for the waspish little boat emerged from the deluge she had raised and, steaming swiftly on, turned round and retraced her track. On reaching about the same position as to the *Nettle*, she repeated the experiment with her second torpedo.

"Splendid!" exclaimed young Naranovitsch, whose military ardour was aroused.

"It means, does it not," said Bella, "a splendid ship destroyed, and some hundreds of lives lost?"

"Well—yes—" said Nicholas, hesitatingly; "but of course it does not always follow, you know, that so *many* lives—"

He paused, and smiled with a perplexed look. Bella smiled dubiously, and shook her head, for it did not appear to either of them that the exact number of lives lost had much to do with the question. A sudden movement of the visitors to the other side of the ship stopped the conversation.

They were now preparing to show the effect of a gun-cotton hand-grenade; in other words, a species of bomb-shell, meant to be thrown by the hand into an enemy's boat at close-quarters. This really tremendous weapon was an innocent-looking disc or circlet of gun-cotton, weighing not more than eight ounces. Innocent it would, in truth, have been but for the little detonator in its heart, without which it would only have burned, not exploded. Attached to this disc was an instantaneous fuse of some length, so that an operator could throw the disc into a passing boat, and then fire the fuse, which would *instantly* explode the disc.

All this was carefully explained by Firebrand to my astonished mother, while the disc, for experimental purposes, was being placed in a cask floating in the water. On the fuse being fired, this cask was blown "into matchwood"—a wreck so complete that the most ignorant spectator could not fail to understand what would have been the fate of a boat and its crew in similar circumstances.

"How very awful!" said my mother. "Pray, Mr Firebrand, what *is* gun-worsted—I mean cotton."

The young lieutenant smiled rather broadly as he explained, in a glib and slightly sing-song tone, which savoured of the Woolwich Military Academy, that, "gun-cotton is the name given to the explosive substance produced by the action of nitric acid mixed with sulphuric acid, on cotton fibre." He was going to add, "It contains carbon, hydrogen, nitrogen, and oxygen, corresponding to—" when my mother stopped him.

"Dear me, Mr Firebrand, is a *popular* explanation impossible?"

"Not impossible, madam, but rather difficult. Let me see. Gun-cotton is a chemical compound of the elements which I have just named—a *chemical compound*, you will observe, not a mechanical *mixture*, like gunpowder. Hence it explodes more rapidly than the latter, and its power is from three to six times greater."

My mother looked perplexed. "What is the difference," she asked, "between a chemical compound and a mechanical mixture?"

Firebrand now in his turn looked perplexed. "Why, madam," he exclaimed, in modulated desperation, "the ultimate molecules of a mixture are only placed *beside* each other, so that an atom of gunpowder may be saltpetre, charcoal, or sulphur, dependent on its fellow-atoms for power to act; whereas a chemical compound is such a perfect union of substances, that each ultimate molecule is complete in its definite proportions of the four elements, and therefore an *independent* little atom."

"Now, the next experiment," continued Firebrand, glad to have an opportunity of changing the subject, "is meant to illustrate our method of countermining. You must know that our enemies may sometimes sink torpedoes at the entrance of their harbours, to prevent our ships of war entering. Such torpedoes consist usually of casks or cases of explosives, which are fired either by electric wires, like the telegraph, when ships are seen to be passing over them, or by *contact*. That is to say, an enemy's ship entering a harbour runs against something which sets something else in motion, which explodes the torpedo and blows it and the ship into what natives of the Green Isle call smithereens. This is very satisfactory when it happens to an enemy, but not when it happens to one's-self, therefore when *we* have to enter an enemy's harbour we *countermine*. This operation is now about to be illustrated. The last experiments exhibited the power of offensive torpedoes. There are several different kinds, such as Mr Whitehead's fish-torpedo, the Harvey torpedo, and others."

"Dear me," said my mother, with a perplexed air, "I should have thought, Mr Firebrand, that all torpedoes were offensive."

"By no means; those which are placed at the entrance of harbours and navigable rivers are defensive. To protect ourselves from the offensive weapon, we use crinolines."

My mother looked quickly up at her polite young mentor. "You play with the ignorance of an old woman, sir," she said, with a half-jocular air.

"Indeed I do not, madam, I assure you," returned Firebrand, with much earnestness. "Every iron-clad is provided with a crinoline, which is a powerful iron network, hung all round the ship at some distance from her, like—pardon me—a lady's crinoline, and is intended to intercept any torpedo that may be discharged against her."

Attention was called, at this point, to the counter-mining experiments.

It may be said, in regard to these, that they can be conducted in various ways, but always with the same end in view, namely, to destroy an enemy's mines by exploding others in their midst.

For the sake of illustration, it was supposed that the surrounding sea-bottom was studded with invisible torpedoes, and that the *Nettle* was a warship, determined to advance into the enemy's harbour. To effect this with safety, and in order to clear away the supposed sunken torpedoes, a counter-torpedo was floated between two empty casks, and sent off floating in the desired direction by means of the tide. This countermine consisted of an iron cylinder, containing 300 pounds of powder, and was electrically connected with the *Nettle*. A small charge of gun-cotton was fixed to the suspender that held the torpedo to its casks. When at a safe distance from the ship, this charge was fired. It cut the suspender and let the torpedo sink to the bottom. There it was exploded with terrific violence, as was quickly shown by the mighty fountain of mud, water, and smoke that instantly shot up into the air. It has been proved by experiment that 500 pounds of gun-cotton exploded below water, will destroy all the torpedoes that lie within a radius of 120 yards. It is obvious, therefore, that a warship could advance into the space thus cleared and then send a second countermine ahead of her in the same way. If neither tide, current, nor wind will serve to drift the casks, the operation might be accomplished by a small boat, which could back out of danger after laying each torpedo, and thus, step by step, or shot by shot, the advance could be made in safety through the enemy's defences.

After this, twelve small charges of gun-cotton were sunk in various directions, each representing a countermine of 500 pounds. These were discharged simultaneously, to demonstrate the possibility of extending the operations over a wide area. These miniature charges were sent down in small nets, and were quite unprotected from the water, so that the gun-cotton was wet when fired.

This fact caught the attention of my mother at once.

"How can it go off when *wet*?" she exclaimed, turning her bright little eyes in astonishment on her young companion.

"Ha, that is one of the strange peculiarities of gun-cotton," replied Firebrand, with an amused look; "you don't require to keep it dry like powder. It is only necessary that there should be one small lump of dry gun-cotton inside the wet stuff, with a detonator in its heart. A detonator, you must know—"

"Oh, I know what a detonator is," said my mother, quickly.

"Well then," continued Firebrand, "the exploding of the detonator and the dry disc causes the wet gun-cotton also to go off, as you have seen. Now they are going to exhibit one of the modes of defending harbours. They have sunk four mines, of 300 pounds of gunpowder each, not far from where you see yon black specks floating on the water. The black specks are buoys, called *circuit-closers*, because they contain a delicate contrivance—a compound of mechanism and galvanism—which, when the buoys are bumped, *close* the electric circuit and cause the mine to explode. Thus when a ship-of-war sails against one of these circuit-closers, she is immediately blown up."

"Is not that rather a sneaking way of killing one's enemies?" asked my mother.

Young Firebrand laughed, and admitted that it was, but pleaded that everything was fair in love and war.

In actual warfare the circuit-closers are placed just over the mines which they are designed to explode, but for safety on this occasion they were placed at a safe distance from their respective mines. A steam-launch was used to bump them, and a prodigious upheaval of water on each explosion showed clearly enough what would have been the fate of an iron-clad if she had been over the mine.

"Oh, shade of Nelson!" I could not help exclaiming, "how shocked you must be if you are permitted to witness such methods of conducting war."

"Ah, yes!" sighed Firebrand; "the bubble reputation, you see, is being transferred from the cannon's mouth to the torpedo."

I made no reply, for my mind reverted to my laboratory in Devonshire, where lay the working-model of the terrible weapon I had spent so much time in perfecting. It seemed strange to me now, that, in the eager pursuit of a scientific object, I had scarcely ever, if at all, reflected on the dire results that the use of my torpedo involved, and I felt as if I were really guilty of the intent to murder. Just before leaving home I had charged my model, which was quite a large one, capable of holding about 50 pounds of dynamite, in the hope that I might prevail on the First Lord of the Admiralty and some of his colleagues to come down and see it actually fired. I now resolved to throw the dynamite into the sea, break up my model, and have done with explosives for ever.

While my mind was running on this, I was startled by an explosion close alongside. On turning towards the side of the ship, I found that it was caused by the rending of a huge iron chain, the links of which were more than one and a quarter inch in thickness. This powerful cable, which could have held an iron-clad, was snapped in twain like a piece of thread by the explosion *against* it of only two and a half pounds of gun-cotton.

"Very well done," I said to Firebrand, "but I think that a much smaller quantity of dynamite would have done it as effectively."

"Now, Mrs Childers," said the young lieutenant, "the last experiment is about to be made, and I think it will interest you even more than the others. See, they are about to send off the electrical steam-pinnace."

As he spoke, a boat was being prepared alongside the ship.

"Why!" exclaimed my mother, almost speechless with surprise, "they have forgotten to send its crew in it."

"No, madam," said Firebrand, with one of his blandest smiles, "they have not forgotten her crew, but there are services so dangerous, that although the courage of the British sailor will of course enable him to face *anything*, it has been thought advisable not to put it to too severe a test, hence this automatic boat has been invented. It is steered, and all its other operations are performed, by means of electricity, applied not on board the boat but on board of the *Nettle*."

This was indeed the case. The electric pinnace went off as he spoke, her steam-engines, steering-gear, and all the other apparatus being regulated by electric wires, which were "paid out" from the ship as the boat proceeded on her mission of supposed extreme danger. Right under the withering fire of the imaginary enemy's batteries she went, and having scorned the rain of small shot that swept over her like hail, and escaped the plunging heavy shot that fell on every side, she dropped a mine over her stern, exploded it by means of a slow fuse, turned round and steamed back in triumph, amid the cheers of the spectators.

This last was really a marvellous sight, and the little boat seemed indeed to deserve the encomiums of Firebrand, who said, that, "If cool, calm pluck, in the face of appalling danger, merited anything, that heroic little steam-pinnace ought to receive the Victoria Cross."

I was still meditating on this subject, and listening to the animated comments going on around me, when I myself received a shock, compared to which all the explosions I had that day witnessed were as nothing.

It suddenly recurred to my memory that I had left a compound in my laboratory at home in a state of chemical preparation, which required watching to prevent its catching fire at a certain part of the process. I had been called away from that compound suddenly by Nicholas, just before we left for London, and I had been so taken up with what he had to tell me, that I had totally forgotten it. The mere burning of this compound would, in itself, have been nothing, for my laboratory was an old out-house, quite unconnected with the dwelling; but in the laboratory also lay my torpedo! The worst of it was that I had inserted a detonator and affixed a fuse, feeling quite secure in doing so, because I invariably locked the door and carried the key in my pocket.

My face must have turned very pale, for Nicholas, who came up at the moment, looked at me with anxious surprise, and asked if I were ill.

"No," said I, hurriedly; "no, not ill—but—yes—it is a slow process at best, and not always certain—sometimes takes a day or two to culminate. The fusion may not have been quite completed, or it may have failed altogether. Too late, I fear, too late, but I cannot rest till I know. Tell my mother I'm off home—only business—don't alarm her."

Regardless of the amazed looks of those who stood near me, I broke from the grasp of Nicholas, leaped into one of the boats alongside, seized the oars, and rowed ashore in mad haste.

Fortune favoured me. The train had not left, though it was just in motion. I had no time to take a ticket, but leaping upon the moving footboard, I wrenched open a carriage-door and sprang in.

It was an express. We went at full sixty miles an hour, yet I felt as if we moved like a snail. No words can adequately explain the state of my mind and body—the almost uncontrollable desire I felt to spring out of the train and run on ahead. But I was forced to sit still and think. I thought of the nearness of the laboratory to our kitchen windows, of the tremendous energy of the explosive with which the model-torpedo was charged, of the mass of combustibles of all kinds by which it was surrounded, of the thousand and one possibilities of the case, and of my own inexcusable madness in not being more careful.

At last the train pulled up at the town from which our residence is about two miles distant. It was now evening; but it was summer, and the days were long. Hiring a horse at the nearest hotel, I set off at a break-neck gallop.

The avenue-gate was open. I dashed in. The laboratory was not visible from that point, being at the back of the house. At the front door I pulled up, sprang to the ground, let the horse go, and ran forward.

I was met by Lancey coming round the corner. I saw at once that all was over! His face and hands had been scorched, and his hair singed! I gasped for breath.

"No one killed?" I asked.

"No, sir, nobody killed, but most of us 'orribly scared, sir."

"Nobody hurt, Lancey?" I asked again, leaning against the side of the house, and wiping my forehead.

"No, sir, nor 'urt," continued my faithful groom, hastening to relieve my mind; "you've no need to alarm yourself, sir, for we're all alive and 'earty, though I must say it's about the wust buster, sir, that you've yet turned out of 'ands. It sent in the kitchen winders as if they'd bin made of tissue paper, sir, an' cook she went into highstericks in the coal-bunker, Margaret she swounded in the scullery, and Mary went into fits in the wash'us. But they're all right again, sir,—only raither skeery ever since. We 'ad some trouble in puttin' it out, for the cumbustibles didn't seem to care much for water. We got it under at last, early this morning."

"This morning?"

"Yes, sir. It blow'd up about two hours arter you left for London, an' we've bin at it ever since. We *was* so glad your mother was away, sir, for it *did* make an uncommon crack. I was just sayin' to cook, not 'alf an hour since, the master would have enjoyed that, he would; it was *such* a crusher."

"Any of—of—the torpedo left, Lancey?" I asked, with some hesitation.

"The torpedo, sir. Bless your 'art, it went up to the 'eavens like a sky-rocket, an' blowed the out-'ouse about to that extent that you couldn't find a bit big enough to pick your teeth with."

On hearing this I roused myself, and hastened to the scene of devastation.

One glance sufficed. The spot on which my laboratory had stood was a blackened heap of rubbish!

"Now, mother," said I next day, after relieving her mind by a full and rapid account of what had happened, "there is nothing that I know of to detain me at home. I will therefore see to having the yacht got ready, and we shall all go to sea without delay."

Chapter Five
Terrible Torpedo Tales, Followed
By Overturned Plans

Change of scene has almost always an invigorating effect on the mind. Whatever be the nature of your mind, variety, rest assured, will improve its condition.

So we thought, my mother and I, Nicholas and Bella, as we lay, one beautiful morning, becalmed in the English Channel.

The yacht turned out to be a most charming vessel. Schooner-rigged, with two cabins, one of which formed our *salon* during the day, and the gentlemen's bed-room by night, the other being set apart entirely for the ladies. It was quite full. My mother and Bella filled it. Another female would have caused it to overflow.

Contrary to all expectation, my mother turned out a capital sailor; better even than Bella, on whom she attended during the first part of the voyage when the latter was ill.

"D'you think we shall have a good passage across the far-famed Bay of Biscay?" asked Nicholas, as he sat on the cabin skylight, smoking a mild cigar. Talking of that, smoking was the only thing in which I could not join my future brother-in-law. I know not how it is, but so it is that I cannot smoke. I have often tried to, but it invariably makes me sick, for which, perhaps, I ought to be thankful.

"It is to be hoped we shall," I replied to his question; "but I am not a judge of weather. What think you, Mr Whitlaw?" I said, addressing my skipper.

"I hope we shall, sir," replied the skipper, with a deferential touch of his cap, and a glance round the horizon; "but I don't feel sure."

Mr Whitlaw was an American, and a splendid specimen of the nation to which he belonged,—tall, lanky, broad-shouldered, gentlemanly, grave, self-possessed, prompt, good-humoured: I have seldom met a more agreeable man. He had been in the Northern navy of America during the last war, and had already introduced some of the discipline, to which he had been accustomed, amongst my small crew.

Bella was up on deck enjoying the sunset; so was my mother. Lancey was busy cleaning my fowling-piece, near the companion-hatch.

"It is charming," exclaimed my mother.

"So calm," said Bella.

"And settled-looking," remarked Nicholas, flipping the end of his cigar over the side.

"Mr Whitlaw does not appear to think so favourably of the weather," I remarked.

The skipper, looking gravely at a particular point on the horizon, said, in a quiet tone—

"The clouds are heavy."

"From which you judge that the fine weather may not last?"

"It may be so, but the indications are not certain," was his cautious reply.

That night we were in a perfect chaos of wind and water. The storm-fiend seemed to have reserved all his favours in order to give us a befitting reception. The sea roared, the wind yelled, the yacht—but why repeat the oft-told tale that invariably ends with "Biscay, O!" A week later and we were in a dead calm, revelling in warmth, bathed in sunshine, within the straits of Gibraltar.

It was evening. All sail was set. Not a puff of wind rendered that display available. The reef-points pattered as the yacht rolled gracefully from side to side on the gentle heave of the Mediterranean's bosom.

Sitting on a rug on the deck, between my mother and Nicholas, Bella said, in a low quiet tone, "This is perfect felicity."

"Agreed," said Nicholas, in a similar tone, with a puff from his cigar.

Bella referred to the calm, of course!

A sea-captain, sitting astride the bulwarks of his ship in the "Doldrums," far far away from Bella, said, in reference to a similar calm which had beset him for three weeks, "This is perfectly maddening," with many other strong expressions which we would rather not record; but Bella, of course, did not know that, and could not be expected to reflect on it. She was taken up with her own comforts at the time.

"My dear," said Mrs Childers, "I think I shall go to bed. Come with me. Good-night, Nicholas. Will you keep the skylight off to-night, Jeffry? It was too hot in our cabin last night."

"Of course I will," said I; "why did you not ring, and let me know that you would like fresh air? But I shall see to it to-night."

About eleven o'clock that night, I lay on one of the lockers of the main cabin, in a wakeful mood. Nicholas lay on the other locker, in that profound slumber which is so characteristic of healthy youth. His regular breathing was the only sound I heard, except the soft footfall of our skipper, as he slowly paced the deck.

Presently I heard another step. It advanced, and a low "Fine night, sir," apprised me that it was Lancey, who had come on deck to air himself after the culinary and other labours of the day, for he served in the capacity of cook and steward to the yacht.

"I wish you'd tell me about that expedition you was speakin' off to the master this morning," said Lancey.

"With pleasure," replied the skipper; "sit down here, and I'll spin it off to you right away."

I knew by the sound of their motions that they had seated themselves at the foot of the main-mast, just between the skylights of the two cabins, and feared that their talk might disturb my mother; but, reflecting that she must have got to sleep long ago, I thought it better not to disturb them, unless their talk should become too loud. As for myself, in my wakeful mood, their converse could not annoy me. After a time it began to interest me deeply.

"It was about the blowing-up of Southern ironclads, was it not?" said the skipper. As he spoke I could distinctly hear the puff, puff, of his pipe between each half-dozen words.

"*Just* so," replied Lancey. "The master is uncommon fond of blowin's-up and inquirin' into the natur' of things. I never know'd another except one as beat 'im at inwestigation, but that one beat everybody I ever seen or heard of. He was a Scotch boy, named Sandy—"

"What was his other name?" asked the skipper.

"'Aven't a notion," replied Lancey. "We never called 'im anythink else. I don't believe he 'ad any other name. He said he was the son of an apothecary. No doubt the schoolmaster knew 'is other name, if he 'ad one, but he never used it, and we boys were content with Sandy. That boy, sir, seemed to me to know everythink, and was able, I believe, to do hanythink. He was a tremendous fighter, too, though not out o' the way as regards size. He could lick the biggest boy in the school, and when he made up his mind to do a thing, nothin' on earth could stop him a-doin' of it."

"Good," said the skipper, with an emphatic puff; "that's what we Americans call the power to go ahead. Did Sandy become a great man?"

"Don't know," answered Lancey. "He went a'ead too fast for me to foller. One day the master gave 'im a lickin'. He vowed he'd be revenged. Next mornin' early he got up an' smashed the school winders, redooced the master's desk to matchwood, an' walked away whistlin'. I never seed 'im since."

"Nor heard of him?"

"Nor 'eard of 'im."

"That was a pity," said the skipper, with a prolonged whiff.

"It was. But go on, Mister Whitlaw, with your hanecdotes. I couldn't rightly hear all you said to the master."

"It was about torpedo warfare we were talking," said the skipper. "You know that sort o' thing is only in its infancy, but the Americans, as usual, had the honour of starting it fairly into being."

"The 'honour,' eh?" said Lancey; "h'm! well, I'm not so sure about the honour, but go on."

"Well, whether it be an honour or no, I won't dispute," returned the skipper, with a puff; "but of this I am sure, that during the late war between the North and South in America, torpedo practice was regularly brought into play for the first time, and the case which I brought before Mr Childers yesterday is only one of many which I could describe. I'll not relate the same story, but another and a better.

"About the beginning of the war, in 1862, the Confederates—these were the Southern men—blew up our ironclad, the *Cairo*, in which I lost one of my most intimate friends; and in 1864 they attempted to blow up the *Wabash*, and myself along with it. The *Cairo* business was caused by sunk torpedoes. She was going up the Yazoo river at the time, and had lowered a boat to search for torpedoes, which were known to be sunk there. They succeeded in fishing up one, which was found to be an exploded one. Meanwhile the *Cairo*, having got rather too close in shore, backed out towards the middle of the stream, when two explosions occurred in quick succession, one close to the port-quarter, the other under the port-bow. The effect was tremendous. Some of the heavy guns were actually lifted from the deck. The captain instantly shoved the *Cairo* on the bank, and got a hawser out to a tree to keep her, if possible, from sinking in deep water. The pumps, steam and hand, were set going immediately; but her whole frame, ironclad though she was, had been so shattered, that nothing could save her. Twelve minutes afterwards she slipped down into six fathoms water, giving them barely time to get out the boats and save the sick men aboard, and the arms. My friend was one of the sick, and the moving was ultimately the death of him, though no lives were lost at the time."

"You're not tellin' me crackers, are you?" said Lancey, in an incredulous tone.

"My good fellow," returned the skipper, "I wish that I were. The story is only too true, and I would it were the only one of the sort I had to tell. You can find a book in London, (see note 1) if you like, which tells all about this and the other torpedo work done during the late American war."

"Well, then," said Lancey, in the tone of an eager listener, while, by the tapping on the combings of the hatchway, I could distinguish that he was emptying his pipe, with a view, no doubt, to the enjoyment of another, "and what happened when they tried to blow *you* up?"

"Well, you must know," resumed the skipper, "it was long afterwards, near the end of the war. I was in the US steamer *Wabash* at the time. We were at anchor off Charleston, and we kept a sharp look-out at that time, for it was a very different state of things from the wooden-wall warfare that Nelson used to carry on. Why, we never turned in a night without a half sort of expectation of being blown into the sky before morning. It was uneasy work, too, for although American sailors are as good at *facing* death as any men, they don't like the notion of death coming in on them, like a sneak below the waterline, and taking them in the dark while asleep. We were always on the alert, and doubly so at that time, for only a short while previously, the Confederates had sunk another of our ironclads, the *Housatonic*, with one of their torpedo-Davids,—little boats that were so called because, compared with the great ironclads they were meant to attack, they somewhat resembled David when he went out against Goliath.

"Well, as I said, the *Wabash* was at anchor, and it was night—not very late, about ten; but it was very dark.

"Fortunately the deck was in charge that night of a young officer named Craven, and never was an officer worse named or better deserving to be called Courage. He had his wits about him. At the hour I have named, he observed something on the starboard-quarter, about 150 yards off. It resembled a plank on the water. In reality it was a torpedo-David. It was opposite the main-mast when first observed, going rapidly against the tide. At that moment it turned and made straight for the ship. Craven was up to the mark. He commenced with volleys of musketry; beat the gong for the crew to assemble at quarters; rang four bells for the engine to go ahead; opened fire with the watch and the starboard battery; and gave orders to slip the cable.

"His orders, you may be sure, were obeyed with promptitude. The gong sent every man from his hammock as if he had received an electric shock. Jack-in-the-box never came out of his box more promptly than each man shot up the hatchway. An exaggerated idea of the effect of torpedoes—if that were possible—had got possession of us. We were at our quarters in a moment; the ship moved ahead; the chain slipped; and the torpedo-boat passed us about forty yards astern. A round shot from us at the same moment appeared to strike it. We cheered. A second shot was fired, and appeared to send it to the bottom, for we saw it no more.

"But now *our* turn came," continued the skipper, refilling his pipe. "Puff! you see we were not so well situated as the Southerners for the use of this weapon, for we had to go in to attack their forts, while they had only to defend themselves, which they did largely with sunk torpedoes.

"We had long been desirous of revenging their attacks in a similar fashion, and at last we were successful on the 27th of October. I had the good luck to be one of the expedition. It was risky work, of course. We all knew that, but where is the nation worthy of the name that will not find men for risky work? People talk about the difference of courage in nations. In my opinion that is all gammon. Most nations that lie near to one another are pretty much alike as to courage. In times of trial among all nations, the men of pluck come to the front, and the plucky men, be they American, English, French, German, Russian, or Turk, do pretty much the same thing—they fight like heroes till they conquer or die."

"Better if they didn't fight at all," remarked Lancey.

"That's true, but if you're attacked you *must* fight. Anyhow, on this particular occasion we attacked the Confederate ironclad ram *Albemarle*, and sent her to the bottom. I had volunteered for the duty with some other men from the squadron, and we started in a steam-launch under Lieutenant Cushing. The distance from the mouth of the river to where the ram lay was about eight miles, the stream averaging 200 yards in width, and being lined with the enemy's pickets, so that we had to proceed with the utmost possible caution. We set out in the dead of night. There was a wreck on our way, which was surrounded by schooners, and we knew that a gun was mounted there to command the bend of the river. We had the good luck, however, to pass the pickets and the wreck without being discovered, and were not hailed until seen by the look-out of the ram itself.

"Without replying to the hail, we made straight at her under a full head of steam. The enemy sprang their rattles, rang their bell, and commenced firing. The *Albemarle* was made fast to a wharf, with a defence of logs around her about thirty feet from her side. A chance fire on the shore enabled us to see this, although the night was intensely dark, and raining.

"From the report afterwards published by the commander of the *Albemarle*, it seems that a good look-out had been kept. The watch also had been doubled, and when we were seen (about three in the morning) they were all ready. After hailing, a brisk fire was opened on us both by small arms and large guns; but the latter could not be brought to bear, owing to our being so close, and we partially disturbed the aim of the former by a dose of canister at close range. Paymaster Swan, of the *Otsego*, was wounded near me, and some others. My own jacket was cut in many places, and the air seemed full of bullets.

"Our torpedo-boom was out and ready. Passing close to the *Albemarle*, we made a complete circle round her, so as to strike her fairly. Then Lieutenant Cushing gave the order, and we went straight at her, bows on. In a moment we struck the logs, just abreast of the quarter-port, with such force that we leaped half over them, at the same time breasted them in. The boom was lowered at once. 'Now, lads, a vigorous pull!' said Cushing.

"We obeyed, and sent the torpedo right under the overhang of the ship. It exploded. At the same instant the *Albemarle's* great-gun was fired. A shot seemed to go crashing through the boat, and a dense mass of water rushed in from the torpedo. It seemed to me as if heaven and earth had come together. Smoke and yells, with continued firing at only fifteen feet range, followed, in the midst of which I heard the commander of the ironclad summon us to surrender. I heard our lieutenant twice refuse, and then, ordering the men to save themselves, he jumped into the water. I followed him, and for some time swam in the midst of a shower-bath caused by plunging shot and bullets, but not one of them struck me. At last I reached the shore, and escaped.

"At the time I thought we must have failed in our purpose, but I was mistaken. Though we had lost one boat and some of our men, many of them being captured, I learned that the *Albemarle* had sunk in fifteen minutes after the explosion of the torpedo, only her shield and smoke-stack being left out of the water to mark the spot where a mighty iron-clad had succumbed to a few pounds of well-applied gunpowder!"

"If that be so," said Lancey, after a pause and deep sigh, "it seems to me no manner of use to build ironclads at all, and that it would be better, as well as cheaper, in time to come, to fight all our battles with torpedo-boats."

"It may be so," replied the skipper, rising, "but as that is a subject which is to be settled by wiser heads than ours, and as you have to look after the ladies' breakfast to-morrow morning, I'd strongly advise you to turn in."

Lancey took the hint, and as he slept in a berth close to the cabin, I quickly had nasal assurance that he had thrown care and torpedoes to the dogs.

It was not so with myself. Much of the information which Mr Whitlaw had unconsciously conveyed to me was quite new, for although I had, as a youth, read and commented on the late American war while it was in progress, I had not given to its details that amount of close study which is necessary to the formation of a reasonable judgment. At first I could not resist the conviction that my skipper must have been indulging in a small amount of exaggeration, especially when I reflected on the great strength and apparent invulnerability of such massive vessels as our *Thunderer*; but knowing the sedate and truthful character of Mr Whitlaw, I felt perplexed. Little did I think at the time that I should live to see, and that within the year, the truth of his statements corroborated with my own eyes. I meditated long that night on war and its results, as well as the various processes by which it is carried on; and I had arrived at a number of valuable conclusions, which I would have given worlds to have been able to jot down at the moment, when I was overtaken by that which scattered them hopelessly to the winds: I fell sound asleep!

The rest of this delightful voyage I am compelled to pass over, in order that I may come to matters of greater importance.

We had reached the neighbourhood of the beautiful town of Nice, when my dear mother, to my surprise and mortification, suddenly announced that she could not endure the sea any longer. She had kept pretty well, she admitted, and had enjoyed herself, too, except when listening to those dreadful stories of the captain about the American war, which had travelled to her down the after-cabin skylight, during wakeful hours of the night. Despite appearances, she said she had suffered a good deal. There was something, she declared, like a dumpling in her throat, which always seemed about to come up, but wouldn't, and which she constantly tried to swallow, but couldn't.

In these circumstances, what could I do? We had meant to land at Nice in passing. I now resolved to leave my mother and sister there and proceed eastward—it might be to Egypt or the Black Sea—with Naranovitsch. The latter had ordered his letters to be forwarded to Nice; we therefore ran into the port, and, while my mother and sister and I drove to "the Château" to see the splendid view from that commanding position, he went off to the post-office.

On returning to the yacht, we found poor Nicholas in deep distress. He had received a letter announcing the death of his father, and requiring his immediate return to Russia. As the circumstances admitted of no delay, and as my mother could not be prevailed on to go farther in the yacht, it was hastily arranged that she and Bella should return through France to England, and that Nicholas should take charge of them.

Our plans being fixed, they were at once carried into effect, and the same evening I found myself alone in my yacht, with no one but the skipper and crew and the faithful Lancey, to keep me company.

The world was now before me where to choose. After a consultation with my skipper, I resolved to go on a cruise in the Black Sea, and perhaps ascend the Danube, in spite of the rumours of possible war between the Russians and Turks.

Note 1. "A Treatise on Coast-Defence ... Compiled from official reports of officers of the United States. By Von Scheliha, Lieutenant-Colonel and chief engineer of the department of the Gulf of Mexico of the army of the late Confederate States of America."

Chapter Six
Turk and Bulgarian—A Wrestling Match and a Dispute

River navigation is, to my mind, most captivating; but space forbids that I should enlarge on it, and on many other points of interest in this eventful voyage. I shall therefore pass over the Dardanelles and the Bosporus, leaving the great and classic Stamboul itself behind untouched, and transport the reader at once to one of those "touches of nature" which "make the whole world kin."

It is a little village on the Danube river—the mighty Danube, which bears the fleets of the world on its ample breast.

We had been a considerable time in the river, for we took things very leisurely, before reaching the village to which I refer. It was named Yenilik. While I had been rejoicing in the varied scenery—the lagoons and marshes of the several mouths of the great river, and the bolder prospects of hill and dale higher up—I had not been idling my time or making entire holiday of it, for I had devoted myself to the study of the Turkish language.

My powers as a linguist may not perhaps be above the average, nevertheless I confess to a considerable facility in the acquisition of languages. Russian I already knew very well, having, as before intimated, spent a considerable time in St. Petersburg.

Desiring to perfect myself in Turkish, I undertook to teach my man Lancey. Not that I had much opinion of his ability—far from it; but I entertain a strong belief in the Scriptural idea that two are better than one. Of course I do not hold that two fools are better than one wise man; but two men of average ability are, in nearly all circumstances, better than one, especially if one of them is decidedly and admittedly superior to the other. Lancey's powers were limited, but his ambition was not so, and I am bound to add that his application was beyond all praise. Of course his attainments, like his powers, were not great. His chief difficulty lay in his tendency to drop the letter *h* from its rightful position in words, and to insert it, along with *r* and *k*, in wrong places. But my efforts to impress Lancey's mind had the satisfactory effect of imbedding minute points of the language deeply in my own memory.

The village to which I have referred was in Bulgaria—on the right or southern shore of the Danube. It was a pretty spot, and the bright sunny weather lent additional charms to water, rock, and tree, while the twittering of birds, to say nothing of the laughter and song of men, women, and children working in the fields, or engaged in boisterous play, added life to it.

Towards the afternoon I landed, and, accompanied by Lancey, went up to the chief store or shop of the village. It was a primitive store, in which the most varied and incongruous articles were associated.

The owner of the shop was engaged in bargaining with, I think, one of the finest specimens of manhood I ever saw. His name I accidentally learned on entering, for the shopman, at that moment, said—

"No, Dobri Petroff, I cannot let you have it for less."

The shopman spoke in the Bulgarian tongue, which, being a kindred dialect of the Russian language, I understood easily.

"Too dear," said Petroff, as he turned over the article, a piece of calico, with a good-humoured affectation of contempt.

Dobri Petroff was a young man, apparently not more than twenty-five, tall, broad, deep-chested, small-waisted—a perfect study for an Apollo. Both dress and language betokened him an uneducated man of the Bulgarian peasantry, and his colour seemed to indicate something of gipsy origin; but there was an easy frank deportment about him, and a pleasant smile on his masculine countenance, which told of a naturally free, if not free-and-easy, spirit. Although born in a land where tyranny prevailed, where noble spirits were crushed, independence destroyed, and the people generally debased, there was an occasional glance in the black eye of Dobri Petroff which told of superior intelligence, a certain air of natural refinement, and a strong power of will.

"No, Dobri, no; not a rouble less," repeated the shopman.

Petroff smiled, and shook back his black curly hair, as a lion might in sporting with an obstinate cub.

At that moment a Turk entered. His position in society I could not at the time guess, but he had the overbearing manner of one who might have been raised by favour from a low to a high station. He pushed Petroff rudely out of his way, and claimed the entire attention of the shopman, which was at once and humbly accorded.

A fine expression of fierce contempt flashed across Petroff's countenance; but to my surprise, he at once drew aside.

When the Turk was served and had gone out, the shopman turned to me.

"After Petroff," I said, bowing towards the man.

The surprise and pleasure of Petroff was evidently great, but he refused to take advantage of my courtesy, and seemed so overwhelmed with modest confusion at my persisting that he should be served before me, that he ultimately left the shop, much to my regret, without making his purchase.

To my inquiries, the shopman replied that Dobri was the blacksmith of the place, and one of its best and steadiest workmen.

After completing my purchases I left, and strolled through the village towards its further extremity.

"The Turks seem to 'ave it all their own way ere, sir," said Lancey, as we walked along.

"If the treatment we have seen that man receive were the worst of it," I replied, "the Bulgarians would not have very much to complain of, though insolence by superiors to inferiors is bad enough. They have, however, more than that to bear, Lancey; the story of Bulgarian wrongs is a long and a very sad one."

As we strolled beyond the village, and were engaged in earnest converse on this subject, we suddenly came on a group of holiday-makers. A number of the peasantry were assembled in a field, engaged in dances, games, and athletic sports. We mingled with the crowd and looked on. They were engaged at the time in a wrestling match. Little notice was taken of our appearing, so intent were they on the proceedings. Two strong men were engaged in what I may call a tremendous hug. Each was stripped to the waist. Their muscles stood out like those of Hercules, as they strained and tugged. At last they went down, one being undermost, with both shoulder-blades touching the ground, and a loud cheer greeted the victor as he stood up.

He was a splendid animal, unquestionably—over six feet, with immense chest and shoulders, and modest withal; but a man of about five feet eight stepped into the ring, and overthrew him with such ease that a burst of laughter mingled with the cheer that followed. The triumph of the little man was, however, short-lived, for a Bulgarian giant next made his appearance—evidently a stranger to those present—and after a prolonged struggle, laid the little man on his back.

For some time this giant strutted about defiantly, and it appeared as if he were to remain the champion, for no one seemed fit or willing to cope with him. At last some gipsy girls who were sitting in front of the ring, urged one of their tribe, a tall, strong, young fellow, to enter the lists against the giant.

The youth consented, and entered the ring; but a quick throw from the giant sent him sprawling, to the great disappointment of his brunette friends.

Amongst the girls present, there sat a remarkably pretty young woman, whom the others endeavoured to urge to some course of action, to which she at first objected. After a little persuasion, however, she appeared to give in, and, rising, left the circle. Soon after she returned with a magnificent specimen of humanity, whom she pushed into the ring with evident pride.

It was Dobri Petroff. The villagers greeted him by name with a ringing cheer as he advanced.

With a modest laugh he shook his huge antagonist by the hand.

He stripped to the waist, and each man presented a rounded development of muscular power, which would have done credit to any of the homeric heroes; but there was a look of grand intelligence and refinement in Petroff's countenance, which would probably have enlisted the sympathies of the villagers even if he had been an utter stranger.

Having shaken hands, the wrestlers began to walk round each other, eagerly looking for a chance to get the "catch." It seemed at first as if neither liked to begin, when, suddenly, the Bulgarian turned sharp on Petroff, and tried a favourite throw; but with the lithe easy motion of a panther, the blacksmith eluded his grasp. The excitement of the spectators became intense, for it now seemed as if the two huge fellows were well-matched, and that a prolonged struggle was about to take place. This, however, was a mistake. The villagers apparently had underrated the powers of their own champion, and the gipsy girls looked anxious, evidently fearing that the hitherto victorious stranger would again triumph.

For some moments the cautious walk-round continued, then there was a sudden exclamation of surprise from the crowd, for the blacksmith seized his adversary by the waist, and with a quick throw, caused him to turn almost a somersault in the air, and to come down on his back with stunning violence.

While the heavy fellow lay, as if slightly stunned, on the ground, Petroff stooped, again shook hands with him, and then lifting him high in the air, as though he had been but a boy, set him on his feet, and turned to resume his jacket, amid the enthusiastic cheers of the people.

Petroff's jacket was handed to him by a pretty dark-eyed girl of about five years of age, who bore so strong a resemblance to the young woman who had brought the blacksmith on the scene, that I at once set them down as sisters. The child looked up in the champion's face with such innocence that he could not resist the temptation to stoop and kiss her. Then, taking the little one's hand, he pushed through the crowd and left the ring. I observed that the young woman also rose and went with them.

Feeling interested in these people. Lancey and I followed, and overtook them before they had quitted the field. I said in Russian:—

"Good-day, Petroff; you overthrew that fellow with greater ease than I had expected."

The blacksmith gave me a look of pleased recognition as he returned my salutation.

"Well, sir," he said, "it was not difficult. The man is strong enough, but does not understand the art well. You are an Englishman, I think."

"I am," said I, somewhat surprised as well by the question as by the superior manner and address of the man.

"It was a man from your land," returned Petroff, with a grave earnest look, "who taught me to wrestle,—a man from Cornwall. He was a sailor—a stout fellow, and a good man. His vessel had been anchored off our village for some time, so that we saw a good deal of him. They had a passenger on board, who landed and went much about among the people. He was a German, and called himself a colporteur. He taught strange doctrines, and gave away many Bibles, printed in the Bulgarian tongue."

"Ah," said I, "no doubt he was an agent of the British and Foreign Bible Society."

"Perhaps so," returned Petroff, with a somewhat perplexed look, "but he said nothing about that. His chief desire seemed to be to get us to listen to what he read out of his Bible. And some of us did listen, too. He gave one of the Bibles to my wife here, and she has been reading it pretty eagerly ever since."

"What! this, then, is your wife?" I exclaimed.

"Yes, Marika is my wife, and Ivanka is my daughter," replied Petroff, with a tender glance at the little girl that trotted by his side.

"Perhaps, Marika, your Cornish friend may have taught you to speak English," said I, in my native tongue, turning to the woman.

Marika shook her pretty head, laughed, and blushed. She seemed to understand me, but would not consent to reply in English.

"The colporteur of whom you have spoken," said I, turning to the blacksmith, and again speaking Russian, "did you a great service when he gave your wife the Word of God."

Dobri Petroff assented, but a frown for a minute overspread his face. "Yes," he said, "I admit that, but he also taught me to think, and it might have been better for me—for many of us in this land—if we did not think; if we could eat and sleep and work like the brutes that perish."

I feared that I knew too well what the man referred to, and would gladly have dropped the subject, but could not do so without appearing rude.

"It is always well to think," said I, "when we think rightly, that is, in accordance with the teachings of the Bible, about which we have just been speaking. Marika has read much of it to you, no doubt?"

"She has," said the blacksmith, with a touch of sternness, "and among other things, she has read to me that 'oppression driveth even a wise man mad.' Am I to understand that as merely stating the fact, or justifying the madness?"

Without waiting for a reply to the question, he went on, hurriedly—

"You saw that Turk to-day, who pushed me aside as if I had been a dog? That showed you the *spirit* of the men in power here, but you little know their practices—"

"Petroff," said I, interrupting, and looking at the man earnestly, "forgive me if I say that we had better not discuss the subject now. I have just arrived in your land, and know little about it yet. When I have seen and heard and thought much, I will be better able to understand you."

Petroff admitted with ready grace that I was right, and thrusting his fingers through the wild clustering curls of his black hair, as if to let the air circle more freely about his head, he turned sharp round, and pointed to a cottage which stood at a short distance from the high-road, at the entrance to the village.

"That is our home, sir; we shall feel happy if you will enter it."

I willingly complied, and turned with them into the by-path that led to it.

The cottage was a mere hut, long and low, one end of which constituted the forge, the other end, divided into three compartments, being the dwelling-house. Here I found the hand of Marika very evident, in the neatness and cleanliness of everything in and around the place. The owners were very poor, but there was sufficient for comfort and health. On a shelf in a corner lay the Bible which the family had received from the colporteur. It was the only book in the house, and evidently a cherished treasure.

In another corner, on a rudely-made but warm couch, lay a treasure of a different stamp—a boy, apparently about two years of age. As I looked at the curly black hair, the well-shaped nose, the firm, rosy lips, and the broad brow, I turned to Petroff with a smile, and said—

"I need not ask if that boy is yours."

The man did not at once reply, but seized the child, which our entrance had awakened, and raised it high above his head.

"Do you hear that, little Dob? The gentleman knows who you are by your mother's eyes."

"Nay," said I, with a laugh, "by its father's nose. But now that you mention the eyes, I do recognise the mother's plainly. How old is he?"

This was the first of a series of questions which opened the hearts of these people to me. On the strength of these jet-black eyes and the well-shaped nose, to say nothing of the colporteur and the Bible, Lancey and I struck up quite an intimate friendship, insomuch that at parting, little Dob gave me a familiar dab on the face, and Ivanka turned up her sweet little mouth to be kissed—quite readily and of her own accord. There is nothing on earth so captivating as a trustful child. My heart was knit to little Ivanka on the spot, and it was plain that little Dob and Lancey were mutually attracted.

I remained at that village several days longer than I had intended, in order to cultivate the acquaintance of the blacksmith's family. During that time I saw a good deal of the other villagers, and found that Petroff was by no means a typical specimen. He was above his compeers in all respects, except in his own opinion; one of Nature's gentlemen, in short, who are to be found, not numerously perhaps, but certainly, in almost every land, with unusual strength of intellect, and breadth of thought, and power of frame, and force of will, and nobility of aspiration. Such men in free countries, become leaders of the good and brave. In despotic lands they become either the deliverers of their country or the pests of society—the terror of rulers, the fomentors of national discord. Doubtless, in many cases, where right principles are brought to bear on them, they learn to submit, and, sometimes, become mitigators of the evils which they cannot cure.

Most of the other inhabitants of this village, some of whom were Mohammedans, and some Christians of the Greek Church, were sufficiently commonplace and uninteresting. Many of them appeared to be simply lazy and inert. Others were kindly enough, but stupid, and some were harsh, coarse, and cruel, very much as we find the peasantry in other parts of the world where they are ill-treated or uncared for.

While staying here I had occasion to go on shore one morning, and witnessed a somewhat remarkable scene in a café.

Lancey and I, having made a longer excursion than usual and the day being rather hot, resolved to refresh ourselves in a native coffee-house. On entering we found it already pretty well filled with Bulgarians, of whom a few were Moslems. They were apparently of the poorer class. Most of them sat on low stools, smoking chibouks—long pipes, with clay heads and amber mouth-pieces—and drinking coffee. The Christians were all engrossed, at the moment of our arrival, with a stranger, who from his appearance and the package of books which lay open at his side, I at once judged to be a colporteur. Dobri Petroff, I observed, was near him, and interested so deeply in what was going on, that he did not at first perceive us.

Having selected some New Testaments and Bibles from his pack, the colporteur handed them round for inspection. These, I found, were printed in the modern Bulgarian tongue. The people greatly admired the binding of the volumes, and began to evince considerable interest in what the colporteur said about them. At last he proposed to read, and as no objection was made, he read and commented on several passages. Although a German, he spoke Bulgarian fluently, and ere long had aroused considerable interest, for the people had little or no knowledge of the Bible; the only one to which they had access being that which lay on the pulpit of the Greek Church of the village, and which, being written in the ancient Slavic language, was incomprehensible by them.

The priests in the Greek Church there are generally uneducated men, and their intoned services and "unknown tongue" do not avail much in the way of enlightenment. The schoolmasters, I was told by those who had good opportunity of judging, are much better educated than the priests. I observed that one of these, who had on a former visit been pointed out to me by my friend Dobri, sat not far from the colporteur smoking his chibouk with a grave critical expression of countenance.

At last the colporteur turned to the 115th Psalm, and I now began to perceive that the man had a purpose, and was gradually leading the people on.

It is well known that the Greek Church, although destitute of images in its religious buildings, accords the same reverence, or homage, to pictures which the Romish Church does to the former. At first, as the colporteur read, the people listened with grave attention; but when he came to the verses that describe the idols of the heathen as being made of, "silver and gold, the work of men's hands," with mouths that could not speak, and eyes that could not see, and ears that could not hear, several of the more earnest listeners began to frown, and it was evident that they regarded the language of the colporteur's book as applicable to their sacred pictures, and resented the implied censure. When he came to the eighth verse, and read, "They that make them are like unto them, so is every one that trusteth in them," there were indignant murmurs; for these untutored peasants, whatever their church might teach about such subtleties as worshipping God *through* pictures, accepted the condemnatory words in simplicity.

"Why are you angry?" asked the colporteur, looking round.

"Because," answered a stern old man who sat, close to me, "your words condemn *us* as well as the heathen. They make out the pictures of our saints to be idols—images and pictures being one and the same thing."

"But these are not *my* words," said the colporteur, "they are the words of God."

"If these words are true," returned the old man, with increasing sternness, "then *we* are all wrong; but these words are not true—they are only the words of *your* Bible, about which we know nothing."

"My friends," returned the colporteur, holding up the volume from which he had been reading, "this is not only my Bible, it is also yours, the same that is read in your own churches, only rendered into your own modern tongue."

At this point Dobri Petroff, who, I observed, had been listening keenly to what was said, started up with vehemence, and exclaimed—

"If this be true, we can prove it. Our Bible lies in the neighbouring church, and here sits our schoolmaster who reads the ancient Slavic like his mother-tongue. Come, let us clear up the matter at once."

This proposal was heartily agreed to. The Bulgarians in the café rose *en masse*, and, headed by the village schoolmaster, went to the church, where they found the Bible that the priests were in the habit of reading, or rather intoning, and turned up the 115th Psalm. It was found to correspond exactly with that of the colporteur!

The result was at first received in dead silence, and with looks of surprise by the majority. This was followed by murmuring comments and some disputes. It was evident that the seeds of an inquiring spirit had been sown that day, which would bear fruit in the future. The colporteur, wisely forbearing to press his victory at that time, left the truth to simmer. (See note 1.)

I joined him as he went out of the church, and, during a brief conversation, learned from him that an extensive work is being quietly carried on in Turkey, which, although not attracting much attention, is nevertheless surely undermining the huge edifice of Error by means of the lever of Truth.

Among other things, he said that in the year 1876 so many as twenty-eight thousand Bibles, translated into the modern native tongue, had been circulated in the Turkish Empire and in Greece by the British and Foreign Bible Society, while the Americans, who are busily engaged in the blessed work in Armenia, had distributed twenty thousand copies.

Leaving the village of Yenilik and my Bulgarian friends with much regret, I continued the voyage up the Danube, landing here and there for a day or two and revelling in the bright weather, the rich prospects and the peaceful scenes of industry apparent everywhere, as man and beast rejoiced in the opening year.

Time passed rapidly as well as pleasantly. Sometimes I left the yacht in charge of Mr Whitlaw, and in company with my trusty servant travelled about the country, conversing with Turks wherever I met them, thus becoming more and more versed in their language, and doing my best, without much success, to improve Lancey in the same.

Note 1. The facts on which the above is founded were given to the author by the Reverend Doctor Thomson, who has resided in Turkey as the agent of the British and Foreign Bible Society for upwards of thirty years.

Chapter Seven
The Black Clouds Gather

While I was enjoying myself thus, among the towns and villages on the banks of the Danube, admiring the scenery, cultivating the acquaintance of the industrious rural population of the great river, and making an occasional trip into the interior, the dogs of war were let loose, and the curtain rose on the darkest tragedy of the nineteenth century.

The comic and the tragic are inextricably mingled in this world. I believe that this is no accident, but, like everything else, a special arrangement. "All fun makes man a fool," but "all sorrow" makes him a desperado. The feeling of anxiety aroused by the war news was, I may say, mitigated by the manner of its announcement.

"Sir," cried Lancey, bursting into the cabin one afternoon while I was preparing for a trip ashore, "the Roossians 'as declared war, an' the whole country is gettin' hup in harms!"

Of course I had been well aware for some time past that there was a prospect, nay, a probability, of war; but I had not allowed myself to believe it, because I have a strong natural tendency to give civilised men credit for more sense than they appear to possess. That Russia would really draw the sword, and sacrifice millions of treasure, and thousands of her best young lives, to accomplish an object that could be more easily and surely attained by diplomacy, with the expenditure of little money and no bloodshed, seemed to me incredible. That the other European nations should allow this state of things to come to pass, seemed so ridiculous that I had all along shut my eyes to facts, and proceeded on my voyage in the confidence of a peaceful solution of the "Eastern question."

"In days of old," I said to my skipper, in our last conversation on this subject, which we were fond of discussing, "the nations were less educated than now, and less imbued perhaps with the principles of the peace-teaching gospel, which many of them profess to believe; but now the Christian world is almost out of its teens; intercommunication of ideas and interests is almost miraculously facile. Thought is well-nigh instantaneously flashed from hemisphere to hemisphere, if not from pole to pole; commerce is so highly cultivated that international exhibitions of the raw material and the fabrics of all nations are the order of the day; while good-will between man and man—to say nothing of woman—is so prevalent, that I really find it hard to believe in the possibility of a great European war."

"Nevertheless," replied Mr Whitlaw, in a tone of cynicism, to which at times he gave pretty free indulgence, "the Crimean war occurred in the nineteenth century, and the American civil war, and the young widows of the Franco-Prussian war are not yet grey-haired, while their children have scarcely reached their teens. Truly, civilisation and the progress of knowledge, which men boast of so much, seem to be of little value."

I pointed out to Mr Whitlaw that he was wrong in supposing that civilisation is of little value. "If you compare the condition of the United States or England," I said, "with that of the Red Indians of your own land, or with the semi-barbarous states of Asia, you must allow that civilisation has done much. It seems to me that the fault of mankind lies in expecting too much of that condition. Civilisation teaches man how to make the world most comfortable to himself and to his fellows; but there is a higher attainment than that, and it is only Christianity which can teach man how to sacrifice himself for others, and, in so doing, to attain the same ends as those arrived at by civilisation, with more important and lasting ends in addition."

"Well, then, on that principle," objected the skipper, "you ought to expect war just now, for there is very little Christianity going that I can see, though plenty of civilisation."

"On these points we differ, Mr Whitlaw," said I, "for there seems to me very little civilisation at present, considering the age of the world; and, on the other hand, there is much genuine Christianity,—more, I believe, than meets the careless or the jaundiced eye. However, now that war *has* been declared, it becomes necessary that we should get out of the Danube as fast as possible."

Accordingly, the yacht's head was turned eastward, and we descended rapidly with the stream. My intention was good, but the result was disastrous; not an unwonted state of things, the best intentions in human affairs being frequently doomed to miscarry.

I must ask the reader now to turn aside with me from my own personal adventures, to events which had occurred near the banks of the Pruth,—the river that divides Russia from Turkey.

Here, on Tuesday, the 24th of April 1877, a scene of the utmost animation and excitement prevailed. The Emperor of "all the Russias" was about to review his troops previous to the declaration of war on Turkey. Up to that time, of course, war had been expected—as regards the army, eagerly desired; but no declaration had absolutely been made.

Ungheni, where the railway crosses the Pruth, and not far from Kischeneff, the capital of Bessarabia, was fixed on as the spot where the grand review should take place.

Great were the preparations for the reception of his Majesty, for whether "majesty" be right or wrong, majesty must be honoured and cheered. Majesty, male or female, represents *power*, and power *must* be treated with respect, nay, ought to be so treated—when it behaves itself!

There is something overwhelmingly grand in multitude. Humanity cannot resist the influence. It is quite clear that the human race were meant to be gregarious. What were the orator without his multitude? I might go further, and ask, What were the multitude without its orator? Flags and banners waved, and ribbons rippled that day in Bessarabia, for the serried legions of Russia marched in almost unending columns towards Ungheni, on the Roumanian frontier, and, after they had passed, the Emperor himself made for the same point with the Grand Duke Nicholas, and the Czarewitch, and General Ignatieff, and the Minister of War, and many other dignitaries of the empire, with a numerous and gorgeous staff.

The day was magnificent. The people who streamed out to see the review were enthusiastic. Perhaps, if they had been Bulgarian peasantry, and had been able to foresee the future, their enthusiasm would not have been so great. Yet I do not say that their enthusiasm was misplaced. They saw a nation's chivalry assembled to fight and die, if need be, in the nation's cause, with its Emperor to patronise, and its nobles to lead the legions on, in all of which there was ground for real enthusiasm.

Among the regiments that marched that day to Ungheni was one to which I would draw special attention. It was not much better, perhaps, than the others, but it was a good typical Russian regiment, and had a commander at its head who looked as if he could do it justice. They marched at a smart pace, four miles an hour, with a long, dogged, steady tramp that was clumsy to look at, but seemed likely to last. Few of the men were tall, but they were burly, square-set fellows, broad of shoulder, deep of chest, and smart of limb. They wore a French-like blue cap, with a red band round it, and a blue tunic, with loose blue trousers stuffed into boots that reached the knee. Their knapsacks were hairy, and their belts black, the latter suggesting deliverance from that absurdity of old, pipeclay. Their great-coats, heavy and brown, were worn in a roll over the left shoulder, and each man carried his own kettle, the latter being suggestive of tea and tuck-in, followed by tobacco and turn-in.

Among these warriors, in his proper position, marched a noteworthy young lieutenant. He was my old college chum and brother-in-law to be, Nicholas Naranovitsch, head and shoulders over his fellows, straight as a poplar, proud as a peacock, and modest as an untried man ought to be.

The spot for the review was well chosen, on a gentle undulating hillside, which enabled the spectators to see the whole army at once. The weather was bright and sunny, as I have said, and the glitter of uniforms and thousands of bayonets with the broad blaze reflected from a long line of polished field-pieces, sent a thrill through many a heart, suggesting "glory." There were a few hearts also, no doubt, to whom they suggested the natural end for which these glorious things were called together—blood and murder, national ruination, broken constitutions, desolated homes, and sudden death.

Holiday reviews are common enough all over the world, but this was no holiday review. Every one knew that it was the prelude to war, and there was an appropriate gravity and silence in the conduct of spectators. It was deeply impressive, too, to watch the long lines and masses of troops,—each unit full of youth, strength, energy, enthusiasm, hope,—standing perfectly silent, absolutely motionless, like statues, for full an hour and a half. Their deep silence and immobility seemed to produce a sympathetic condition in the spectators. There was no laughing, jesting, or "chaff" among them.

Even when the Emperor arrived there was no cheering. A greater than the Emperor had overawed them. They merely swayed open and took off hats deferentially as he passed. It was not till he began to ride round the lines with his brilliant staff that the silence was broken by music and cheers.

Of the review itself I will not speak. That, and the three-quarters of an hour mass which followed, being over, a murmur of expectation ran through the crowd and along the ranks like a solemn growl. Then there was a deep, intense silence, which was faintly broken by the Bishop of Kischeneff reading the manifesto. He had not read far, when sobs were heard. It was the voice of the Emperor Alexander, who prided himself on the fact that the glory of his reign had hitherto been its peaceful character. They say that it had been his boast and hope that he should finish it without a war. Previously he had said to the troops: "I have done everything in my power to avoid war and bloodshed. Nobody can say we have not been patient, or that the war has been of our seeking. We have practised patience to the last degree, but there comes a time when even patience must end. When that time comes, I know that the young Russian army of to-day will not show itself unworthy of the fame which the old army won in days gone by."

What the "young army" thought of the fame of its elder brother, as well as of the sobs of its present Emperor, may be gathered from the fact that it went all but mad with enthusiasm! When the Bishop finished reading, there went up a wild and universal shout of joy of exultation, of triumph, of relief, as though a great weight of suspense had been lifted from the hearts of the multitude. It spread through the army like light, and was raised again and again, until the very vault of heaven seemed to thunder, while the soldiers tossed their caps in the air, or twirled them on their bayonets for several minutes.

Then the *ordre du jour* of the Grand Duke Nicholas, commander-in-chief of the army, was read to every battalion, squadron, and battery, and the day's work was done. The right was legally and constitutionally granted to some hundreds of thousands of young men to go forth and slaughter, burn, and destroy, to their hearts' content—in other words, to "gather laurels."

It was a sad day's work—sad for Turkey, sad for Russia, sad for Europe, and especially sad for the women, children, and old people of the theatre of the future war. It was a good day's work for nobody and for nothing; but it was the legitimate outcome of work that had been going on for years before.

In pondering over the matter since, I have often been led to ask myself with considerable surprise, Why did this war occur—who wanted it? It is quite plain that Europe did not, equally plain that Turkey did not, still more plain that the Emperor Alexander did not, for he wept at the prospect of it "like a child." Who, then, *did* desire and cause it? There are some things in this remarkable world that no man can understand. At all events I cannot. When I put the same question, long afterwards, to my dear and ever-sagacious mother, she replied, "Do you not think, Jeff; that perhaps the men in power, somewhere, wanted it and caused it? There are some countries, you know, where the *people* are mere chessmen, who have nothing whatever to do or say in the management of their own affairs, and are knocked about, wisely or foolishly as the case may be, by the *men in power*. England herself was in that sad case once, if we are to believe our school histories, and some of the European nations seem to be only now struggling slowly out of that condition, while others are still in bondage."

I think my mother was right. After much consideration, I have come to the conclusion that war is usually, though not always, caused by a few ambitious men in power at the head of enslaved or semi-enslaved nations. Not always, I repeat, because free nations, being surrounded by savage, barbarous, and semi-free, are sometimes wheedled, dragged, or forced into war in spite of themselves.

After the review some of the regiments started directly for the frontier.

Nicholas Naranovitsch was summoned to the presence of his colonel. Nicholas was very young and inexperienced; nevertheless, during the brief period in which he had served, he had shown himself possessed of so much ability and wisdom that he was already selected to go on a secret mission. What that mission was he never told me. One result of it, however, was, that he and I had a most unexpected meeting on the Danube in very peculiar circumstances.

Chapter Eight
Treats of Torpedoes, Terrible Catastrophe, Unexpected Meetings, and Such Like

To return to my personal experiences. It now became a matter of the deepest importance that we should get out of the river before the Russian army reached its banks and stopped the navigation. The weather, however, was against us. It rained a great deal, and the nights were very dark. The swollen current, it is true, was in our favour; nevertheless, as we had already spent several weeks in ascending the river, it was clear that we should have to race against time in retracing our course.

One dark night about the end of May, as we were approaching the Lower Danube, and speculating on the probability of our getting out in time, I gave orders to run into a creek and cast anchor, intending to land and procure a supply of fresh meat, of which we had run short.

"Better wait for daylight, sir," suggested my skipper. "It's not unlikely, in these days of torpedoes, that the entrance to places may be guarded by them."

The skipper was so far right. The entrance to unimportant creeks, indeed, had not been guarded, but the Russians had already laid down many torpedoes in the river to protect them from Turkish ironclads while engaged in constructing their pontoon bridges. He had scarcely made the remark, when I was half stunned by a shock under my feet, which seemed to rend the yacht asunder. There followed a terrific report, and the deck was instantly deluged with water. There could be no doubt what had occurred. We had touched a torpedo, and the yacht was already sinking. We rushed to our little boat in consternation, but before we could lower it, our trim little vessel went down, stern foremost.

For a few moments there was a horrible rushing sound in my ears, and I felt that I could hold my breath no longer when my head rose above the surface. I struck out with a gasp of relief, which was, as it were, echoed close to me. I looked round, as well as darkness and water would allow, and observed an object floating near me. I pushed towards it, and just as I caught hold, I heard a panting voice exclaim—

"'Eaven be praised!"

"Amen," said I; "is that you, Lancey?"

"It is, sir, an' I'm right glad to 'ear your voice. Cetch a tight 'old, sir; it's big enough for two."

"What is it?" I asked.

"One of the 'en-coops," said Lancey.

"It's too small for two, I fear," said I, seizing hold of it.

"Hall right, sir; it'll 'old us both. I can swim."

Clinging to our frail support we were hurried by the rapid current we knew not whither, for, although the moon was in the sky, it was so covered with black clouds that we could not see whether we were being swept towards the shore or into the middle of the stream. Besides this, the wind was driving the rain and dashing the water into our eyes continuously.

"Lancey," I gasped, "it is u—useless to let ourselves be—swe—swept about at the will of chance currents. The river is very wi-wide. Let us place ourselves side by side—and—strike—out—in—the—same—d'rection. Uniformity of action—necessary—in desp'r't situations!"

Lancey at once acted on my suggestion, gasping that, "Haction of—of—hany kind would tend to—to—k–p limbs warm."

We proceeded in silence for some minutes, when I observed the masts and rigging of several vessels drawn faintly against the dark sky. They were considerably to our right, and the current was evidently bearing us away from them.

"A strong effort now, Lancey," said I, "and we may reach them."

I could feel, as well as see, that my faithful servant exerted himself to the utmost.

As we approached the vessels, their huge black hulls loomed up out of the dark surroundings, and were pictured against the sky, which, dark though it was, had not the intense blackness of the vessels themselves.

We passed the nearest one within twenty yards.

"Let go, sir, and swim for it," cried Lancey.

"No, no!" I cried earnestly, "never let go your—"

I stopped, for Lancey had already let go, and made a dash for the nearest ship. I heard him hail, and saw the flashing of lights for a moment, then all was dark again and silent, as I was hurried onward. The feeling of certainty that he could not have been saved with so rapid a current sweeping him past, filled my mind with intense anxiety. Just then I felt a shock. The hen-coop had been driven against another vessel, which I had not observed.

I tried to grasp her, but failed. I uttered a loud cry, not with the expectation that the crew of the vessel could save me,—that I knew to be impossible,—but in the hope that they might be ready for Lancey should he be carried close to them.

Then I was dragged onward by the powerful current, and tossed like a cork on the river. I had observed in passing that the vessel was a Turkish ironclad, and came to the conclusion that I had passed the Turkish flotilla, which I knew was at that time lying near the fortress of Matchin.

At the very time that I was being thus driven about by the wild waters, and praying to God for the deliverance of my comrades and myself— sometimes audibly, more frequently in spirit—another and a very different scene was taking place, not far off, on the Roumanian shore.

The wind had fallen; the clouds that covered the moon had just thinned enough to render darkness visible, and nothing was to be heard save the continual croaking of the frogs, which are very large and numerous in the marshes of the Danube, when four boats pushed off and proceeded quickly, yet quietly, up the river.

No men were visible in these boats, no sails, no oars. They were "steam launches," and were destined for a night attack on the flotilla which I had just passed. Their crews were covered nearly from stem to stern by iron bullet-proof awnings, which, as well as the boats, were painted black. The engines were so constructed as to make the least possible amount of noise, and when speed was reduced no sound was heard save a dull throbbing that was almost drowned by the croaking frogs.

It was a little after midnight when these boats set out—two being meant to attack, and two to remain in support. They had seven miles of river to traverse before reaching the enemy, and it was while they were in the midst of their voyage that I chanced to meet them, clinging to my hen-coop. They came so straight at me that I was on the point of being run down by the leading boat, when I gave a sharp "halloo!"

It was replied to by one that indicated surprise, and was decidedly English in tone. Next moment the launch scraped violently against my raft, and I saw a hand extended. Grasping it, I was drawn quickly into the boat. Another hand instantly covered my mouth, and I was thrust down into the bottom of the boat with considerable violence. Being allowed to raise myself a little, the chink of a dark lantern was opened, and the light streamed full upon me. It at the same time lighted up several faces, the inquiring eyes of which gazed at me intently. A stern voice demanded who I was.

Just then a gleam of light fell on a countenance which gazed at me with open-mouthed and open-eyed amazement. It was that of Nicholas Naranovitsch! I was just going to answer, when the sight of him struck me dumb.

Nicholas touched the officer who had questioned me on the shoulder, and whispered in his ear. He at once closed the lantern, leaving us all in total darkness, while Nicholas caught me by the arm, and, making me sit down on a box of some kind beside him, gave vent to his surprise in hurried, broken whispers.

A short time sufficed to explain how it was that I came to be there. Then he began to tell me about his being sent on a secret expedition, and his having obtained leave to join in this midnight attack by torpedo-boats, when a low stern order to be silent compelled him to stop.

From that moment he and I remained perfectly quiet and observant.

After an hour's steaming the Russian launches came to the immediate neighbourhood of the enemy's flotilla, and the engines were slowed.

Each boat was armed with two torpedoes attached to the end of two long spars, which moved on pivots, and could also be dipped so that the torpedoes should be sunk ten feet under water at any moment. These torpedoes—each being about twenty inches long, by about fifteen in diameter—had a double action. They could be fired by "contact," or, in the event of that failing, by electricity. The latter mode could be accomplished by an electric battery in a little box in the stern of each boat, with which a long cable, a quarter of an inch thick, of fine wires twisted together, connected each torpedo.

All this, of course, I learned afterwards. At the time, sitting in almost total darkness, I knew nothing more than that we were bound on a torpedo expedition. I could scarcely persuade myself that it was not a dream, but my numbed frame and drenched garments were too real to be doubted, and then I fancied it must be a special judgment to punish me for the part I had taken in the improvement of these terrible implements of war.

Despite the slowing of the engines, and the dead silence that prevailed, the boats were observed by the Turkish sentinels as we approached.

"Who goes there?" was demanded in the Turkish language.

The launch in which I sat was the first to approach, but the officer in command took no notice and made no reply.

Again the sentinel challenged—perhaps doubting whether in the darkness his eyes had not deceived him as well as his ears. Still no answer was given.

The darkness was not now quite so intense, and it was evident that longer concealment was impossible; when, therefore, the challenge was given a third time, our Russian commander replied, and I thought I observed a grim smile on his countenance as he said in Turkish, "Friends!"

The sentinel, however, seeing that we continued to advance, expressed his disbelief in our friendship by firing at us.

Then there began an uproar the like of which I had never before conceived. Being very near the Turkish monitor at the time, we distinctly heard the clattering of feet, the shout and rush of sailors, and the hurried commands to prepare for action. There was no lack of promptitude or energy on board the vessel. There was some lack of care or discipline, however, for I heard the order for the bow gun to be fired given three times, and heard the click of the answering hammer three times in little more than as many seconds, betokening a determined miss-fire. But if the bow gun *had* gone off, and sent one of us to the bottom, there would still have been three boats left to seal the vessel's fate.

At the fourth order a globe of flame leaped from the iron side of the monitor and a heavy shot went harmlessly over our heads. Shouts and lights in the other vessels showed that the entire flotilla was aroused.

I observed that the launch next to ours drew off and we advanced alone, while the other two remained well behind, ready to support. A sharp fusillade had now been opened on us, and we heard the bullets pattering on our iron screen like unearthly hail, but in spite of this the launch darted like a wasp under the monitor's bow. The torpedoes were arranged so as to be detached from their spars at any moment and affixed by long light chains to any part of an attacked ship. Round a rope hanging from the bow of the vessel one of these chains was flung, and the torpedo was dropped from the end of the spar, while the launch shot away, paying out the electric cable as she went. But this latter was not required. The torpedo swung round by the current and hit the ship with sufficient violence. It exploded, and the column of water that instantly burst from under the monitor half filled and nearly swamped us as we sped away. The noise was so great that it nearly drowned for an instant the shouts, cries, and firing of the Turks. The whole flotilla now began in alarm to fire at random on their unseen foes, and sometimes into each other.

Meanwhile the launches, like vicious mosquitoes, kept dodging about, struck often, though harmlessly, by small shot, but missed by the large guns.

Our commander now perceived that the monitor he had hit was sinking, though slowly, at the bows. He shouted, therefore, to the second launch to go at her. She did so at once; slipped in, under the fire and smoke that belched from her side, and fixed another torpedo to her stern in the same manner as the former. The officer in charge perceived, however, that the current would not drive it against the ship. He therefore shot away for a hundred yards,—the extent of his electric cable,—and then fired the charge. A terrible explosion took place. Parts of the ship were blown into the air, and a huge plank came down on the Russian launch, like an avenging thunderbolt, pierced the iron screen, which had so effectually resisted the bullets, and passed between two sailors without injuring either. It did no further damage, however, and when the crew turned to look at their enemy, they saw the great ironclad in the act of sinking. In a few minutes nothing of her was left above water except her masts. The crew were drowned, with the exception of a few who escaped by swimming.

By this time it was daybreak, and our danger, within near range of the other monitors, of course became very great. Just then an incident occurred which might have proved fatal to us. Our screw fouled, and the boat became unmanageable. Observing this, a Turkish launch from one of the monitors bore down upon us. One of our sailors, who chanced to be a good diver, jumped over the side and cleared the screw. Meanwhile the men opened so heavy fire on the enemy's launch that she veered off, and a few minutes later we were steaming down the Danube towards the place from which the boats had set forth on their deadly mission.

"That was gloriously done, wasn't it?" said Nicholas to me with enthusiasm, after the first blaze of excitement began to abate;—"one of the enemy's biggest ironclads sent to the bottom, with all her crew, at the trifling expense of two or three hundred pounds' weight of powder, and not a man injured on our side!"

I looked earnestly in my friend's handsome face for a few seconds.

"Yes," said I, slowly; "many thousands of pounds' worth of human property destroyed, months of human labour and ingenuity wasted, and hundreds of young lives sacrificed, to say nothing of relatives bereaved and souls sent into eternity before their time—truly, if *that* is glory, it has been gloriously done!"

"Bah! Jeff," returned Nicholas, with a smile; "you're not fit to live in this world, you should have had a special one created for yourself. But come, let me hear how you came to be voyaging *à la Boyton* on the Danube."

We at once began a rapid fire of question and reply. Among other things, Nicholas informed me that the two boats which had accomplished this daring feat were commanded by Lieutenants Dubasoff and Thestakoff, one with a crew of fourteen, the other of nine, men.

"The world is changing, Nicholas," said I, as we landed. "That the wooden walls of Old England have passed away has long been acknowledged by every one, but it seems to me now that her iron walls are doomed to extinction, and that ere long the world's war-navies will consist of nothing but torpedo-boats, and her wars will become simply tournaments therewith."

"It may be so," said Nicholas gaily, as he led the way to his quarters. "It may be that extremes shall meet at last, and we shall be reduced by sheer necessity to universal peace."

"That would be glorious indeed," said I, "though it would have the uncomfortable effect of leaving you without employment."

"Well, in the meantime," he rejoined, "as you are without employment just now, you must consider yourself my prisoner, for of course you cannot remain among us without passport, profession, purpose, or business of any kind. To be shot for a spy is your legitimate due just now. But we shall want surgeons soon, and newspaper correspondence is not a bad business in these times; come, I'll see what can be done for you."

Chapter Nine
In which Lancey is Tried, Suspected, Blown Up, Captured, Half-Hanged, Delivered, and Astonished

We must turn now to poor Lancey, from whom I parted in the waters of the Danube, but with whose fate and doings I did not become acquainted until long afterwards.

As I had anticipated, he missed the vessel of the Turkish flotilla towards which he had struck out, but fortunately succeeded in grappling the chain cable of that which lay next to it, and the crew of which, as the reader will recollect, I had roused by a shout in passing.

Lancey soon let the Turks know where he was. A boat being lowered, he was taken on board, but it was clear to him that he was regarded with much suspicion. They hurried him before the officer in charge of the deck, who questioned him closely. The poor fellow now found that his knowledge of the Turkish language was much slighter than, in the pride of his heart, while studying with me, he had imagined. Not only did he fail to understand what was said to him, but the dropping of h's and the introduction of r's in wrong places rendered his own efforts at reply abortive. In these circumstances one of the sailors who professed to talk English was sent for.

This man, a fine stalwart Turk, with a bushy black beard, began his duties as interpreter with the question—

"Hoosyoo?"

"Eh? say that again," said Lancey, with a perplexed look.

"Hoosyoo?" repeated the Moslem, with emphasis.

"Hoosyoo," repeated Lancey slowly. "Oh, I see," (with a smile of sudden intelligence,) "who's you? Just so. I'm Jacob Lancey, groom in the family of Mrs Jeff Childers, of Fagend, in the county of Devonshire, England."

This having been outrageously misunderstood by the Turk, and misinterpreted to the officer, the next question was—

"Wessyoocumfro?"

"Wessyoocumfro?"

Again Lancey repeated the word, and once more, with a smile of sudden intelligence, exclaimed, "Ah, I see: w'ere's you come from? Well, I last come from the water, 'avin' previously got into it through the hupsettin' of our boat."

Lancey hereupon detailed the incident which had left him and me struggling in the water, but the little that was understood by the Turks was evidently not believed; and no wonder, for by that time the Russians had been laying down torpedoes in all directions about the Danube, to prevent the enemy from interfering with their labours at the pontoon bridges. The Turkish sailors were thus rendered suspicious of every unusual circumstance that came under their notice. When, therefore, a big, powerful, and rather odd-looking man was found clinging to one of their cables, they at once set him down as an unsuccessful torpedoist, and a careful search was instantly made round the vessel as a precaution.

Meanwhile Lancey was led rather roughly down to the cabin to be questioned by the captain.

The cabin, although very luxurious in its fittings, was not so richly ornate as had been anticipated by the English groom, whose conceptions of everything had been derived from the Arabian Nights' Entertainments, or rather from a fanciful imagination fed by that romantic work. The appearance of the Turkish captain, however, and the brightly-coloured costume of an officer who sat by his side, were sufficiently striking and Oriental.

On Lancey being placed before him, the captain turned and said a few words to the officer at his side, who was a splendid fellow, in the prime of life, with a square bony frame and red beard, which harmonised, if it did not contrast, with his scarlet fez and blue tassel. A rich Eastern shawl encircled his waist, from the folds of which peeped the handles of a brace of pistols.

He looked at the dripping Englishman earnestly and sternly for a few moments, and the slightest tinge of a smile lighted his grave countenance as he said in broken, but sufficiently fluent English—

"The captin do want you to repeat vat you have say on deck."

Lancey repeated it, with a considerable number of additions, but no variations.

After translating it all, and listening to something in reply, the officer turned again to Lancey.

"The captin," he said, with quiet gravity, "bids me tell to you that you is a liar."

Lancey flushed deeply. "I would tell *you*," he said, with a frown, "to tell the captain that 'e's another, on'y that would show I was as bad-mannered as 'imself."

"If I do tells him zat," returned the officer, "you should have your head cutted off immediately."

Lancey's indignation having already half-cooled, and his memory being refreshed just then with some vivid remembrances of the Eastern mode of summoning black slaves by the clapping of hands, followed by the flying off of heads or the prompt application of bowstrings to necks, he said, still however with an offended air—

"Well then, tell 'im what you like, hall I've got to say is that I've told the plain truth, an' 'e's welcome to believe it or not as 'e likes."

Without the slightest change in his grave countenance, or his appearing in the least degree offended by Lancey's free-and-easy manner, the red-bearded officer again turned to address the captain. Lancey now observed that the latter replied with a degree of deferential respect which seemed unnatural in mere brother officers.

"You is regarded as a spy," said the red-beard, turning once more to Lancey, and fixing his cold grey eye intently on him, as if to read his thoughts.

"No, I ain't a spy," returned the unfortunate man, somewhat bitterly, "nor never mean to be. 'Ang me if you like. I've nothink more to say."

Neither the captain nor the red-bearded officer replied, but the former waved his hand, and the two sailors who had led Lancey to the cabin again seized him and led him away, more roughly than before. The free spirit of my poor servant resented this unnecessary rudeness, and he felt a strong inclination to fight, but discretion, or some faint remembrance of scimitars and bowstrings, induced him to submit.

Full well did he know what was the fatal doom of a spy, and a sinking of the heart came over him as he thought of immediate execution. At the very least, he counted on being heavily ironed and thrust into the darkest recesses of the hold. Great, then, was his surprise when the man who had at first acted as interpreter took him below and supplied him with a dry shirt and a pair of trousers.

Thankfully accepting these, and standing between two guns, he put them on.

"Who is the hofficer with the red beard?" he asked, while thus engaged.

The interpreter seemed unwilling to answer at first, but, on a repetition of the question replied—

"Pasha."

"Pasha, eh? Ah, that accounts for the respect of the cap'n—rather shorter in the legs these 'ere than I could 'ave wished; 'owever, beggars, they say, mustn't be—well, they're wide enough anyhow.—A Pasha, is 'e? Don't look like a sailor, though. Is 'e a sailor?"

"No," replied the interpreter sharply.

"Well, well, no offence meant," said Lancey, buttoning his shirt. "If you don't feel commoonicative *I* won't trouble you, no more than to thank 'ee for the shirt an' trousers, which the latter bein' dry is a blessin', though they air a trifle short in the legs an' wide in the 'ips."

After this Lancey was supplied with food.

While he was eating it he was startled by sudden rushing and shouting, which was immediately followed by the discharge of musketry on deck. He sprang up, and seeing that the Turkish sailors were grasping their arms and swarming up the hatchways, he mingled with one of the streams. No one paid any attention to him. At that moment he felt a shock which he afterwards described as resembling an earthquake or the blowing up of a powder-magazine. Part of the planking near to where he stood was shattered. Some of the guns appeared almost to leap for an instant a few inches into the air. Gaining the deck he ascertained that an attack of Russian torpedo-boats was going on. It was, in fact, the attack which I have already described, the monitor by which Lancey was rescued being that which had been selected by the Russian commander as his victim.

When the second torpedo exploded, as already described, Lancey was standing near the gangway, and saw that the men were lowering the boats in urgent haste, for the vessel was evidently sinking.

"Yoos know 'bout dat," said a stern voice near him. At the same moment he was seized by the interpreter and another man, who made an effort to hurl him into the sea. But Lancey was strong, and tenacious of life. Before a third sailor, who was about to aid his comrades, could act, the red bearded officer appeared with the captain and was about to descend into the boat when he observed Lancey struggling in the grasp of the sailors.

"Spy!" he exclaimed in the Turkish tongue, "you must not escape. Get into the boat."

The sailors fell back. Lancey, not sure whether to regard this as temporary deliverance or his death-warrant, hesitated, but at a sign from the Pasha he was collared by five or six men and hurled into the bottom of the boat, where he lay, half-stunned, while they rowed towards the shore. Before reaching it, however, he was still doomed to rough handling, for one of the shots from the large guns, which were fired almost at random from the flotilla, accidentally struck the boat and sent it to the bottom.

Lancey was a good swimmer. The cold water restored him to full vigour, and he struck out boldly for the shore. He soon left the boat's crew behind, with the exception of one man who kept close to his side all the way. As they neared the shore, however, this man suddenly cried out like one who is drowning. A second time he cried, and the gurgling of his voice told its own tale. The stout Englishman could not bear to leave a human being to perish, whether friend or foe. He swam towards the drowning man and supported him till their feet touched bottom.

Then, perceiving that he was able to stagger along unassisted, Lancey pushed hurriedly from his side in the hope of escaping from any of the crew who might reach land, for they were evidently the reverse of friendly.

He landed among a mass of bulrushes. Staggering through them, and nearly sinking at every step, he gradually gained firmer footing.

"Ah, Jacob," he muttered to himself, pausing for a few minutes' rest, "little did you think you'd git into such an 'orrible mess as this w'en you left 'ome. Sarves you right for quittin' your native land."

With this comforting reflection he pushed on again, and soon found himself on a road which led towards a town, or village, whose lights were distinctly visible.

What should he do? The village was on the Bulgarian side, and the natives, if not enemies, would of course become so on learning from any of the saved men of the monitor who he was. To swim across the Danube he felt was, after his recent exertions, impossible. To remain where he was would be to court death among the frogs.

Lancey was a prompt man. Right or wrong, his conclusions were soon come to and acted on. He decided to go straight to the village and throw himself on the hospitality of the people. In half an hour he found himself once more a prisoner! Worse than that; the interpreter, who was among the men saved from the wreck, chanced to discover him and denounced him as a spy. The mood in which the Turks then were was not favourable to him. He was promptly locked up, and about daybreak next morning was led out to execution.

Poor Lancey could scarcely credit his senses. He had often read of such things, but had never fully realised that they were true. That he, an innocent man, should be hung off-hand, without trial by jury or otherwise, in the middle of the nineteenth century, was incredible! There was something terribly real, however, in the galling tightness of the rope that confined his arms, in the troop of stern horsemen that rode on each side of him, and in the cart with ropes, and the material for a scaffold, which was driven in front towards the square of the town. There was no sign of pity in the people or of mercy in the guards.

The contrivance for effecting the deadly operation was simple in the extreme,—two large triangles with a pole resting on them, and a strong rope attached thereto. There was no "drop." An empty box sufficed, and this was to be kicked away when the rope was round his neck.

Even up to the point of putting the rope on, Lancey would not believe.

Reader, have you ever been led out to be hanged? If not, be thankful! The conditions of mind consequent on that state of things is appalling. It is also various.

Men take it differently, according to their particular natures; and as the nature of man is remarkably complex, so the variation in his feeling is exceedingly diverse.

There are some who, in such circumstances, give way to abject terror. Others, whose nervous system is not so finely strung and whose sense of justice is strong, are filled with a rush of indignation, and meet their fate with savage ferocity, or with dogged and apparent indifference. Some, rising above sublunary matters, shut their eyes to all around and fix their thoughts on that world with which they may be said to be more immediately connected, namely, the next.

Lancey went through several of these phases. When the truth first really came home to him he quailed like an arrant coward. Then a sense of violated justice supervened. If at that moment Samson's powers had been his, he would have snapped the ropes that bound him like packthread, and would have cut the throat of every man around him. When he was placed upon the substitute for a "block," and felt by a motion of his elbows his utter powerlessness, the dogged and indifferent state came on, but it did not last. It could not. His Christian training was adverse to it.

"Come," he mentally exclaimed, "it is God's will. Quit you like a man, Jacob—and die!"

There is no doubt that in this frame the brave fellow would have passed away if he had not been roused by the loud clattering of horses' feet as a cavalcade of glittering Turkish officers dashed through the square. In front of these he observed the red-bearded officer who had acted as interpreter in the cabin of the Turkish monitor.

There came a sudden gush of hope! Lancey knew not his name, but in a voice of thunder he shouted—

"'Elp! 'elp! 'allo! Pasha! Redbeard!—"

The executioner hastened his work, and stopped the outcry by tightening the rope.

But "Redbeard" had heard the cry. He galloped towards the place of execution, recognised the supposed spy, and ordered him to be released, at the same time himself cutting the rope with a sweep of his sword.

The choking sensation which Lancey had begun to feel was instantly relieved. The rope was removed from his neck, and he was gently led from the spot by a soldier of the Pasha's escort, while the Pasha himself galloped coolly away with his staff.

If Lancey was surprised at the sudden and unexpected nature of his deliverance, he was still more astonished at the treatment which he thereafter experienced from the Turks. He was taken to one of the best hotels in the town, shown into a handsome suite of apartments, and otherwise treated with marked respect, while the best of viands and the choicest of wines were placed before him.

This made him very uncomfortable. He felt sure that some mistake had occurred, and would willingly have retired, if possible, to the hotel kitchen or pantry; but the waiter, to whom he modestly suggested something of the sort, did not understand a word of English and could make nothing of Lancey's Turkish. He merely shook his head and smiled respectfully, or volunteered some other article of food. The worthy groom therefore made up his mind to hold his tongue and enjoy himself as long as it lasted.

"When I wakes up out o' this remarkable and not unpleasant dream," he muttered, between the whiffs of his cigarette, one evening after dinner, "I'll write it out fair, an' 'ave it putt in the *Daily Noos* or the *Times*."

But the dream lasted so long that Lancey began at last to fear he should never awake from it. For a week he remained at that hotel, faring sumptuously, and quite unrestrained as to his movements, though he could not fail to observe that he was closely watched and followed wherever he went.

"Is it a Plenipotentiary or a furrin' Prime Minister they take me for?" he muttered to himself over a mild cigar of the finest quality, "or mayhap they think I'm a Prince in disguise! But then a man in disguise ain't known, and therefore can't be follered, or, if he was, what would be the use of his disguise? No, I can't make it out, no'ow."

Still less, by any effort of his fancy or otherwise, could he make out why, after a week's residence at the village in question, he was ordered to prepare for a journey.

This order, like all others, was conveyed to him by signs. Some parts of his treatment had been managed otherwise. When, for instance, on the night of his deliverance, it had been thought desirable that his garments should be better and more numerous, his attendants or keepers had removed his old wardrobe and left in its place another, which, although it comprehended trousers, savoured more of the East than the West. Lancey submitted to this, as to everything else, like a true philosopher. Generally, however, the wishes of those around him were conveyed by means of signs.

On the morning of his departure, a small valise, stuffed with the few articles of comfort which he required, and a change of apparel, was placed at his bed-side. The hotel attendant, who had apparently undertaken the management of him, packed this up in the morning, having somewhat pointedly placed within it his *robe de nuit*. Thereafter the man bowed, smiled gravely, pointed to the door, beckoned him to follow, and left the room.

By that time Lancey had, as it were, given himself up. He acted with the unquestioning obedience of a child or a lunatic. Following his guide, he found a native cart outside with his valise in it. Beside the cart stood a good horse, saddled and bridled in the Turkish fashion. His hotel-attendant pointed to the horse and motioned to him to mount.

Then it burst upon Lancey that he was about to quit the spot, perhaps for ever, and, being a grateful fellow, he could not bear to part without making some acknowledgment.

"My dear Turk, or whatever you are," he exclaimed, turning to his attendant, "I'm sorry to say good-bye, an' I'm still more sorry to say that I've nothin' to give you. A ten-pun-note, if I 'ad it, would be but a small testimony of my feelin's, but I do assure you I 'av'n't got a rap."

In corroboration of this he slapped his empty pockets and shook his head. Then, breaking into a benignant smile, he shook hands with the waiter warmly, turned in silence, mounted his horse and rode off after the native cart, which had already started.

"You don't know where we're goin' to, I s'pose?" said Lancey to the driver of the cart.

The man stared, but made no reply.

"Ah, I thought not!" said Lancey; then he tried him in Turkish, but a shake of the head intimated the man's stupidity, or his interrogator's incapacity.

Journeying in silence over a flat marshy country, they arrived about mid-day at a small village, before the principal inn of which stood a number of richly-caparisoned chargers. Here Lancey found that he was expected to lunch and join the party, though in what capacity he failed to discover. The grave uncommunicative nature of the Turks had perplexed and disappointed him so often that he had at last resigned himself to his fate, and given up asking questions, all the more readily, perhaps, that his fate at the time chanced to be a pleasant one.

When the party had lunched, and were preparing to take the road, it became obvious that he was not regarded as a great man travelling incognito, for no one took notice of him save a Turk who looked more like a servant than an aristocrat. This man merely touched him on the shoulder and pointed to his horse with an air that savoured more of command than courtesy.

Lancey took the hint and mounted. He also kept modestly in rear. When the cavalcade was ready a distinguished-looking officer issued from the inn, mounted his charger, and at once rode away, followed by the others. He was evidently a man of rank.

For several days they journeyed, and during this period Lancey made several attempts at conversation with the only man who appeared to be aware of his existence—who, indeed, was evidently his guardian. But, like the rest, this man was taciturn, and all the information that could be drawn out of him was that they were going to Constantinople.

I hasten over the rest of the journey. On reaching the sea, they went on board a small steamer which appeared to have been awaiting them. In course of time they came in sight of the domes and minarets of Stamboul, the great city of the Sultans, the very heart of Europe's apple of discord.

It was evening, and the lights of the city were everywhere glittering like long lines of quivering gold down into the waters of the Bosporus. Here the party with which Lancey had travelled left him, without even saying good-bye,—all except his guardian, who, on landing, made signs that he was to follow, or, rather, to walk beside him. Reduced by this time to a thoroughly obedient slave, and satisfied that no mischief was likely to be intended by men who had treated him so well, Lancey walked through the crowded streets and bazaars of Constantinople as one in a dream, much more than half-convinced that he had got somehow into an "Arabian Night," the "entertainments" of which seemed much more real than those by which his imagination had been charmed in days of old.

Coming into a part of the city that appeared to be suburban, his keeper stopped before a building that seemed a cross between a barrack and a bird-cage. It was almost surrounded by a wall so high that it hid the building from view, except directly in front. There it could be seen, with its small hermetically-closed windows, each covered with a wooden trellis. It bore the aspect of a somewhat forbidding prison.

"Konak—palace," said the keeper, breaking silence for the first time.

"A konak; a palace! eh?" repeated Lancey, in surprise; "more like a jail, I should say. 'Owever, customs differ. Oos palace may it be, now?"

"Pasha; Sanda Pasha," replied the man, touching a spring or bell in the wall; "you goes in."

As he spoke, a small door was opened by an armed black slave, to whom he whispered a few words, and then, stepping back, motioned to his companion to enter.

"Arter you, sir," said Lancey, with a polite bow.

But as the man continued gravely to point, and the black slave to hold the door open, he forbore to press the matter, and stepped in. The gate was shut with a bang, followed by a click of bolts. He found, on looking round, that the keeper had been shut out, and he was alone with the armed negro.

"You're in for it now, Jacob my boy," muttered Lancey to himself, as he measured the negro with a sharp glance, and slowly turned up the wristband of his shirt with a view to prompt action. But the sable porter, far from meditating an assault, smiled graciously as he led the way to the principal door of the palace, or, as the poor fellow felt sure it must be, the prison.

Chapter Ten
Involves Lancey in Great Perplexities, which Culminate in a Vast Surprise

No sooner did the dark and unpretending door of Sanda Pasha's konak or palace open than Lancey's eyes were dazzled by the blaze of light and splendour within, and when he had entered, accustomed though he was to "good society" in England, he was struck dumb with astonishment. Perhaps the powerful contrast between the outside and the interior of this Eastern abode had something to do with the influence on his mind.

Unbridled luxury met his eyes in whatever direction he turned. There was a double staircase of marble; a court paved with mosaic-work of brilliant little stones; splendid rooms, the walls of which were covered with velvet paper of rich pattern and colour. Gilding glittered everywhere—on cornices, furniture, and ceilings, from which the eyes turned with double zest to the soft light of marble sculpture judiciously disposed on staircase and in chambers. There were soft sofas that appeared to embrace you as you sank into them; pictures that charmed the senses; here a bath of snow-white marble, there gushing fountains and jets of limpid water that appeared to play hide-and-seek among green leaves and lovely flowers, and disappeared mysteriously,—in short, everything tasteful and beautiful that man could desire. Of course Lancey did not take all this in at once. Neither did he realise the fact that the numerous soft-moving and picturesque attendants, black and white, whom he saw, were a mere portion of an army of servants, numbering upwards of a thousand souls, whom this Pasha retained. These did not include the members of his harem. He had upwards of a hundred cooks and two hundred grooms and coachmen. This household, it is said, consumed, among other things, nearly 7000 pounds of vegetables a day, and in winter there were 900 fires kindled throughout the establishment. (See note 1.)

But of all this, and a great deal more, Lancey had but a faint glimmering as he was led through the various corridors and rooms towards a central part of the building.

Here he was shown into a small but comfortable apartment, very Eastern in its character, with a mother-of-pearl table in one corner bearing some slight refreshment, and a low couch at the further end.

"Eat," said the black slave who conducted him. He spoke in English, and pointed to the table; "an' sleep," he added, pointing to the couch. "Sanda Pasha sees you de morrow."

With that he left Lancey staring in a bewildered manner at the door through which he had passed.

"Sanda Pasha," repeated the puzzled man slowly, "will see me 'de morrow,' will he? Well, if 'de morrow' ever comes, w'ich I doubt, Sanda Pasha will find 'e 'as made a most hegragious mistake of some sort. 'Owever that's 'is business, not mine."

Having comforted himself with this final reflection on the culminating event of the day, he sat down to the mother-of-pearl table and did full justice to the Pasha's hospitality by consuming the greater part of the viands thereon, consisting largely of fruits, and drinking the wine with critical satisfaction.

Next morning he was awakened by his black friend of the previous night, who spread on the mother-of-pearl table a breakfast which in its elegance appeared to be light, but which on close examination turned out, like many light things in this world, to be sufficiently substantial for an ordinary man.

Lancey now expected to be introduced to the Pasha, but he was mistaken. No one came near him again till the afternoon, when the black slave reappeared with a substantial dinner. The Pasha was busy, he said, and would see him in the evening. The time might have hung heavily on the poor man's hands, but, close to the apartment in which he was confined there was a small marble court, open to the sky, in which were richly-scented flowers and rare plants and fountains which leaped or trickled into tanks filled with gold-fish. In the midst of these things he sat or sauntered dreamily until the shades of evening fell. Then the black slave returned and beckoned him to follow.

He did so and was ushered into a delicious little boudoir, whose windows, not larger than a foot square, were filled with pink, blue, and yellow glass. Here, the door being softly shut behind him, Lancey found himself in the presence of the red-bearded officer whom he had met on board the Turkish monitor.

Redbeard, as Lancey called him, mentally, reclined on a couch and smoked a chibouk.

"Come here," he said gravely, in broken English. Lancey advanced into the middle of the apartment. "It vas you what blew'd up de monitor," he said sternly, sending a thick cloud of smoke from his lips.

"No, your—." Lancey paused. He knew not how to address his questioner, but, feeling that some term of respect was necessary, he coined a word for the occasion—

"No, your Pashaship, I did nothink of the sort. I'm as hinnocent of that ewent as a new-born babe."

"Vat is your name?"

"Lancey."

"Ha! your oder name."

"Jacob."

"Ho! *My* name is Sanda Pasha. You have hear of me before?"

"Yes, on board the Turkish monitor."

"Just so; but before zat, I mean," said the Pasha, with a keen glance.

Lancey was a bold and an honest man. He would not condescend to prevaricate.

"I'm wery sorry, your—your Pashaship, but, to tell the plain truth, I never *did* 'ear of you *before* that."

"Well, zat matters not'ing. I do go now to sup vid von friend, Hamed Pasha he is called. You go vid me. Go, get ready."

Poor Lancey opened his eyes in amazement, and began to stammer something about having nothing to get ready with, and a mistake being made, but the Pasha cut him short with another "Go!" so imperative that he was fain to obey promptly.

Having no change of raiment, the perplexed man did his best by washing his face and hands, and giving his hair and clothes an extra brush, to make himself more fit for refined society. On being called to rejoin the Pasha, he began to apologise for the style of his dress, but the peremptory despot cut him short by leading the way to his carriage, in which they were driven to the konak or palace of Hamed Pasha.

They were shown into a richly-furnished apartment where Hamed was seated on a divan, with several friends, smoking and sipping brandy and water, for many of these *eminent* followers of the Prophet pay about as little regard to the Prophet's rules as they do to the laws of European society.

Hamed rose to receive his brother Pasha, and Lancey was amazed to find that he was a Nubian, with thick lips, flat nose, and a visage as black as coal. He was also of gigantic frame, insomuch that he dwarfed the rest of the company, including Lancey himself.

Hamed had raised himself from a low rank in society to his present high position by dint of military ability, great physical strength, superior intelligence, reckless courage, and overflowing animal spirits. When Sanda Pasha entered he was rolling his huge muscular frame on the divan, and almost weeping with laughter at something that had been whispered in his ear by a dervish who sat beside him.

Sanda introduced Lancey as an Englishman, on hearing which the black Pasha seized and wrung his hands, amid roars of delight, and torrents of remarks in Turkish, while he slapped him heartily on the shoulder. Then, to the amazement of Lancey, he seized him by the collar of his coat, unbuttoned it, and began to pull it off. This act was speedily explained by the entrance of an attendant with a pale blue loose dressing-gown lined with fur, which the Pasha made his English guest put on, and sit down beside him.

Having now thoroughly resigned himself to the guidance of what his Turkish friends styled "fate," Lancey did his best to make himself agreeable, and gave himself up to the enjoyment of the hour.

There were present in the room, besides those already mentioned, a Turkish colonel of cavalry and a German doctor who spoke Turkish fluently. The party sat down to supper on cushions round a very low table. The dervish, Hadji Abderhaman, turned out to be a gourmand, as well as a witty fellow and a buffoon. The Pasha always gave the signal to begin to each dish, and between courses the dervish told stories from the Arabian Nights' Entertainments, or uttered witticisms which kept the Nubian Pasha in roars of laughter. They were all very merry, for the host was fond of boisterous fun and practical jokes, while his guests were sympathetic. Lancey laughed as much as any of them, for although he could not, despite his previous studies, follow the conversation, he could understand the pantomime, and appreciated the viands highly. His red-bearded friend also came to his aid now and then with a few explanatory remarks in broken English.

At such times the host sat with a beaming smile on his black face, and his huge mouth half-expanded, looking from one to another, as if attempting to understand, and ready at a moment's notice to explode in laughter, or admiration, or enthusiasm, according to circumstances.

"Hamed Pasha wants to know if you is in do army," said Sanda Pasha.

"Not in the regulars," replied Lancey, "but I 'ave bin, in the militia."

The Nubian gave another roar of delight when this was translated, and extended his great hand to one whom he thenceforth regarded as a brother-in-arms. Lancey grasped and shook it warmly.

"Let the Englishman see your sword," said Sanda in Turkish to Hamed.

Sanda knew his friend's weak point. The sword was at once ordered in for inspection.

Truly it was a formidable weapon, which might have suited the fist of Goliath, and was well fitted for the brawny arm that had waved it aloft many a time in the smoke and din of battle. It was blunt and hacked on both edges with frequent use, but its owner would not have it sharpened on any account, asserting that a stout arm did not require a keen weapon.

While the attention of the company was taken up with this instrument of death, the dervish availed himself of the opportunity to secure the remains of a dish of rich cream, to which he had already applied himself more than once.

The Nubian observed the sly and somewhat greedy act with a twinkling eye. When the dervish had drained the dish, the host filled a glass full to the brim with vinegar, and, with fierce joviality, bade him drink it. The poor man hesitated, and said something about wine and a mistake, but the Pasha repeated "Drink!" with such a roar, and threw his sword down at the same time with such a clang on the marble floor, that the dervish swallowed the draught with almost choking celerity.

The result was immediately obvious on his visage; nevertheless he bore up bravely, and even cut a sorry joke at his own expense, while the black giant rolled on his divan, and the tears ran down his swarthy cheeks.

The dervish was an adventurer who had wandered about the country as an idle vagabond until the war broke out, when he took to army-contracting with considerable success. It was in his capacity of contractor that he became acquainted with the boisterous black Pasha, who greatly appreciated his low but ready wit, and delighted in tormenting him. On discovering that the dervish was a voracious eater, he pressed—I might say forced—him with savage hospitality to eat largely of every dish, so that, when pipes were brought after supper, the poor dervish was more than satisfied.

"Now, you are in a fit condition to sing," cried Hamed, slapping the over-fed man on the shoulder; "come, give us a song: the Englishman would like to hear one of your Arabian melodies."

Redbeard translated this to Lancey, who protested that, "nothink would afford 'im greater delight."

The dervish was not easily overcome. Despite his condition, he sang, well and heartily, a ditty in Arabic, about love and war, which the Nubian Pasha translated into Turkish for the benefit of the German doctor, and Sanda Pasha rendered into broken English for Lancey.

But the great event of the evening came, when the English guest, in obedience to a call, if not a command, from his host, sang an English ballad. Lancey had a sweet and tuneful voice, and was prone to indulge in slow pathetic melodies. The black Pasha turned out to be intensely fond of music, and its effect on his emotional spirit was very powerful. At the first bar of his guest's flowing melody his boisterous humour vanished: his mouth and eyes partly opened with a look of pleased surprise; he evidently forgot himself and his company, and when, although unintelligible to him, the song proceeded in more touching strains, his capacious chest began to heave and his eyes filled with tears. The applause, not only of the host, but the company, was loud and emphatic, and Lancey was constrained to sing again. After that the colonel sang a Turkish war-song. The colonel's voice was a tremendous bass, and he sang with such enthusiasm that the hearers were effectively stirred. Hamed, in particular, became wild with excitement. He half-suited his motions, while beating time, to the action of each verse, and when, as a climax in the last verse, the colonel gave the order to "charge!" Hamed uttered a roar, sprang up, seized his great sabre, and caused it to whistle over his friends with a sweep that might have severed the head of an elephant!

At this point, one of the attendants, who appeared to be newly appointed to his duties, and who had, more than once during the feast, attracted attention by his stupidity, shrank in some alarm from the side of his wild master and tumbled over a cushion.

Hamed glared at him for a moment, with a frown that was obviously not put on, and half-raised the sabre as if about to cut him down. Instantly the frown changed to a look of contempt, and almost as quickly was replaced by a gleam of fun.

"Stand forth," said Hamed, dropping the sabre and sitting down.

The man obeyed with prompt anxiety.

"Your name?"

"Mustapha."

"Mustapha," repeated the Pasha, "I observe that you are a capable young fellow. You are a man of weight, as the marble floor can testify. I appoint you to the office of head steward. Go, stand up by the door."

The man made a low obeisance and went.

"Let the household servants and slaves pass before their new superior and do him honour."

With promptitude, and with a gravity that was intensely ludicrous—for none dared to smile in the presence of Hamed Pasha—the servants of the establishment, having been summoned, filed before the new steward and bowed to him. This ceremony over, Mustapha was ordered to go and make a list of the poultry. The poor man was here obliged to confess that he could not write.

"You can draw?" demanded the Pasha fiercely.

With some hesitation the steward admitted that he could—"a little."

"Go then, draw the poultry, every cock and hen and chicken," said the Pasha, with a wave of his hand which dismissed the household servants and sent the luckless steward to his task.

After this pipes were refilled, fresh stories were told, and more songs were sung. After a considerable time Mustapha returned with a large sheet of paper covered with hieroglyphics. The man looked timid as he approached and presented it to his master.

The Pasha seized the sheet. "What have we here?" he demanded sternly.

The man said it was portraits of the cocks and hens.

"Ha!" exclaimed the Pasha, "a portrait-gallery of poultry—eh!"

He held the sheet at arm's-length, and regarded it with a fierce frown; but his lips twitched, and suddenly relaxed into a broad grin, causing a tremendous display of white teeth and red gums.

"Poultry! ha! just so. What is this?"

He pointed to an object with a curling tail, which Mustapha assured him was a cock.

"What! a cock? where is the comb? Who ever heard of a cock without a comb, eh? And that, what is that?"

Mustapha ventured to assert that it was a chicken.

"A chicken," cried the Pasha fiercely; "more like a dromedary. You rascal! did you not say that you could draw? Go! deceiver, you are deposed. Have him out and set him to cleanse the hen-house, and woe betide you if it is not as clean as your own conscience before to-morrow morning—away!"

The Pasha shouted the last word, and then fell back in fits of laughter; while the terrified man fled to the hen-house, and drove its occupants frantic in his wild attempts to cleanse their Augean stable.

It was not until midnight that Sanda Pasha and Lancey, taking leave of Hamed and his guests, returned home.

"Come, follow me," said the Pasha, on entering the palace.

He led Lancey to the room in which they had first met, and, seating himself on a divan, lighted his chibouk.

"Sit down," he said, pointing to a cushion that lay near him on the marble floor.

Lancey, although unaccustomed to such a low seat, obeyed.

"Smoke," said the Pasha, handing a cigarette to his guest.

Lancey took the cigarette, but at this point his honest soul recoiled from the part he seemed to be playing. He rose, and, laying the cigarette respectfully on the ground, said —

"Sanda Pasha, it's not for the likes o' me to be sittin' 'ere smokin' with the likes o' you, sir. There's some mistake 'ere, hobviously. I've been treated with the consideration doo to a prince since I fell into the 'ands of the Turks, and it is right that I should at once correct this mistake, w'ich I'd 'ave done long ago if I could 'ave got the Turks who've 'ad charge of me to understand Hinglish. I'm bound to tell you, sir, that I'm on'y a groom in a Hinglish family, and makes no pretence to be hanythink else, though circumstances 'as putt me in a false position since I come 'ere. I 'ope your Pashaship won't think me ungracious, sir, but I can't a-bear to sail under false colours."

To this speech Sanda Pasha listened with profound gravity, and puffed an enormous cloud from his lips at its conclusion.

"Sit down," he said sternly.

Lancey obeyed.

"Light your cigarette."

There was a tone of authority in the Pasha's voice which Lancey did not dare to resist. He lighted the cigarette.

"Look me in the *face*," said the Pasha suddenly, turning his piercing grey eyes full on him guest.

Supposing that this was a prelude to an expression of doubt as to his honesty, Lancey did look the Pasha full in the face, and returned his stare with interest.

"Do you see this cut over the bridge of my nose?" demanded the Pasha.

Lancey saw it, and admitted that it must have been a bad one.

"And do you see the light that is blazing in these two eyes?" he added, pointing to his own glowing orbs with a touch of excitement.

Lancey admitted that he saw the light, and began to suspect that the Pasha was mad. At the same time he was struck by the sudden and very great improvement in his friend's English.

"But for *you*," continued the Pasha, partly raising himself, "that cut had never been, and the light of those eyes would now be quenched in death!"

The Pasha looked at his guest more fixedly than ever, and Lancey, now feeling convinced of his entertainer's madness, began to think uneasily of the best way to humour him.

"Twenty years ago," continued the Pasha slowly and with a touch of pathos in his tone, "I received this cut from a boy in a fight at school," (Lancey thought that the boy must have been a bold fellow), "and only the other day I was rescued by a man from the waters of the Danube." (Lancey thought that, on the whole, it would have been well if the man had left him to drown.) "The name of the boy and the name of the man was the same. It was Jacob Lancey!"

Lancey's eyes opened and his lower jaw dropped. He sat on his cushion aghast.

"Jacob Lancey," continued the Pasha in a familiar tone that sent a thrill to the heart of his visitor, "hae ye forgotten your auld Scotch freen' and school-mate Sandy? In Sanda Pasha you behold Sandy Black!"

Lancey sprang to his knees—the low couch rendering that attitude natural—grasped the Pasha's extended hand, and gazed wistfully into his eyes.

"Oh Sandy, Sandy!" he said, in a voice of forced calmness, while he shook his head reproachfully, "many and many a time 'ave I prophesied that you would become a great man, but little did I think that you'd come to this—a May'omedan and a Turk."

Unable to say more, Lancey sat down on his cushion, clasped his hands over his knees, and gazed fixedly at his old friend and former idol.

"Lancey, my boy—it is quite refreshing to use these old familiar words again,—I am no more a Mohammedan than you are."

"Then you're a 'ypocrite," replied the other promptly.

"By no means,—at least I hope not," said the Pasha, with a smile and a slightly troubled look. "Surely there is a wide space between a thoroughly honest man and an out-and-out hypocrite. I came here with no religion at all. They took me by the hand and treated me kindly. Knowing nothing, I took to anything they chose to teach me. What could a youth do? Now I am what I am, and I cannot change it."

Lancey knew not what to reply to this. Laying his hand on the rich sleeve of the Pasha he began in the old tone and in the fulness of his heart.

"Sandy, my old friend, as I used to all but worship, nominal May'omedan though you be, it's right glad I am to—" words failed him here.

"Well, well," said the Pasha, smiling, and drawing a great cloud from his chibouk, "I'm as glad as yourself, and not the less so that I've been able to do you some small service in the way of preventing your neck from being stretched; and that brings me to the chief point for which I have brought you to my palace, namely, to talk about matters which concern yourself, for it is obvious that you cannot remain in this country in time of war with safety unless you have some fixed position. Tell me, now, where you have been and what doing since we last met in Scotland, and I will tell you what can be done for you in Turkey."

Hereupon Lancey began a long-winded and particular account of his life during the last twenty years. The Pasha smoked and listened with grave interest. When the recital was finished he rose.

"Now, Lancey," said he, "it is time that you and I were asleep. In the morning I have business to attend to. When it is done we will continue our talk. Meanwhile let me say that I see many little ways in which you can serve the Turks, if you are so minded."

"Sandy Black," said Lancey, rising with a look of dignity, "you are very kind—just what I would 'ave expected of you—but you must clearly understand that I will serve only in works of 'umanity. In a milingtary capacity I will serve neither the Turks nor the Roossians."

"Quite right, my old friend, I will not ask military service of you, so good-night. By the way, it may be as well to remind you that, except between ourselves, I am not Sandy Black but Sanda Pasha,—you understand?"

With an arch smile the Pasha laid down his chibouk and left the room, and the black attendant conducted Lancey to his bedroom. The same attendant took him, the following morning after breakfast, to the Pasha's "Selamlik" or "Place of Salutations," in order that he might see how business matters were transacted in Turkey.

The Selamlik was a large handsome room filled with men, both with and without turbans, who had come either to solicit a favour or a post, or to press on some private business. On the entrance of the Pasha every one rose. When he was seated, there began a curious scene of bowing to the ground and touching, by each person present, of the mouth and head with the hand. This lasted full five minutes.

Sanda Pasha then received a number of business papers from an officer of the household, to which he applied himself with great apparent earnestness, paying no attention whatever to his visitors. Lancey observed, however, that his absorbed condition did not prevent a few of these visitors, apparently of superior rank, from approaching and whispering in his ear. To some of them he was gracious, to others cool, as they severally stated the nature of their business. No one else dared to approach until the reading of the papers was finished. Suddenly the Pasha appeared to get weary of his papers. He tossed them aside, ordered his carriage, rose hastily, and left the room. But this uncourteous behaviour did not appear to disconcert those who awaited his pleasure. Probably, like eels, they had got used to rough treatment. Some of them ran after the Pasha and tried to urge their suits in a few rapid sentences, others went off with a sigh or a growl, resolving to repeat the visit another day, while Sanda himself was whirled along at full speed to the Sublime Porte, to hold council with the Ministers of State on the arrangements for the war that had by that time begun to rage along the whole line of the Lower Danube—the Russians having effected a crossing in several places.

After enjoying himself for several days in the palace of his old school-mate, my worthy servant, being resolved not to quit the country until he had done his utmost to discover whether I was alive or drowned, accepted the offer of a situation as cook to one of the Turkish Ambulance Corps. Having received a suitable change of garments, with a private pass, and recommendations from the Pasha, he was despatched with a large body of recruits and supplies to the front.

Note 1. A similar establishment to this was, not long ago, described by the "correspondent" of a well-known Journal.

Chapter Eleven
Refers to two Important Letters,
and a Secret Mission

It is a curious coincidence that, about the very time when my servant was appointed to serve in the Turkish Ambulance Corps, I received permission to act as a surgeon in the Russian army. Through the influence of Nicholas Naranovitsch, I was attached to his own regiment, and thus enjoyed the pleasure of his society for a considerable time after the breaking out of the war.

I preferred this course to that of returning home, because, first, I could not bear the thought of leaving the country without making every possible exertion to ascertain the fate of my yacht's crew, and rendering them succour if possible; and, secondly, because I felt an irresistible desire to alleviate, professionally, the sufferings of those who were certain to be wounded during the war. I also experienced much curiosity to know something more of the power and influence of modern war-engines. Perhaps some people will think this latter an unworthy motive. It may have been so; I cannot tell. All I can say is that it was a very secondary one, and would not, of itself, have been sufficient to induce me to remain for an hour to witness the horrors and carnage of battle-fields. Still, putting the various motives together, I felt justified in remaining.

In order that I might render still more effective service to the cause of humanity, I wrote, immediately after my appointment as surgeon, to an intimate friend, north of the Tweed, offering my services as war correspondent to a paper of which he was editor, namely, the *Scottish Bawbee*.

That celebrated journal,—well known on the east, west, and north coasts of Scotland, and extensively circulated in the centre and south of the country, including England,—is liberal in its principles, conservative in reference only to things that are good, and violently radical when treating of those that are bad. It enjoys the credit of being curt in its statements, brief in the expression of its opinions, perfectly silent in reference to its surmises, distinctly repudiative of the gift of prophecy, consistently averse to the attribution of motives, persistently wise in giving the shortest possible account of murders and scandalous cases, and copious in its references to literature, art, and religious progress, besides being extremely methodical in its arrangement.

In regard to the latter quality, I cannot refrain from referring to its sensible mode of treating births, marriages, and deaths, by putting the Christian and surname of the born, married, or defunct as the *first* words in each announcement, so that one's digestion at breakfast is aided by reading with some comfort of the joys and sorrows of one's friends, instead of having incipient dyspepsia engendered by a painful search for the main facts in confusing sentences.

The editor's reply came by return of post. It contained the acceptance of my services, and a proposal of extremely liberal terms, allowing me, besides a handsome retaining fee, two horses, and such travelling attendants as might be found necessary. There were also certain emphatic stipulations which are worth recording. I was not, on any pretext whatever, to attempt the divination, much less the revelation, of the future. I was never, upon any consideration, to be seduced into lengthy descriptions of things that I did not see, or minute particulars about matters which I did not know. I was utterly to ignore, and refuse to be influenced by, personal predilections or prejudices in regard to either combatant. I was to say as little about scenery as was consistent with a correct delineation of the field of war, and never to venture on sentimental allusions to sunsets, moonlights, or water-reflections of any kind. I was not to forget that a newspaper was a vehicle for the distribution of news, the announcement of facts and the discussion thereof, not a medium for the dissemination of fancies and fiddledededee. Above all, I was never to write a column and a half of speculation as to the possible and *probable* movements of armies; to be followed "in our next" by two columns of the *rumoured* movements of armies; to be continued "in our next" by two columns and a half of the *actual* movements of armies; to wind up "in our next" with three columns of retrospective consideration as to what might, could, would, or *should* have been the movements of armies; but that I was, on the contrary, to bear in remembrance the adage about "brevity" being the "soul of wit," and, when I had nothing to write, to write nothing. By so doing, it was added, I should please the editor and charm the public, one of whose minor griefs is, as regards newspapers, that it is brought into a state of disgust with every event of this life long before it has happened, and thoroughly nauseated with it long after it is past,—to say nothing of the resulting mental confusion.

In case any gentleman of the press should feel injured by these statements, I must remind him that I am not responsible for them. They are the sentiments of the *Scottish Bawbee*, which must be taken for what they are worth. It is true, I heartily agree with them, but that is an entirely different subject, on which I do not enter.

I readily agreed to fall in with the wishes of the editor, and thenceforward devoted myself, heart and soul, to correspondence and surgery. In both fields of labour I found ample scope for all the powers of body and mind that I possessed.

Just about this time I received a letter from my dear mother, who was aware of my plans. It cost me some anxiety, as it was utterly impossible that I should comply with the injunctions it contained. "Jeffry, my dear boy," she wrote, "let me entreat you, with all the solemnity of maternal solicitude, to take care of your health. Let Russians and Turks kill and expose themselves as they please, but ever bear in remembrance that it is your duty to avoid danger. Whatever you do, keep your feet dry and your— I need not go further into particulars; medical allusions cannot always be couched in language such as one desires. Never sleep on damp ground, nor, if possible, without a roof or a covering of some sort over your head. Even a parasol is better than nothing. If, despite your precautions, you should catch cold, tie a worsted sock—one of the red and black striped ones I have knitted for you—round your neck, and take one drop of aconite—only one, remember—before going to bed. I know how, with your allopathic notions, you will smile at this advice, but I assure you, as your mother, that it will prove an infallible cure. Never sit in a draught when you can avoid it. If you ever come under fire, which I trust you never may, be sure to get behind a house, or a wall, or a stone, if possible; if you cannot do so, get behind a soldier, one larger than yourself would be preferable of course, but if you have not the opportunity of doing this, then turn your side to the enemy, because in that position you are a much narrower target, and more likely to escape their bullets. I need not caution you not to run away. I would rather see you, dear boy, in a premature grave, than hear that you had run away. But you *could not* run away. No Childers ever did so—except from school.

"Let the phial of globules which I gave you at parting be your bosom friends, till their friendship is required in another and a lower region. They are a sovereign remedy against rheumatism, catarrh, bronchitis, dyspepsia, lumbago, nervous affections, headaches, loss of memory, debility, monomania, melancholia, botherolia, theoretica, and, in short, all the ills that flesh is heir to, if only taken in time."

It struck me, as I folded my mother's letter and that of the editor, that there never was a man who went into any course of action better guarded and advised than myself. At the moment when this thought occurred to me, my friend Nicholas burst into my room in a state of unusual excitement.

"Come, Jeff," he said, "I'm detailed for another secret duty. People seem to have inordinate faith in me, for all my duties are secret! Are you willing to go with me?"

"Go where?" I asked.

"That I may not tell," he replied; "anywhere, or nowhere, or everywhere. All I can say is, that if you go, it will be to act as surgeon to a squadron of cavalry. I see you have letters. Good news from home—eh? What of Bella?"

"Yes" I replied, "good news and good advice—listen."

I reopened the letters and read them aloud.

"Capital!" exclaimed Nicholas, "just the thing for you. No doubt my expedition will furnish a column and a half, if not more, of unquestionable facts for the *Scottish Bawbee*. Get ready, my boy; I start in half-an-hour."

He swung off in the same hearty, reckless manner with which he had entered; and I immediately set about packing up my surgical instruments and note-books, and making other preparations for a journey of unknown extent and duration.

Chapter Twelve
My First Experience of Actual War, and my Thoughts Thereon

We set out by the light of the moon. Our party consisted of a small force of Russian light cavalry. The officer in command was evidently well acquainted with our route, for he rode smartly ahead without hesitation or sign of uncertainty for several hours.

At first Nicholas and I conversed in low tones as we cantered side by side over hill and dale, but as the night advanced we became less communicative, and finally dropped into silence. As I looked upon village and hamlet, bathed in the subdued light, resting in quietness and peace, I thought sadly of the evils that war would surely bring upon many an innocent and helpless woman and child.

It was invariably in this course that my thoughts about war flowed. I was, indeed, quite alive to the national evils of war, and I will not admit that any man-of-peace feels more sensitively than I do the fact that, in war, a nation's best, youngest, and most hopeful blood is spilled, while its longest lives and most ardent spirits are ruthlessly, uselessly sacrificed— its budding youths, its strapping men, its freshest and most muscular, to say nothing of mental, manhood. Still, while contemplating war and its consequences, I have always been much more powerfully impressed with the frightful consequences to women and children, than anything else. To think of our wives, our little ones, our tender maidens, our loving matrons, and our poor helpless babes, being exposed to murder, rapine, torture, and all the numerous and unnameable horrors of war, for the sake of some false, some fanciful, some utterly ridiculous and contemptible idea, such as the connection of one or two provinces of a land with this nation or with that, or the "integrity of a foreign empire," has always filled me with sensations of indignation approaching to madness, not unmingled, I must add, with astonishment.

That savages will fight among themselves is self-evident; that Christian nations shall defend themselves from the assaults of savages is also obvious; but that two Christian nations should go to war for anything, on any ground whatever, is to my mind inexplicable and utterly indefensible.

Still, they do it. From which circumstance I am forced to conclude that the Christianity as well as the civilisation and common-sense of one or the other of such nations is, for the time, in abeyance.

Of course I was not perplexed in regard to the Turks. Their religion is not Christian. Moreover, it was propagated by the sword, and teaches coercion in religious matters; but I could not help feeling that the Russians were too ready to forsake diplomacy and take to war.

"My dear fellow," said Nicholas, rousing himself, when I stated my difficulty, "don't you see that the vacillating policy of England has driven us to war in spite of ourselves? She would not join the rest of Europe in compelling Turkey to effect reforms which she—Turkey—had promised to make, so that nothing else was left for us but to go to war."

"My dear fellow," I retorted, somewhat hotly, "that Turkey has behaved brutally towards its own subjects is a well-known fact. That she has treated the representatives of all the great powers of Europe with extreme insolence is another well-known fact, but it is yet to be proved that the efforts of diplomacy were exhausted, and even if they were, it remained for Europe, not for Russia, to constitute herself the champion of the oppressed."

"Jeff, my boy," returned Nicholas, with a smile, "I'm too sleepy to discuss that subject just now, further than to say that I don't agree with you."

He did indeed look sleepy, and as we had been riding many hours I forbore to trouble him further.

By daybreak that morning we drew near to the town of Giurgevo, on the Roumanian—or, I may say, the Russian—side of the Danube, and soon afterwards entered it.

Considerable excitement was visible among its inhabitants, who, even at that early hour, were moving hurriedly about the streets. Having parted from our escort, Nicholas and I refreshed ourselves at the Hôtel de l'Europe, and then went to an hospital, where my companion wished to visit a wounded friend—"one," he said, "who had lately taken part in a dashing though unsuccessful expedition."

This visit to Giurgevo was my first introduction to some of the actual miseries of war. The hospital was a clean, well-ventilated building. Rows of low beds were ranged neatly and methodically along the whitewashed walls. These were tenanted by young men in every stage of suffering and exhaustion. With bandaged heads or limbs they sat or reclined or lay, some but slightly wounded and still ruddy with the hue of health on their young cheeks; some cut and marred in visage and limbs, with pale cheeks and blue lips, that told of the life-blood almost drained. Others were lying flat on their backs, with the soft brown moustache or curly brown hair contrasting terribly with the grey hue of approaching death.

In one of the beds we found the friend of Nicholas.

He was quite a youth, not badly wounded, and received us with enthusiasm.

"My dear Nicholas," he said, in reply to a word of condolence about the failure of the expedition, "you misunderstand the whole matter. Doubtless it did not succeed, but that was no fault of ours, and it was a glorious attempt. Come, I will relate it. Does your friend speak Russian?"

"He at all events understands it," said I.

On this assurance the youth raised his hand to his bandaged brow as if to recall events, and then related the incident, of which the following is the substance.

While the Russians were actively engaged in preparing to cross the Danube at a part where the river is full of small islands, the Turks sent monitors and gunboats to interrupt the operations. The Russians had no vessels capable of facing the huge ironclads of the enemy. Of the ten small boats at the place, eight were engaged in laying torpedoes in the river to protect the works, and two were detailed to watch the enemy. While they were all busily at work, the watchers in a boat named the *Schootka* heard the sound of an approaching steamer, and soon after descried a Turkish gunboat steaming up the river. Out went the little *Schootka* like a wasp, with a deadly torpedo at the end of her spar. The gun-boat saw and sought to evade her, put on full steam and hugged the Turkish shore, where some hundreds of Circassian riflemen kept up an incessant fire on the Russian boat. It was hit, and its commander wounded, but the crew and the second in command resolved to carry out the attack. The *Schootka* increased her speed, and, to the consternation of the Turks, succeeded in touching the gun-boat just behind the paddle-boxes, but the torpedo refused to explode, and the *Schootka* was compelled to haul off, and make for shelter under a heavy fire from the gun-boat and the Circassian riflemen, which quite riddled her. While she was making off a second Turkish gun-boat hove in sight. The *Schootka* had still another torpedo on board, one on the Harvey principle. This torpedo may be described as a somewhat square and flat case, charged with an explosive compound. When used it is thrown into the sea and runs through the water on its edge, being held in that position by a rope and caused to advance by pulling on it sidewise. Anglers will understand this when I state that it works on the principle of the "otter," and, somewhat like the celebrated Irish pig going to market, runs ahead the more it is pulled back by the tail. With this torpedo the daring Russians resolved to attack the second gunboat, but when they threw it overboard it would not work; something had gone wrong with its tail, or with the levers by which, on coming into contact with the enemy, it was to explode. They were compelled therefore to abandon the attempt, and seek shelter from the Turkish fire behind an island.

"So then," said I, on quitting the hospital, "torpedoes, although *terrible* in their action, are not always *certain*."

"Nothing is always certain," replied Nicholas, with a smile, "except the flight of time, and as the matter on which I have come requires attention I must now leave you for a few hours. Don't forget the name of our hotel. That secure in a man's mind, he may lose himself in any town or city with perfect safety—*au revoir*."

For some time I walked about the town. The morning was bright and calm, suggesting ideas of peace; nevertheless my thoughts could not be turned from the contemplation of war, and as I wandered hither and thither, looking out for reminiscences of former wars, I thought of the curiously steady way in which human history repeats itself. It seems to take about a quarter of a century to teach men to forget or ignore the lessons of the past and induce them to begin again to fight. Here, in 1829, the Russians levelled the fortifications which at that time encircled the town; here, in 1854, the Russians were defeated by the Turks; and here, in 1872, these same Russians and Turks were at the same old bloody and useless game—ever learning, yet never coming to a knowledge of the great truth, that, with all their fighting, nothing has been gained and nothing accomplished save a few changes of the men on the chess-board, and the loss of an incalculable amount of life and treasure.

As the day advanced it became very sultry. Towards the afternoon I stopped and gazed thoughtfully at the placid Danube, which, flowing round the gentle curve of Slobosia, reflected in its glittering waters the white domes and minarets of the opposite town of Rustchuk. A low, rumbling sound startled me just then from a reverie. On looking up I perceived a small puff of smoke roll out in the direction of the Turkish shore. Another and another succeeded, and after each shot a smaller puff of smoke was seen to hang over the Turkish batteries opposite.

A strange conflicting rush of feelings came over me, for I had awakened from dreaming of ancient battles to find myself in the actual presence of modern war. The Russian had opened fire, and their shells were bursting among the Turks. These latter were not slow to reply. Soon the rumbling increased to thunder, and I was startled by hearing a tremendous crash not far distant from me, followed by a strange humming sound. The crash was the bursting of a Turkish shell in one of the streets of the town, and the humming sound was the flying about of ragged bits of iron. From the spot on which I stood I could see the havoc it made in the road, while men, women, and children were rushing in all directions out of its way.

Two objects lay near the spot, however, which moved, although they did not flee. One was a woman, the other a boy; both were severely wounded.

I hurried through the town in the direction of the Red-Cross hospital, partly expecting that I might be of service there, and partly in the hope of finding Nicholas. As I went I heard people remarking excitedly on the fact that the Turks were firing at the hospital.

The bombardment became furious, and I felt an uncomfortable disposition to shrink as I heard and saw shot and shell falling everywhere in the streets, piercing the houses, and bursting in them. Many of these were speedily reduced to ruins.

People hurried from their dwellings into the streets, excited and shouting. Men rushed wildly to places of shelter from the deadly missiles, and soon the cries and wailing of women over the dead and wounded increased the uproar. This was strangely and horribly contrasted with the fiendish laughter of a group of boys, who, as yet unhurt, and scarcely alive to the real nature of what was going on, had taken shelter in an archway, from which they darted out occasionally to pick up the pieces of shells that burst near them.

These poor boys, however, were not good judges of shelter-places in such circumstances. Just as I passed, a shell fell and burst in front of the archway, and a piece of it went singing so close past my head that I fancied at the first moment it must have hit me. At the same instant the boys uttered an unearthly yell of terror and fled from under the archway, where I saw one of their number rolling on the ground and shrieking in agony.

Hastening to his assistance, I found that he had received a severe flesh wound in the thigh. I carried him into a house that seemed pretty well protected from the fire, dressed his wound, and left him in charge of the inmates, who, although terribly frightened, were kind and sympathetic.

Proceeding through the marketplace, I observed a little girl crouching in a doorway, her face as pale as if she were dead, her lips perfectly white, and an expression of extreme horror in her eyes. I should probably have passed her, for even in that short sharp walk I had already seen so many faces expressing terror that I had ceased to think of stopping, but I observed a stream of blood on her light-coloured dress.

Stooping down, I asked—

"Are you hurt, dear?"

Twice I repeated the question before she appeared to understand me; then, raising a pair of large lustrous but tearless eyes to my face, she uttered the single word "Father," and pointed to something that lay in the gloom of the passage beyond her. I entered, lifted the corner of a piece of coarse canvas, and under it saw the form of a man, but there was no countenance. His head had been completely shattered by a shell. Replacing the canvas, I returned to the child. Her right hand was thrust into her bosom, and as she held it there in an unnatural position, I suspected something, and drew it gently out. I was right. It had been struck, and the middle finger was hanging by a piece of skin. A mere touch of my knife was sufficient to sever it. As I bandaged the stump, I tried to console the poor child. She did not appear to care for the pain I unavoidably caused her, but remained quite still, only saying now and then, in a low voice, "Father," as she looked with her tearless eyes at the heap that lay in the passage.

Giving this hapless little one in charge of a woman who seemed to be an inhabitant of the same building, I hurried away, but had not gone a hundred yards when I chanced to meet Nicholas.

"Ha! well met, my boy!" he exclaimed, evidently in a state of suppressed excitement; "come along. I expected to have had a long hunt after you, but fortune favours me, and we have not a moment to lose."

"Where are you going?" I asked.

"Just think," he said, seizing my arm and hurrying me along, but taking no heed of my question; "we are fairly over the Danube in force! The night before last three thousand men, Cossacks and infantry, crossed from Galatz in boats and rafts, and gained the heights above Matchin. Zoukoff has beaten the enemy everywhere, and Zimmermann is reported to have driven them out of Matchin—in fact we have fairly broken the ice, and all that we have now to do is to go in and win."

I saw by the flush on his handsome countenance that the martial ardour of Nicholas was stirred to its depths. There was a noble look of daring in his clear grey eye, and a smile of what seemed like joy on his lips, which I knew well were the expression of such sentiments as love of country, desire to serve, like a brave son, that Emperor whom he regarded as a father, hatred of oppression, belief in the righteousness of the cause for which he fought, and delight in the prospect of wild animal excitement. He was full of high hopes, noble aspirations, superabundant energy, and, although not a deep thinker, could tell better than most men, by looking at it, whether the edge of a grindstone were rough or smooth.

We walked smartly to our hotel, but found that our servant had fled, no one knew whither, taking our horses with him. The landlord, however, suggested the railway station, and thither we ran.

A train was entering when we arrived. It was full of Russian soldiers. On the platform stood a Jew, to whom Nicholas addressed himself. The Jew at first seemed to have difficulty in understanding him, but he ultimately said that he had seen a man who must be the one we were in search of, and was about to tell us more, when a Turkish shell burst through the roof of the station, and exploded on the platform, part of which it tore up, sending splinters of iron and wood in all directions. The confused noise of shout and yell that followed, together with the smoke, prevented my observing for a moment or two what damage had been done, but soon I ascertained that Nicholas and myself were unhurt; that the Jew had been slightly wounded, and also several of the people who were waiting the arrival of the train.

The groans of some of the wounded, and the cursing and shouting of the soldiers just arrived, made a powerful impression on me.

"Come, I see our fellow," cried Nicholas, seizing me suddenly by the arm and hurrying me away.

In a few minutes we had caught our man, mounted our horses, rejoined our cavalry escort, which awaited us in the marketplace, and galloped out of the town.

It is a fact worthy of record that of all the people killed and hurt during this bombardment of Giurgevo, not one was a Russian! This arose from the fact that the soldiers were under the safe cover of their batteries. The Turkish shells did not produce any real damage to works or men. In short, all that was accomplished in this noisy display of the "art of war" was the destruction of many private houses, the killing and maiming of several civilians, including women and children, and a shameful waste of very expensive ammunition, partly paid for by the sufferers. In contemplating these facts, the word "glory" assumed a very strange and quite a new meaning in my mind.

Soon we were beyond the reach of Turkish missiles, though still within sound of the guns. Our pace showed that we were making what I suppose my military friends would style a forced march. Nicholas was evidently unwilling to converse on the object of our march, but at length gave way a little.

"I see no harm," he said, "in telling you that we are about to cross the Danube not far from this, and that at least one of my objects is to secure a trustworthy intelligent spy. You know—perhaps you don't know—that such men are rare. Of course we can procure any number of men who have pluck enough to offer themselves as spies, for the sake of the high pay, just as we can get any number of men who are willing to jump down a cannon's throat for the honour and glory of the thing."

"Yes," said I, interrupting, "men like our friend Nicholas Naranovitsch!"

"Well, perhaps," he replied, with a light laugh, "but don't change the subject, Jeff, you've got a bad tendency to do so. I say there is no difficulty in getting spies; but it is not easy to find men well qualified for such work. Now one has been heard of at last, and, among other things, I am commissioned to secure him for the purpose of leading our troops across the Balkans."

"The Balkans!" said I, in surprise; "you are a long way from that range."

"The length of any way, Jeff, depends not so much upon the way as on the spirit of him who measures it. Ten miles to one man is a hundred miles to another, and *vice versa*."

I could make no objection to that, for it was true. "Nevertheless," said I, after a pause, "there may be spirits among the Turks who could render that, which is only a few days' journey in ordinary circumstances, a six months' business to the Russians."

"Admitted heartily," returned Nicholas, with animation; "if the Turk were not a brave foe, one could not take so much interest in the war."

This last remark silenced me for a time. The view-point of my future kinsman was so utterly different from mine that I knew not what to reply. He evidently thought that a plucky foe, worthy of his steel, was most desirable, while to my mind it appeared obvious that the pluckier the foe the longer and more resolute would be the resistance, and, as a consequence, the greater the amount of bloodshed and of suffering to the women, children, and aged, the heavier the drain on the resources of both empires, and of addition to the burdens of generations yet unborn.

When, after a considerable time, I put the subject in this light before Nicholas, he laughed heartily, and said—

"Why, Jeff, at that rate you would knock all the romance out of war."

"That were impossible, Nick," I rejoined quickly, "for there is no romance whatever in war."

"No romance?" he exclaimed, opening his eyes to their widest, and raising his black brows to their highest in astonishment.

"No," said I, firmly, "not a scrap. All the romance connected with war is in spite of it, and by no means the result of it. The heroism displayed in its wildest sallies is true heroism undoubtedly, but it would be none the less heroism if it were exercised in the rescue of men and women from shipwreck or from fire. The romance of the bivouac in the dark woods or on the moonlit plains of foreign lands, with the delights of fresh air and life-giving exercise and thrilling adventure, is not the perquisite of the warrior; it is the privilege, quite as much, if not more, of the pioneer in the American backwoods and prairies, and of the hunter in the wilds of Africa. The romance of unexpected meetings with foreign 'fair ones' in out-o''-the-way circumstances, with broken bones, perhaps, or gunshot wounds, to lend pathos to the affair, and necessitate nursing, which may lead to love-making,—all that is equally possible to the Alpine climber and the chamois-hunter, to the traveller almost anywhere, who chooses to indulge in reckless sport, regardless of his neck.—Of course," I added, with a smile, for I did not wish to appear too cynical in my friend's eyes, "the soldier has a few advantages in which the civilian does not quite come up to him, such as the glorious brass band, and the red coat, and the glittering lace."

"Jeff," said Nicholas, somewhat gravely, "would you then take all the glory out of war, and reduce soldiers to a set of mere professional and legalised cut-throats, whose duty it is callously to knock over so many thousand men at the command of governments?"

"Bear with me a little," said I, "and hear me out. You misunderstand me. I speak of war, not of warriors. As there is no 'romance,' so there is no 'glory' in war. Many a glorious deed may be, and often is, done *in connection with* war. Such a deed is done when a handful of brave men sacrifice their lives at the call of duty, and in defence of country, as at Thermopylae. Such a deed is done when a wounded Prussian soldier, dying of thirst on the battle-field, forgets the accursed custom—war—which has brought him to that pass, and shares the last drops of his water-flask with a so-called French enemy. And such a deed is done, still more gloriously, when a soldier, true to his Queen and country, is true also to his God, and preaches while he practises the principles and gospel of the Prince of Peace, in the presence of those with whom he acts his part in this world's drama. There is indeed much that is glorious in the conduct of many warriors, but there is no glory whatever in war itself. The best that can be said of it is, that sometimes it is a stern yet sad necessity."

We dropped the subject here, having reached the point of the river where our party was to cross to the Turkish shore.

The passage was soon accomplished by means of rafts, and many thousands of Russians having already preceded us we experienced no opposition. It was daylight when we rode into a village on the Bulgarian shore, and I looked up sleepily at the cottages as we passed.

"We halt here," said Nicholas, with a yawn as he drew rein.

The officer in command of our party had already halted his men, who, gladly quitting their saddles, streamed after us into the courtyard of the village.

Chapter Thirteen
Shews what Sometimes Happens in the Track of Troops

"Why, Nicholas," I exclaimed, looking round the inn, "I have been here before. It is—it must be—the very place where, on my way up, I saw a famous wrestling-match. Did I ever tell you about it?"

"Never; but come along, I must finish one part of my duty here without delay by paying a visit. You can tell me about the wrestling-match as we walk together."

I described the match with great interest, for my heart warmed towards the chief actor and his family, and as I proceeded with the narration I observed with some satisfaction that the road we were following led in the direction of the cottage of Dobri Petroff. As we drew near to the path that diverged to it I resolved, if possible, to give Nicholas, who was evidently interested in my narrative, a surprise by confronting him unexpectedly with the blacksmith and his family.

"Nicholas," I said, "you see that cottage on the hillside? I have a great desire to pay its inmates a visit. Have you any objection to turn aside just for a few minutes?"

Nicholas gave me a look of surprise and laughed.

"None in the world, Jeff, for it happens that I particularly wish to visit the cottage myself."

"You do? Why—what—"

"Well, finish your question, Jeff; why should it seem strange to you that I want to visit a Bulgarian family?"

"Why, because, Nick, this is the cottage of the very blacksmith about whom I have been speaking, and I wanted to give you a surprise by introducing him to you."

"His name?" asked Nicholas quickly.

"Dobri Petroff."

"The very man. How strange! You have already given me a surprise, Jeff, and will now add a pleasure and a service by introducing me to him, and, perhaps, by using your powers of suasion. It is no breach of confidence to tell you that part of my business here is to secure the services of this man as a guide over the Balkans, with the passes of which we have been told he is intimately acquainted. But it is said that he is a bold independent fellow, who may dislike and refuse the duty."

"He won't dislike it at all events," said I. "He has no love for the Turks, who have treated him shamefully, just because of that same bold and independent spirit."

"Well, come, we shall see," rejoined my friend.

In a few minutes we had come to a turn in the path which brought the cottage full into view, and I experienced a sudden shock on observing that part of it—that part which had been the forge—was a blackened ruin. I was at the same moment relieved, however, by the sight of Ivanka and little Dobri, who were playing together in front of the uninjured part of the cottage.

Next moment the tall handsome form of the blacksmith appeared stooping under the doorway as he came out to receive us. I noticed that there was an expression of trouble on his countenance, mingled with a look of sternness which was not usual to him. He did not recognise me at first, and evidently eyed Nicholas—as a Russian officer—with no favour.

As we drew near, the stern look vanished, and he sprang forward with a glad smile to seize and shake my hand. At the same moment Ivanka's black eyes seemed to blaze with delight, as she ran towards me, and clasped one of my legs. Little Dobri, bereft of speech, stood with legs and arms apart, and mouth and eyes wide open, gazing at me.

"All well?" I asked anxiously.

"All well," said the blacksmith; then, with a glance at the forge—"except the—; but that's not much after all.—Come in, gentlemen, come in."

We entered, and found Marika as neat and thrifty as ever, though with a touch of care about her pretty face which had not been there when I first met her.

A few words explained the cause of their trouble.

"Sir," said Petroff, addressing me, but evidently speaking at Nicholas, "we unfortunate Bulgarians have hard times of it just now. The Turk has oppressed and robbed and tortured and murdered us in time past, and now the Russian who has come to deliver us is, it seems to me, completing our ruin. What between the two we poor wretches have come to a miserable pass indeed."

He turned full on Nicholas, unable to repress a fierce look.

"Friend," said Nicholas gently, but firmly, "the chances of war are often hard to bear, but you ought to recognise a great difference between the sufferings which are caused by wilful oppression, and those which are the unavoidable consequences of a state of warfare."

"Unavoidable!" retorted the blacksmith bitterly. "Is it not possible for the Russians to carry supplies for their armies, instead of demanding all our cattle for beef and all our harvests for fodder?"

"Do we not pay you for such things?" asked Nicholas, in the tone of a man who wishes to propitiate his questioner.

"Yes, truly, but nothing like the worth of what you take; besides, of what value are a few gold pieces to me? My wife and children cannot eat gold, and there is little or nothing left in the land to buy. But that is not the worst. Your Cossacks receive nothing from your Government for rations, and are allowed to forage as they will. Do you suppose that, when in want of anything, they will stop to inquire whether it belongs to a Bulgarian or not? When the war broke out, and your troops crossed the river, my cattle and grain were bought up, whether I would or no, by your soldiers. They were paid for—underpaid, I say—but that I cared not for, as they left me one milch-cow and fodder enough to keep her. Immediately after that a band of your lawless and unrationed Cossacks came, killed the cow, and took the forage, without paying for either. After that, the Moldavians, who drive your waggon-supplies for you—a lawless set of brigands when there are no troops near to watch them,—cleaned my house of every scrap that was worth carrying away. What could I do? To kill a dozen of them would have been easy, but that would not have been the way to protect my wife and children."

The man laid his great hand tenderly on Ivanka's head, while he was speaking in his deep earnest voice; and Nicholas, who was well aware of the truth of his remarks about the Cossacks and the waggon-drivers of the army, expressed such genuine feeling and regret for the sufferings with which the household had been visited, that Petroff was somewhat appeased.

"But how came your forge to be burned?" I asked, desiring to change the drift of the conversation.

The question called up a look of ferocity on the blacksmith's face, of which I had not believed it capable.

"The Turks did it," he hissed, rather than said, between his teeth. "The men of this village—men whom I have served for years—men by whom I have been robbed for years, and to whose insults I have quietly and tamely submitted until now, for the sake of these," (he pointed to his wife and children)—"became enraged at the outbreak of the war, and burned my workshop. They would have burned my cottage too, but luckily there is a good partition-wall between it and the shop, which stayed the flames. No doubt they would have despoiled my house, as they have done to others, but my door and windows were barricaded, and they knew who was inside. They left me; but that which the Turks spared the Russians have taken. Still, sir," (he turned again full on Nicholas), "I must say that if your Government is honest in its intentions, it is far from wise in its methods."

"You hate the Turks, however, and are willing to serve against them?" asked Nicholas.

The blacksmith shook his shaggy locks as he raised his head.

"Ay, I hate them, and as for—"

"Oh, husband!" pleaded Marika, for the first time breaking silence, "do not take vengeance into your own hands."

"Well, as to that," returned Dobri, with a careless smile, "I have no particular desire for vengeance; but the Turks have taken away my livelihood; I have nothing to do, and may as well fight as anything else. It will at all events enable me to support you and the children. We are starving just now."

Nicholas hastened to assure the unfortunate man that his family would be specially cared for if he would undertake to guide the Russian columns across the Balkan mountains. Taking him aside he then entered into earnest converse with him about the object of his mission.

Meanwhile I had a long chat with his wife and the little ones, from whom I learned the sad details of the sufferings they had undergone since we last met.

"But you won't leave us now, will you?" said little Ivanka pitifully, getting on my knee and nestling on my breast; "you will stay with father, won't you, and help to take care of us? I'm *so* frightened!"

"Which do you fear most, dear?" said I, smoothing her hair—"the Turks or the Cossacks?"

The child seemed puzzled. "I don't know" she said, after a thoughtful pause. "Father says the Turks are far, far worst; but mother and I fear them both; they are so fierce—so *very* fierce. I think they would have killed us if father had been away."

Nicholas did not find it hard to persuade the blacksmith. He promised him a tempting reward, but it was evident that his assurance that the wife and family would be placed under the special care of the authorities of the village, had much greater effect in causing the man to make up his mind than the prospect of reward.

It was further arranged that Petroff should accompany us at once.

"Ready," he said, when the proposal was made. "I've nothing left here to pack up," he added, looking sadly round the poor and empty room. In less than an hour arrangements had been made with the chief man of the village for the comfort and safeguard of the family during the blacksmith's absence.

It was bright noontide when we were again prepared to take the road.

"Oh, Dobri," said Marika, as in an angle of the inn-yard she bade her husband farewell, "don't forget the Saviour—Jesus—our one hope on earth."

"God bless you, Marika; I'll never forget *you*," returned Petroff, straining his young wife to his heart.

He had already parted from the children. Next moment he was in the saddle, and soon after was galloping with the troop to which we were attached towards the Balkan mountains.

Chapter Fourteen
Tells More of what Occasionally
Happens in the Track of Troops

As we advanced towards the high lands the scenery became more beautiful and picturesque. Rich fields of grain waved on every side. Pretty towns, villages, and hamlets seemed to me to lie everywhere, smiling in the midst of plenty; in short, all that the heart of man could desire was there in superabundance, and as one looked on the evidences of plenty, one naturally associated it with the idea of peace.

But as that is not all gold which glitters, so the signs of plenty do not necessarily tell of peace. Here and there, as we passed over the land, we had evidences of this in burned homesteads and trampled fields, which had been hurriedly reaped of their golden store as if by the sword rather than the sickle. As we drew near to the front these signs of war became more numerous.

We had not much time, however, to take note of them; our special service required hard riding and little rest.

One night we encamped on the margin of a wood. It was very dark, for, although the moon was nearly full, thick clouds effectually concealed her, or permitted only a faint ray to escape now and then, like a gleam of hope from the battlements of heaven.

I wandered from one fire to another to observe the conduct of the men in bivouac. They were generally light-hearted, being very young and hopeful. Evidently their great desire was to meet with the enemy. Whatever thoughts they might have had of home, they did not at that time express them aloud. Some among them, however, were grave and sad; a few were stern—almost sulky.

Such was Dobri Petroff that night. Round his fire, among others, stood Sergeant Gotsuchakoff and Corporal Shoveloff.

"Come, scout," said the corporal, slapping Petroff heartily on the shoulder, "don't be down-hearted, man. That pretty little sweetheart you left behind you will never forsake such a strapping fellow as you; she will wait till you return crowned with laurels."

Petroff was well aware that Corporal Shoveloff, knowing nothing of his private history, had made a mere guess at the "little sweetheart," and having no desire to be communicative, met him in his own vein.

"It's not that, corporal," he said, with a serious yet anxious air, which attracted the attention of the surrounding soldiers, "it's not that which troubles me. I'm as sure of the pretty little sweetheart as I am that the sun will rise to-morrow; but there's my dear old mother that lost a leg last Christmas by the overturning of a sledge, an' my old father who's been bedridden for the last quarter of a century, and the brindled cow that's just recovering from the measles. How they are all to get on without me, and nobody left to look after them but an old sister as tall as myself, and in the last stages of a decline—"

At this point the scout, as Corporal Shoveloff had dubbed him, was interrupted by a roar of laughter from his comrades, in which the "corporal" joined heartily.

"Well, well," said the latter, who was not easily quelled either mentally or physically, "I admit that you have good cause for despondency; nevertheless a man like you ought to keep up his spirits—if it were only for the sake of example to young fellows, now, like André Yanovitch there, who seems to have buried all his relatives before starting for the wars."

The youth on whom Shoveloff tried to turn the laugh of his own discomfiture was a splendid fellow, tall and broad-shouldered enough for a man of twenty-five, though his smooth and youthful face suggested sixteen. He had been staring at the fire, regardless of what was going on around.

"What did you say?" he cried, starting up and reddening violently.

"Come, come, corporal," said Sergeant Gotsuchakoff, interposing, "no insinuations. André Yanovitch will be ten times the man you are when he attains to your advanced age.—Off with that kettle, lads; it must be more than cooked by this time, and there is nothing so bad for digestion as overdone meat."

It chanced that night, after the men were rolled in their cloaks, that Dobri Petroff found himself lying close to André under the same bush.

"You don't sleep," he said, observing that the young soldier moved frequently. "Thinking of home, like me, no doubt?"

"That was all nonsense," said the youth sharply, "about the cow, and your mother and sister, wasn't it?"

"Of course it was. Do you think I was going to give a straight answer to a fool like Shoveloff?"

"But you *have* left a mother behind you, I suppose?" said André, in a low voice.

"No, lad, no; my mother died when I was but a child, and has left naught but the memory of an angel on my mind."

The scout said no more for a time, but the tone of his voice had opened the heart of the young dragoon. After a short silence he ventured to ask a few more questions. The scout replied cheerfully, and, from one thing to another, they went on until, discovering that they were sympathetic spirits, they became confidante, and each told to the other his whole history.

That of the young dragoon was short and simple, but sad. He had been chosen, he said, for service from a rural district, and sent to the war without reference to the fact that he was the only support of an invalid mother, whose husband had died the previous year. He had an elder brother who ought to have filled his place, but who, being given to drink, did not in any way fulfil his duties as a son. There was also, it was true, a young girl, the daughter of a neighbour, who had done her best to help and comfort his mother at all times, but without the aid of his strong hand that girl's delicate fingers could not support his mother, despite the willingness of her brave heart, and thus he had left them hurriedly at the sudden and peremptory call of Government.

"That young girl," said Petroff, after listening to the lad's earnest account of the matter with sympathetic attention, "has no place *there*, has she?" —he touched the left breast of André's coat and nodded.

The blush of the young soldier was visible even in the dim light of the camp-fire as he started up on one elbow, and said—

"Well, yes; she *has* a place there!"

He drew out a small gilt locket as he spoke, and, opening it, displayed a lock of soft auburn hair.

"I never spoke to her about it," he continued, in a low tone, "till the night we parted. She is very modest, you must know, and I never dared to speak to her before, but I became desperate that night, and told her all, and she confessed her love for me. Oh, Petroff, if I could only have had one day more of—of—but the sergeant would not wait. I had to go to the wars. One evening in paradise is but a short time, yet I would not exchange it for all I ever—" He paused.

"Yes, yes, *I* know all about that," said the scout, with an encouraging nod; "I've had more than one evening in that region, and so will you, lad, after the war is over."

"I'm not so sure of that," returned the dragoon sadly; "however, she gave me this lock of her hair—she is called 'Maria with the auburn hair' at our place—and mother gave me the locket to put it in. I noticed that she took some grey hair out when she did so."

"Keep it, lad; keep it always near your heart," said the scout, with sudden enthusiasm, as the youth replaced and buttoned up his treasure; "it will save you, mayhap, like a charm, in the hour of temptation."

"I don't need *that* advice," returned the soldier, with a quiet smile, as he once more laid his head on his saddle.

Soon the noise in our little camp ceased, and, ere long, every man was asleep except the sentinels.

Towards morning one of these observed a man approaching at full speed. As he came near the sentinel threw forward his carbine and challenged. The man stopped and looked about him like a startled hare, then, without reply, turned sharply to the left and dashed off. The sentinel fired. Of course we all sprang up, and the fugitive, doubling again to avoid another sentinel, almost leaped into the arms of André Yanovitch, who held him as if in a vice, until he ceased his struggles, and sank exhausted with a deep groan.

On being led to one of the fires in a half-fainting condition, it was found that he was covered with blood and wounds. He looked round him at first with an expression of maniacal terror, but the moment he observed Petroff among his captors he uttered a loud cry, and, springing forward seized his hand.

"Why, Lewie," exclaimed the scout, with a gleam of recognition, "what has happened?"

"The Bashi-Bazouks have been at our village!" cried the man wildly, as he wiped the blood out of his eyes.

"Ha!" exclaimed Dobri, with a fierce look; "we can succour—"

"No, no, no," interrupted the man: with a strange mixture of horror and fury in his blood-streaked face; "too late! too late!"

He raised his head, stammered as if attempting to say more, then, lifting both arms aloft, while the outspread fingers clutched the air, uttered an appalling cry, and fell flat on the ground.

"Not too late for revenge," muttered the officer commanding the detachment. "Dress his wounds as quickly as may be, Mr Childers."

He gave the necessary orders to get ready. In a few minutes the horses were saddled, and I had done what I could for the wounded man.

"You know the village he came from, and the way to it?" asked the commanding officer of Petroff.

"Yes, sir, I know it well."

"Take the man up behind you, then, and lead the way."

The troop mounted, and a few minutes later we were galloping over a wide plain, on the eastern verge of which the light of the new day was slowly dawning.

An hour's ride brought us to the village. We could see the smoke of the still burning cottages as we advanced, and were prepared for a sad spectacle of one of the effects of war; but what we beheld on entering far surpassed our expectations. Harvests trampled down or burned were bad enough, so were burning cottages, battered-in doors, and smashed windows, but these things were nothing to the sight of dead men and women scattered about the streets. The men were not men of war; their peasant garbs bespoke them men of peace. Gallantly had they fought, however, in defence of hearth and home, but all in vain. The trained miscreants who had attacked them form a part of the Turkish army, which receives no pay, and is therefore virtually told that, after fighting, their recognised duty is to pillage. But the brutes had done more than this. As we trotted through the little hamlet, which was peopled only by the dead, we observed that most of the men had been more or less mutilated, some in a very horrible manner, and the poor fellow who had escaped said that this had been done while the men were alive.

Dismounting, we examined some of the cottages, and there beheld sights at the mere recollection of which I shudder. In one I saw women and children heaped together, with their limbs cut and garments torn off, while their long hair lay tossed about on the bloody floors. In another, which was on fire, I could see the limbs of corpses that were being roasted, or had already been burnt to cinders.

Not one soul in that village was left alive. How many had escaped we could not ascertain, for the wounded man had fallen into such a state of wild horror that he could not be got to understand or answer questions. At one cottage door which we came to he stood with clasped hands gazing at the dead inside, like one petrified. Some one touched him on the shoulder, when we were ready to leave the place, but he merely muttered, "My home!"

As we could do no good there, and were anxious to pursue the fiends who had left such desolation behind them, we again urged the man to come with us, but he refused. On our attempting to use gentle force, he started suddenly, drew a knife from his girdle, and plunging it into his heart, fell dead on his own threshold.

It was with a sense of relief, as if we had been delivered from a dark oppressive dungeon, that we galloped out of the village, and followed the tracks of the Bashi-Bazouks, which were luckily visible on the plain. Soon we traced them to a road that led towards the mountainous country. There was no other road there, and as this one had neither fork nor diverging path, we had no difficulty in following them up.

It was night, however, before we came upon further traces of them,— several fires where they had stopped to cook some food. As the sky was clear, we pushed on all that night.

Shortly after dawn we reached a sequestered dell. The road being curved at the place, we came on it suddenly, and here, under the bushes, we discovered the lair of the Bashi-Bazouks.

They kept no guard, apparently, but the sound of our approach had roused them, for, as we galloped into the dell, some were seen running to catch their horses, others, scarcely awake, were wildly buckling on their swords, while a few were creeping from under the low booths of brushwood they had set up to shelter them.

The scene that followed was brief but terrible. Our men, some of whom were lancers, some dragoons, charged them in all directions with yells of execration. Here I saw one wretch thrust through with a lance, doubling backward in his death-agony as he fell; there, another turned fiercely, and fired his pistol full at the dragoon who charged him, but missed, and was cleft next moment to the chin. In another place a wretched man had dropped on his knees, and, while in a supplicating attitude, was run through the neck by a lancer. But, to say truth, little quarter was asked by these Bashi-Bazouks, and none was granted. They fought on foot, fiercely, with spear and pistol and short sword. It seemed to me as if some of my conceptions of hell were being realised: rapid shots; fire and smoke; imprecations, shouts, and yells, with looks of fiercest passion and deadly hate; shrieks of mortal pain; blood spouting in thick fountains from sudden wounds; men lying in horrible, almost grotesque, contortions, or writhing on the ground in throes of agony.

"O God!" thought I, "and all this is done for the amelioration of the condition of the Christians in Turkey!"

"Ha! ha–a!" shouted a voice near me, as if in mockery of my thought. It was more like that of a fiend than a man. I turned quickly. It was André Yanovitch, his young and handsome face distorted with a look of furious triumph as he wiped his bloody sword after killing the last of the Bashi-Bazouks who had failed to escape into the neighbouring woods. "*These* brutes at least won't have another chance of drawing blood from women and children," he cried, sheathing his sword with a clang, and trotting towards his comrades, who were already mustering at the bottom of the dell, the skirmish being over.

The smooth-faced, tender-hearted youth, with the lock of auburn hair in his bosom, had fairly begun his education in the art of war. His young heart was bursting and his young blood boiling with the tumultuous emotions caused by a combination of pity and revenge.

The scout also galloped past to rejoin our party. I noticed in the *mêlée* that his sword-sweep had been even more terrible and deadly than that of André, but he had done his fearful work in comparative silence, with knitted brows, compressed lips, and clenched teeth. He was a full-grown man, the other a mere boy. Besides, Dobri Petroff had been born and bred in a land of rampant tyranny, and had learned, naturally bold and independent though he was, at all times to hold himself, and all his powers, well in hand.

Little did the scout imagine that, while he was thus inflicting well-deserved punishment on the Turkish Bashi-Bazouks, the Cossacks of Russia had, about the same time, made demands on the men of his own village, who, resisting, were put to the sword, and many of them massacred. Strong in the belief that the country which had taken up arms for the deliverance of Bulgaria would be able to fulfil its engagements, and afford secure protection to the inhabitants of Yenilik, and, among them, to his wife and little ones, Dobri Petroff went on his way with a comparatively easy mind.

It was evening when we reached another village, where the people had been visited by a body of Russian irregular horse, who had murdered some of them, and carried off whatever they required.

Putting up at the little hostelry of the place, I felt too much fatigued to talk over recent events with Nicholas, and was glad to retire to a small room, where, stretched on a wooden bench, with a greatcoat for a pillow, I soon forgot the sorrows and sufferings of Bulgaria in profound slumber.

Chapter Fifteen
Simtova—New Views of War—Lancey Goes to the Front, and Sees Service, and Gets a Scare

Shortly afterwards our detachment reached the headquarters of General Gourko, who, with that celebrated Russian general, Skobeleff the younger, was pressing towards the Balkans.

Here changes took place which very materially altered my experiences.

Nicholas Naranovitsch was transferred to the staff of General Skobeleff. Petroff was sent to act the part of guide and scout to the division, and I, although anxious to obtain employment at the front, was obliged to content myself with an appointment to the army hospitals at Sistova.

As it turned out, this post enabled me to understand more of the true nature of war than if I had remained with the army, and, as I afterwards had considerable experience in the field, the appointment proved to be advantageous, though at the time I regarded it as a disappointment.

When I had been some weeks at Sistova I wrote a letter to my mother, which, as it gives a fair account of the impressions made at the time, I cannot do better than transcribe:—

"Dearest Mother,—I have been in the hospitals now for some weeks, and it is not possible for you to conceive, or me to convey, an adequate description of the horrible effects of this most hideous war. My opinions on war—always, as you know, strong—have been greatly strengthened; also modified. Your heart would bleed for the poor wounded men if you saw them. They are sent to us in crowds daily, direct from the battle-fields. An ordinary hospital, with its clean beds, and its sufferers warmly housed and well cared for, with which you are familiar enough, gives no idea of an army hospital in time of war.

"The men come in, or are carried in, begrimed with powder, smoke, and dust; with broken limbs and gaping wounds, mortifying and almost unfit for inspection or handling until cleansed by the application of Lister's carbolic acid spray.

Some of these have dragged themselves hither on foot from that awful Shipka Pass—a seven days' journey,—and are in such an abject state of exhaustion that their recovery is usually impossible. Yet some do recover. Some men seem very hard to kill. On the other hand, I have seen some men whose hold on life was so feeble as to make it difficult to say which of their comparatively slight wounds had caused death.

"I am now, alas! familiar with death and wounds and human agony in every form. Day and night I am engaged in dressing, operating, and tending generally. The same may be said of all connected with the hospital. The doctors under Professor Wahl are untiring in their work. The Protestant sisters of mercy, chiefly Germans, and the 'Sanitaires,' who take the weary night-watches, are quite worn out, for the number of sick and wounded who pour in on us has far exceeded the computations formed. Everything in this war has been under-estimated. What do you think of this fact— within the last fifty days 15,000 men have been killed, and 40,000 sick and wounded sent to Russian hospitals? This speaks to 55,000 Russian homes plunged into mourning,—to say nothing of similar losses, if not greater, by the Turks,—a heavy price to pay for improving the condition of Bulgaria,— isn't it?

"There is a strong feeling in my mind that this is a war of extermination. 'No quarter' is too frequently the cry on either side. I do not say that the Russians mean it to be so, but when Bashi-Bazouks torture their prisoners in cold blood, and show fiendish delight in the most diabolical acts of cruelty, even going the length of roasting people alive, is it strange that a brutalising effect is produced on the Russians, and that they retaliate in a somewhat similar spirit at times? The truth is, mother, that one of the direct and most powerful effects of war is to dehumanise, and check the influence of, the good men engaged, while it affords a splendid opportunity to the vicious and brutal to give the rein to their passions, and work their will with impunity.

"But, while this is so with the combatants, many of those outside the ring are stirred to pity and to noble deeds. Witness the self-sacrificing labours of the volunteer heroes and heroines who do their work in an hospital such as this, and the generous deeds evoked from the peoples of other lands, such as the sending of two splendid and completely equipped ambulance trains of twenty-five carriages each, by the Berlin Central Committee of the International Association for the Relief of Sick and Wounded Soldiers in the field, the thousands of pounds that have been contributed by the Russians for the comfort of their sick and wounded, and the thousands contributed by England for that fund which embraces in its sympathies both Russian and Turk. It seems to me that a great moral war is going on just now—a war between philanthropy and selfishness; but I grieve to say that while the former saves its thousands, the latter slays its tens of thousands. Glorious though the result of our labours is, it is as nothing compared with the torrent of evil which has called us out, and the conclusion which has been forced upon me is, that we should—every one of us, man, woman, and child—hold and pertinaciously enforce the precept that war among civilised nations is outrageous and intolerable. Of course we cannot avoid it sometimes. If a man *will* insist on fighting *me*, I have no resource left but to fight *him*; but for two *civilised* nations to go to war for the settlement of a dispute is an unreasonable and childish and silly as it would be for two gentlemen, who should differ in opinion, to step into the middle of a peaceful drawing-room, button up their coats, turn up their wristbands, and proceed to batter each other's eyes and noses, regardless of ladies, children, and valuables. War would be a contemptible farce if it were not a tremendous tragedy."

My mother's reply to this letter was characteristic and brief.

"My dear Jeff," she wrote, "in regard to your strictures on war I have only to say that I agree with you, as I have always done on all points, heart and soul. Don't forget to keep your feet dry when sleeping out at nights, and never omit to take the globules."

While I was busy at Sistova—too busy with the pressing duties of my post to think much of absent friends, my poor servant Lancey was going through a series of experiences still more strange and trying than my own.

As I have said, he had been appointed by Sanda Pasha to a post in connection with a Turkish ambulance corps. He was on his way to the front, when the detachment with which he travelled met with a reverse which materially affected his fortunes for some time after.

There were two Turkish soldiers with whom Lancey was thrown much in contact, and with whom he had become very intimate. There was nothing very particular in the appearance of the two men, except that they formed contrasts, one being tall and thin, the other short and thick. Both were comrades and bosom friends, and both took a strong fancy to their English comrade. Lancey had also taken a fancy to them. It was, in short, the old story of "kindred souls," and, despite the fact that these Turks were to Lancey "furriners" and "unbelievers," while he was to them a "giaour," they felt strong human sympathies which drew them powerfully together. The name of the thick little man was Ali Bobo, that of the tall comrade Eskiwin.

That these two loved each other intensely, although Turks, was the first thing that touched Lancey's feelings. On discovering that Ali Bobo happened to have dwelt for a long time with an English merchant in Constantinople, and could speak a little of something that was understood to be English, he became intimate and communicative.

Not more tender was the love of David and Jonathan than was that of Eskiwin and Ali Bobo. As the screw to the nut, so fitted the one to the other. Eskiwin was grave, his friend was funny. Ali Bobo was smart, his comrade was slow. They never clashed. Jacob Lancey, being quiet and sedate, observed the two, admired each, philosophised on both and gained their esteem. Their friendship, alas! was of short duration.

"You's goodish sorro man," said Ali Bobo to Lancey one evening, as they sat over the camp-fire smoking their pipes in concert.

Lancey made no reply, but nodded his head as if in approval of the sentiment.

"Heskiwin, 'e's a good un too, hain't 'e, Bobo?" asked Lancey, pointing with his thumb to the tall Turk, who sat cross-legged beside him smoking a chibouk.

Ali Bobo smiled in the way that a man does when he thinks a great deal more than he chooses to express.

At that moment the officer in command of the detachment galloped furiously into the camp with the information that the Russians were upon them!

Instantly all was uproar, and a scramble to get out of the way. Eskiwin, however, was an exception. He was a man of quiet promptitude. Deliberately dropping his pipe, he rose and saddled his horse, while his more excitable comrades were struggling hurriedly, and therefore slowly, with the buckles of their harness. Ali Bobo was not less cool, though more active. Lancey chanced to break his stirrup-leather in mounting.

"I say, Bobo," he called to his stout little friend, who was near, "lend a 'and, like a good fellow. This brute won't stand still. Give us a leg."

The little Turk put his hand on Lancey's instep and hoisted him into the saddle. Next moment the whole party was in full retreat. Not a moment too soon either. A scattering volley from the Russians, who were coming on in force, quickened their movements.

The faint moonlight enabled the Turks to distance their pursuers, and soon the chase appeared to be given up. Still, most of the detachment continued its headlong retreat for a considerable time.

Suddenly Eskiwin observed that Ali Bobo swayed from side to side as he rode, and then fell heavily to the ground. He pulled up at once and dismounted. Lancey, who saw what had happened, also dismounted. The rest of the detachment was out of sight in a moment. There was no sound of pursuers, and they found themselves left thus in a lonely spot among the hills.

On examining the fallen Turk it was found that he had been hit by two balls. One had apparently penetrated his shoulder, the other had grazed his temple. It was the latter which had brought him to the ground, but the shoulder-wound seemed to be the more dangerous.

"Dead!" said Lancey solemnly, as he kneeled beside the body.

Eskiwin made no answer, his grave countenance expressed nothing but stern decision. His friend's face was colourless, motionless, and growing cold. He raised Bobo's hand and let it drop as he gazed mournfully into his face.

Just then the sound of the pursuers was heard, as if searching the neighbouring thicket.

Eskiwin rose slowly, and, with his bayonet, began to dig a grave. The soil was soft. A hollow was soon scooped out, and the dead Turk was put therein. But while the two men were engaged in burying it, the Russians were heard still beating about in the thicket, and apparently drawing near. Lancey felt uneasy. Still Eskiwin moved with slow deliberation. When the grave was covered he kneeled and prayed.

"Come, come; you can do that on horseback" said Lancey, with impatience.

Eskiwin took no notice of the irreverent interruption, but calmly finished his prayer, cast one sorrowful glance on the grave, and remounted his charger.

Lancey was about to do the same, being retarded by the broken stirrup-leather, when a tremendous shout caused his horse to swerve, break its bridle, and dash away. At the same moment a band of Don Cossacks came swooping down the gorge. Lancey flung himself flat beneath a mass of underwood. The Cossacks saw only one horseman, and went past the place with a wild yell. Another moment and Lancey was left alone beside the grave.

To find his way out of the thicket was now the poor man's chief care, but this was difficult, for, besides being ignorant of the road, he had to contend with darkness, the moon having become obscured.

It is a well-known fact that when a lost man wanders he does so in a circle. Twice, during that night, did Lancey start with a view to get away from that spot, and twice did he find himself, after two hours' wandering, at the side of Ali Bobo's grave. A third time he set out, and at the end of that effort he not only came back to the same spot, but chanced, inadvertently, to plant his foot over the stomach of the luckless Turk.

This was too much, even for a dead man. Ali Bobo turned in his shallow grave, scattered the sod, and, sitting up, looked round him with an expression of surprise. At that moment the moon came out as if expressly for the purpose of throwing light on the dusty, blood-stained, and cadaverous visage of the Turk.

Jacob Lancey, although a brave man, was superstitious. On beholding the yellow countenance and glaring eyeballs turned full upon him, he uttered a yell of deadly terror, turned sharp round and fled, stumbling over stumps and stones in his blind career. The Don Cossacks heard the yell, and made for the spot. Lancey saw them coming, doubled, and eluded them. Perceiving only a wounded man sitting on the ground, the foremost Cossack levelled his lance and charged. Ali Bobo's stare of surprise developed into a glare of petrified consternation. When the Cossack drew near enough to perceive an apparently dead man sitting up in his grave, he gave vent to a hideous roar of horror, turned off at a tangent, and shot away into the bushes. Those in rear, supposing that he had come on an ambuscade, followed his example, and, in another moment, Ali Bobo was left alone to his moonlight reflections.

That these were of a perplexing nature was evident from his movements. Allowing his eyes to resume their ordinary aspect, he looked round him with a troubled expression, while his fingers played slowly with the loose earth that still covered his legs. Then he shook his head, after that he scratched it, and put on his fez, which had fallen off. Finding, apparently, that meditation was of no avail, he finally heaved a deep sigh, rose, shook off the dust, picked up his rifle and marched away.

He had not gone far when he came upon Lancey, who, having fled with such haste that he could scarcely breathe, had been fain to lie down and rest for a few minutes. Hearing a step behind him, he started up. One glance sufficed. The dead Turk again! With another horrific howl he plunged headlong into the nearest thicket and disappeared.

A humorous smile stole over the features of Ali Bobo as he began to understand the situation. He searched the thicket, but his late companion was not to be found. Continuing his march, therefore, he travelled all night. Next morning he found his detachment, and introduced himself to his friend Eskiwin, whose astonishment, I need scarcely say, was great, but his joy was greater.

Ali Bobo's wounds turned out after all to be slight, and were not permitted by him to interfere long with his service in the field.

Chapter Sixteen
Lancey gets Embroiled in Troubles, and Sees some Peculiar Service

Meanwhile Jacob Lancey, impressed with the belief that the Turkish detachment had taken to the mountains, travelled as rapidly as possible in that direction.

Next morning at daybreak he found himself so thoroughly exhausted as to be unable to proceed. With difficulty he climbed a neighbouring eminence, which, being clear of bushes, gave him a view of the country around. There was a small village, or hamlet, within a stone's throw of him. The sight revived his drooping spirits. He descended to it at once, but found no one stirring—not even a dog. Perceiving a small outhouse with its door ajar, he went to it and peeped in. There were a few bundles of straw in a corner. The temptation was irresistible. He entered, flung himself on the straw, and fell sound asleep almost immediately.

The sun was shining high in the heavens when he was awakened by a rude shake. He started up and found himself in the rough grasp of a Bulgarian peasant.

Lancey, although mentally and morally a man of peace, was physically pugnacious. He grappled at once with the Bulgarian, and being, as we have said, a powerful fellow, soon had him on his back with a hand compressing his windpipe, and a knee thrust into his stomach. It would certainly have fared ill with the Bulgarian that day if a villager had not been attracted to the hut by the noise of the scuffle. Seeing how matters stood, he uttered a shout which brought on the scene three more villagers, who at once overwhelmed Lancey, bound him, and led him before the chief man of the place.

This chief man was a Turk with a very black beard. Lancey of course expected to receive severe punishment without trial. But, on hearing that he had merely attacked a Bulgarian, the Turk seemed rather inclined to favour the prisoner than otherwise. At all events, after ascertaining that he could not communicate with him by any known language, he sent him to his kitchen to obtain a meal, and afterwards allowed him to depart, to the evident indignation of the Bulgarian and his friends, who did not, however, dare to show their feelings.

For some time Lancey wandered about endeavouring to make friends with the people, but without success. As the day advanced, the men, and most of the women, went to work in the fields. Feeling that he had not obtained nearly enough of sleep, our wanderer took an opportunity of slipping into another outhouse, where he climbed into an empty loft. There was a small hole in the loft near the floor. As he lay down and pillowed his head on a beam, he found that he could see the greater part of the village through the hole, but this fact had barely reached his brain, when he had again fallen into the heavy slumber of an exhausted man.

His next awakening was caused by shouts and cries. He raised himself on one elbow and looked out of his hole. A large body of Russian soldiers had entered the village, and were welcomed with wild joy by the Bulgarians, while the Turkish inhabitants—those of them who had not been able or willing to leave—remained quiet, but polite. The column halted. The men swarmed about the place and "requisitioned," as the phrase goes, whatever they wanted—that is, they took what they chose from the people, whether they were willing or not. To do them justice, they paid for it, though in most cases the payment was too little.

There was a good deal of noisy demonstration, and some rough treatment of the inhabitants on the part of those who had come to deliver them, but beyond being "cleaned out," and an insufficient equivalent left in money, they were not greatly the worse of this visit from the regulars.

The loft where Lancey had ensconced himself did not attract attention. He felt, therefore, comparatively safe, and, while he watched the doings of the soldiery, opened his wallet and made a hearty meal on the débris of his rations.

Before he had finished it the trumpets sounded, the troops fell in, and the column left the place.

Then occurred a scene which astonished him not a little. No sooner were the troops out of sight than the Bulgarian population, rising *en masse*, fell upon their Turkish brethren and maltreated them terribly. They did not, indeed, murder them, but they pillaged and burned some of their houses, and behaved altogether in a wild and savage manner. Lancey could not understand it. Perhaps if he had known that these Bulgarians had, for many years, suffered horrible oppression and contemptuous treatment from the Turks under whose misrule they lay, he might have felt less surprise, though he might not have justified the act of revenge. If it be true that the worm turns on the foot that crushes it, surely it is no matter of wonder that human beings, who have long been debased, defrauded, and demoralised, should turn and bite somewhat savagely when opportunity offers!

It had occurred to Lancey, when the Russians had arrived, that it would be well for him to descend and join these troops, so as to get out of his present predicament; but, remembering that he had actually accepted service with the Turks, and that, being clothed in a semi-Turkish costume, he might be taken for a spy, he resolved to remain where he was. The riot in the village after the Russian column had left confirmed him in his intention to remain quiet.

"Your wisest plan, Jacob," he soliloquised, "is to 'old on and bide your time. Don't 'urry yourself on any account."

Scarcely had he made this resolve when, looking through his hole of observation, he observed a body of spearmen galloping along the road that led to the village. The inhabitants also observed them with some anxiety, for by that time they had come to know the difference between regular and irregular troops.

The horsemen proved to be Cossacks. The Bulgarians, of course, regarded them as friends. They formed a portion of the army of deliverers from Turkish misrule. As such they were received with cheers. The cheers were returned heartily—in some cases mingled with laughter—by the gay cavaliers, who had also come to make "requisitions." Their mode of proceeding, however, was quite different from that of their "regular" brethren. Leaping from their saddles, they set about the business without delay. Some went to the fields and cut grain for fodder. Others entered the houses and carried off victuals and wine, while many chased and caught pigs and poultry.

They were evidently in a hurry. So much so, that they had no time to put off in making payment! It was obviously to be regarded as an outstanding debt against them by the villagers. As the rear-guard passed out of the place, the corporal in command observed a fat young pig in the middle of a by-road. He turned aside sharply, charged, picked the pig neatly up on the point of his lance, and galloped after his friends, accompanied by a tune that would have done credit to a Scotch bagpipe.

All this did Lancey see from his secret point of observation, and deeply did his philosophic mind moralise on what he saw.

The village in which he had sought shelter was in the very heart of the district swept by the wave of war. The panorama of incidents commenced to move again at an early hour.

When morning light had just begun to conquer night, Lancey was once more awakened from a refreshing sleep by a noise in the room below. He looked down and saw an old, old woman, with bent form, tottering step, and wrinkled brow. She was searching for something which, evidently, she could not find. Scraping various things, however, and tasting the ends of her thin fingers, suggested that she was in search of food. Lancey was a sympathetic soul. The old woman's visage reminded him of his own mother—dead and gone for many a day, but fresh and beautiful as ever in the memory of her son.

He descended at once. The old woman had flung herself down in despair in a corner of the hovel. Lancey quickly emptied the remnants of food in his wallet into her lap.

It would have saddened you, reader, to have seen the way in which that poor old thing hungrily munched a mouthful of the broken victuals without asking questions, though she glanced her gratitude out of a pair of large black eyes, while she tied up the remainder in a kerchief with trembling haste.

"No doubt," soliloquised Lancey, as he sat on a stool and watched her, "you were a pretty gal once, an' somebody loved you."

It did not occur to Lancey, for his philosophy was not deep, that she might have been loved more than "once," even although she had *not* been a "pretty gal;" neither did it occur to him—for he did not know—that she was loved still by an old, old man in a neighbouring hut, whose supper had been carried off by the Cossacks, and whose welfare had induced her to go out in search of food.

While the two were thus engaged their attention was attracted by a noise outside. Hastening to the door Lancey peeped out and beheld a band of Bashi-Bazouks galloping up the road. The Turks of the village began to hold up their heads again, for they regarded these as friends, but scant was the courtesy they received from them. To dismount and pillage, and to slay where the smallest opposition was offered, seemed the order of the day with these miscreants. For some time none of them came near to the hut where Lancey and the old woman were concealed, as it stood in an out-of-the-way corner and escaped notice.

While the robbers were busy, a wild cheer, accompanied by shots and cries, was heard some distance along the road. The Bashi-Bazouks heard it and fled. A few minutes later Lancey saw Turkish soldiers running into the village in scattered groups, but stopping to fire as they ran, like men who fight while they retreat. Immediately after there was a rush of men, and a column of Turkish infantry occupied the village in force. They were evidently hard pressed, for the men ran and acted with that quick nervous energy which denotes imminent danger.

They swarmed into the houses, dashed open the windows, knocked out loop-holes in the walls, and kept up a furious fusillade, while whistling balls came back in reply, and laid many of them low.

One party of Turks at last made a rush to the hut where Lancey sat with the old woman. There was no weapon of any sort in the hut, and as Lancey's arms had been taken from him when he was captured, he deemed it the wisest policy to sit still.

Leaping in with a rush, the Turks shut and barred the door. They saw Lancey, but had evidently no time to waste on him. The window-frame was dashed out with rifle-butts, and quick firing was commenced by some, while others made loop-holes in the mud walls with their bayonets. Bullets came pinging through the window and brought down masses of plaster from the walls. Suddenly a terrible yell rang in the little room, and the commander of the party, raising both hands above him, dropped his sword and fell with a terrible crash. He put a hand to his side and writhed on the floor in agony, while blood flowed copiously from his wound. The poor fellow's pain lasted but a moment or two. His head fell back suddenly, and the face became ashy pale, while his glaring eyeballs were transfixed in death.

No notice was taken of this except by a man who sat down on the floor beside his dead commander, to bandage his own wounded arm. Before he had finished his task, a shout from his comrades told that danger approached. Immediately the whole party rushed out of the hut by a back door. At the same instant the front door was burst open, and a soldier leaped in.

It was evident to Lancey that, in the midst of smoke and turmoil, a mistake had been made, for the man who appeared was not a Russian but a Turk. He was followed by several companions.

Casting a savage piercing look on Lancey, and apparently not feeling sure, from his appearance, whether he was friend or foe, the man presented his rifle and fired. The ball grazed Lancey's chest, and entering the forehead of the old woman scattered her brains on the wall.

For one moment Lancey stood horror-struck, then uttered a roar of rage, rose like a giant in his wrath, and seized a rifle which had been dropped by one of the fugitive soldiers. In an instant the bayonet was deep in the chest of his adversary. Wrenching it out, he swung the rile round and brought the butt down on the skull of the man behind, which it crushed in like an egg-shell. Staggered by the fury of the onslaught, those in rear shrank back. Lancey charged them, and drove them out pell-mell. Finding the bayonet in his way, he wrenched it off, and, clubbing the rifle, laid about him with it as if it had been a walking-cane.

There can be no question that insanity bestows temporary and almost supernatural power. Lancey was for the time insane. Every sweep of the rifle stretched a man on the ground. There was a wavering band of Turks around him. The cheers of victorious Russians were ringing in their ears. Bullets were whizzing, and men were falling. Shelter was urgently needful. Little wonder, then, that one tall sturdy madman should drive a whole company before him. The Russians saw him as they came on, and cheered encouragingly. He replied with savage laughter and in another moment the Turks were flying before him in all directions.

Then Lancey stopped, let the butt of his rifle drop, leaned against the corner of a burning house, and drew his left hand across his brow. Some passing Russians clapped him on the back and cheered as they ran on to continue the bloody work of ameliorating the condition of the Bulgarian Christians.

Nearly the whole village was in flames by that time. From the windows of every house that could yet be held, a continuous fire was kept up. The Russians replied to it from the streets, rushing, in little bands, from point to point, where shelter could be found, so as to escape from the withering shower of lead. Daring men, with apparently charmed lives, ran straight up in the face of the enemy, sending death in advance of them as they ran. Others, piling brushwood on a cart, pushed the mass before them, for the double purpose of sheltering themselves and of conveying combustibles to the door of the chief house of the town, to which most of the inhabitants, with a company of Turks, had retired.

But the brushwood proved a poor defence, for many of those who stooped behind it, as they ran, suddenly collapsed and dropped, as men are wont to do when hit in the brain. Still, a few were left to push the cart forward. Smoke disconcerted the aim of the defenders to some extent, and terror helped to make the firing wild and non-effective.

Against the town-house of the village some of the Russians had already drawn themselves up so flat and close that the defenders at the windows could not cover them with their rifles. These ran out ever and anon to fire a shot, and returned to reload. Meanwhile the brushwood was applied to the door and set on fire, amid yells of fiendish joy.

Lancey had followed the crowd almost mechanically. He had no enemy—no object. The Turk, as it happened, was, for the time being, his friend.

The Muscovite was not, and never had been, his foe. After the first deadly burst of his fury on seeing the innocent old woman massacred had passed, his rage lost all point. But he could not calm his quivering nerves or check the fierce flow of his boiling blood. Onward he went with the shouting, cheering, yelling, and cursing crowd of soldiery, his clothes cut in many places with bullets, though flesh and bone were spared.

Close to the town-house stood the dwelling of the Turk who had released him, and shown him hospitality when he was seized by the inhabitants. The door of the house was being burst open by clubbed rifles. The memory of a "helping hand," however slight, was sufficient to give direction to the rage of the madman, for such he still undoubtedly was at the moment—like many another man who had become sane enough the following day when the muster-roll was called.

Up to that moment he had been drifting before the gale. He now seized the helm of his rage, and, upsetting two or three of the men who stood in his way, soon drew near to the front. As he came forward the door gave way. A tremendous discharge of fire-arms laid low every man in advance; but of what avail is it to slay hundreds when thousands press on in rear?

Lancey sprang over the dead and was met by the points of half a dozen bayonets,—the foremost man being his deliverer with the black beard.

Grounding his rifle with a crash, and holding up his left hand, he shouted—"A friend!"

At the same moment he was thrown down and leaped over by the soldiers behind, who were stabbed by the Turks and fell on him. But Lancey staggered again to his feet, and using his superior strength to push aside and crush through those in front, he gained an empty passage before the others did, and rushed along towards a door at the end of it.

Opening the door and entering he was arrested by the sight of a beautiful Turkish girl, who stood gazing at him in horror. Before he had time to speak or act, a door at the other end of the room opened, and the Turk with the black beard entered sword in hand. The girl rushed into his arms, with a cry of joy. But this was changed into alarm as the Turk flung her off and ran at Lancey.

There was no time for explanation. The Russians were already heard coming along the passage by which he had reached the apartment. Lancey felt intuitively that a brave man would not stab him in the back. Instead of defending himself he dropped his rifle, turned, and hastily shut and bolted the door, then, turning towards the Turk, held aloft his unarmed hands. The Turk was quick to understand. He nodded, and assisted his ally to barricade the door with furniture, so that no one could force a passage for a considerable time. Then they ran to the other door, which had not yet been menaced. They were almost too late, for shouts and tramping feet were heard approaching.

Lancey caught up his rifle, stepped out of the room, shut the door, and, locking it on the Turk and his daughter, commenced to pace calmly up and down in front of it like a sentinel. Another moment and the Russians rushed up, but halted and looked surprised on beholding a sentinel there, who did not even condescend to stop in his slow measured march, or to bring his arms to the charge to stop them.

One of them advanced to the door, but Lancey grasped his waist with one hand, gently, almost remonstratively, and shook his head. As the man persisted, Lancey gave him a throw which was peculiarly Cornish in its character—he slewed his hip round under the Russian's groin and hurled him back heels over head amongst his comrades, after which feat he resumed the sedate march of a sentinel.

By this time he had been recognised as the man who had routed a whole Turkish company, and was greeted with a laugh and a loud cheer, as the men turned away and ran to effect some other work of destruction.

"Now, my fine fellow," said Lancey, opening the door and entering. "You'll 'ave to defend yourself, for I'm neither a friend o' the Turk nor the Rooshian. They're fools, if not worse, both of 'em, in my opinion; but one good turn desarves another, so now you an' I are quits. Adoo!"

Hurrying out of the house, Lancey picked up a Russian cap and greatcoat as he ran, and put them on, having a vague perception that they might help to prevent his being made prisoner.

He was right. At all events, in the confusion of the moment, he passed through the village, and escaped unnoticed into a neighbouring thicket, whence he succeeded in retiring altogether beyond the range of the assailed position.

Chapter Seventeen
In which some Desperate
Enterprises are Undertaken

At this time the Russians had taken up a strong position in the Balkan mountain range, and entrenched themselves within a short distance of the enemy.

After a night and a day of aimless wandering, Jacob Lancey found himself at last in a rocky defile between the hostile lines. How he got there he could not tell, but there he was, in a position of imminent danger, with the sentinels of the belligerent armies on either side of him.

Evening was setting in when he made this discovery, and recoiled, happily without having been seen, into a narrow rocky place where the fast-failing light had already deepened into gloom. A cold white fog was slowly creeping up from the valleys and covering the hill-sides.

It is in such places and circumstances that men conceive and execute designs, which, according to their nature, are deeds of recklessness or of heroism. Two such ventures were afoot that night.

In the Russian camp preparations were being made for a night attack on a village in possession of the Turks, and out of which, with a view to future movements, it was deemed necessary to drive them. In this village there dwelt a youth, an intimate friend of Dobri Petroff. The two had played with each other in childhood, had roamed about the country together in boyhood, and, when they reached man's estate, had become faster friends than ever, being bound by the ties of intellectual as well as physical sympathy. When this friend, Petko Borronow, left Yenilik at the death of his mother, it was to take charge of the little farm in the Balkan mountains,—the desolate home where his sister Giuana, an invalid, and a beautiful girl, was now left in solitude.

In his capacity of scout, Petroff was always in the neighbourhood of headquarters, and was frequently summoned to the tent of the general commanding, to be interrogated. Thus he chanced to overhear occasional remarks and hints which, when pieced together by his intelligent mind, showed him pretty clearly what was pending.

He sat by the camp-fire that night, buried in meditation, with a series of troubled wrinkles on a brow that was usually open and unclouded. Many a time did he light his pipe and forget to smoke it, and relight it, and again let it die out, until his comrades were impressed by his absence of mind. Well did the scout know by that time the certain fate of a village which was to be fought for by contending armies. To warn his friend Borronow in time to remove his sister from the doomed village became to the scout a duty which must be performed at all hazards, but how to do this without deserting his post, and appearing to go over to the enemy, was the difficulty.

"Something troubles you," said his young friend André Vanovitch, who had for some time sat smoking quietly at his side, gazing into the fire, and thinking, no doubt, of the girl with the auburn hair, far away in the land of the Muscove.

"Yes, I'm troubled about friends," was the scout's laconic answer.

"Oh! they're all right, you may be sure, now that our fellows have crossed the Danube in such force," said André, supposing that the other referred to his family.

"Perhaps!" returned Petroff, and relapsed into silence.

Suddenly it occurred to him that he had overheard some expression among the officers around the General of a desire to know more particularly about the disposition of the Turkish force, and the suggestion that a spy should be sent out. His brow cleared at once; with almost a triumphant look on his countenance, he turned sharply to André, and seized his arm.

"Well, Dobri," said the latter, with a smile and look of surprise, "I have had perfect faith in the strength of your grip without requiring positive proof."

"Listen," said the scout earnestly. "I have a job to do, and a risk to run."

"That is obvious to every one in the division," returned André, with a touch of the smile still curling his young moustache.

"Ay, but I mean a private job, and a great risk—the risk of being shot as a traitor or a spy, and I want you, André, to clear my character with the Russians if it fares ill with me."

Petroff's unwonted energy of action and earnestness of look and tone produced their effect on the young dragoon. He listened intently while his friend told him of his intended plan.

"But why go into the enemy's lines without permission?" objected André. "Why risk being thought a deserter when you have only to go and ask leave? It seems to me they would be only too glad to accept your services as a spy."

"I'm not certain that they would accept them," replied the scout, with a return of the perplexed look; "and if they chanced to refuse leave, my case would be hopeless, because I could not and would not dare to act in opposition to positive orders; whereas, if I go off without leave, I shall only be blamed for undertaking a foolish or reckless act; that is, if I return in safety. If I don't return at all, it won't matter what is said or done, but I should count on you, André, explaining that I did not desert."

"But," returned André, "if you merely go to warn and save your friends, I think the General won't think much of your spying."

"You do me injustice, lad," said Petroff quietly. "I shall enter the enemy's lines as a real spy. I will visit every point of his position, ascertain the number of his troops, count his guns, and bring in such information as will make the General wink, I hope, at my having acted without orders. It would please me better to go with permission, but I cannot allow the lives of my friends to hang upon the chance humour of a Russian general. You must remember, André, that I am not a Russian soldier, and may therefore take upon me to exercise a little more personal liberty than you can. Why, you know," continued the scout, with a touch of humour in his glance, as he rose and made some preliminary preparations, "I might refuse to lead you Russians, or might lead you to your destruction."

"You would be shot if you did," returned the dragoon quietly.

"And what if I am willing to be shot in a good cause? I should be no greater hero than every man in your armies. But now, André, one more shake of your hand. We may never meet again, and I won't part without saying I've taken a fancy to you."

"God knows I can truly say the same to you," cried André, leaping up with enthusiasm, and seizing the scout's hand with a grasp as powerful as his own.

"And don't be angry," added Petroff, in a gentle tone, as he tightened his belt, "if I again urge you to keep the locket always in remembrance. You're not likely ever to forget the auburn hair, but you *may*, lad, you may, for there is no perfection in this world, and soldiering is a dangerous life."

André smiled half-contemptuously. He *felt* that the advice was needless. Petroff also smiled kindly, for he knew that it might be needful.

Neither of these men was very deeply impressed with the fact that keeping before the mental eye the Maker of the "auburn hair," and of all other blessed human influences, was a better and safer refuge. But what matter? Does not our Creator in all His dealings make use of means? Does He not lead us step by step from a lower to a higher level? There are no ready-made human angels in this life, male or female, with full-grown wings to bear them over the troubles of earth to a state of sudden sanctification. We are in a rebel world, and, when lifted from the pit by a Saviour's hand, the steps by which the Spirit of God leads us upwards are numerous as well as varied, including sometimes—I write without irreverence—such footholds as "auburn hair."

Disguised as a Bulgarian rustic, Dobri Petroff left the Russian camp, passed the outposts, and, under cover of the fog, gained the neutral ground between the two armies.

Of course the sentries on both sides were numerous as well as vigilant—especially so on such a night. It therefore behoved him to advance with extreme caution. Creeping from mound to rock, and bush to knoll, he reached a small clump of bushes, into which he entered for the purpose of resting a few minutes and considering well his future movements.

A thrill of excitement ran through his frame when he discovered that he was not alone in this thicket. A man sat there leaning against a tree as if asleep. The scout crouched and drew a revolver. A moment sufficed to show that his arrival had not been observed. No wonder, for his approach had been like that of a cat! He was now in great perplexity. The man was evidently not a sentinel of either belligerent—that was plain, but it was equally plain that he was armed. To shoot him would be impossible without putting the sentries of both sides on the alert. To pass him in so small a thicket, without attracting attention, would be difficult. To draw back would necessitate a long détour, involving loss of precious time and increase of risk. A thought occurred to him. Many a time had he hunted among these mountains, and well accustomed was he to glide with serpentine caution towards his game. He would stalk him! Petroff seldom thought twice in cases of emergency. He unbuckled his sword quietly and hung it on a branch, and leant his carbine against a tree, resolving to trust to his great personal strength alone, for he did not mean to sacrifice life if he could avoid it. In case of being driven to extremity, his knife and revolver would suffice.

Then, sinking down until he became lost among the deep shadows of bush and brake, he began the slow, laborious, and silent process of gliding towards his unconscious victim.

This was one of those ventures to which we have referred as being afoot on that foggy night. The other venture had some points of similarity to it, though the end in view was different.

Let us turn aside for a little to the Turkish camp.

There, round one of the watch-fires, a considerable distance to the rear, stood a group of Turkish soldiers chatting and smoking. Although not so noisy as the Russians round their camp-fires, these Turks were by no means taciturn. There was a touch, now and then, of dry humour in the remarks of some, and a sedate chuckle occasionally. Among them stood Eskiwin and his resuscitated friend Ali Bobo. The latter, although not naturally boastful, had been so nettled by a big comrade underrating his courage and muscular power, in regard to which latter he, Bobo, was rather vain, that he vowed he would prove both by going to the front and bringing in, single-handed, a live Russian sentinel!

The big comrade laughed contemptuously, whereupon Ali Bobo rose to carry out his threat, but was warned by his mates of the danger of being shot by his own commander for going on such an errand without leave. Bobo replied that his captain would forgive him when he presented his Russian prisoner. As it was clear that the angry little man was in earnest, his friend Eskiwin vowed he would go with him, and the big comrade agreed to regard the deed as a sufficient proof of Ali Bobo's strength and prowess if a Russian should be brought in by the two of them. Bobo would have preferred to go alone, but Eskiwin would take no denial.

Accordingly the two adventurous fellows went off and were soon lost in the fog. In a short time they reached the front, and began to move with excessive caution in order to pass their own sentries unobserved.

Ali Bobo, it must be remarked, had not originated this idea of stalking sentinels. Some Albanians in the army had already done so with great success; but these ferocious murderers had done it for the mere pleasure of killing their enemies, without any other end in view. Their method was to creep towards a wearied sentinel, which they did with comparative ease, being expert mountaineers. Each man on reaching his victim sprang on him from behind, clapped a hand on his mouth, crushed his neck, after the manner of garrotters, with his strong left arm, and drawing a long keen knife thrust it into his heart.

But our adventurers had no such murderous design as this. To capture a live Russian was their aim.

The front reached, and the Turkish line of sentries safely passed in the fog, they came unexpectedly on two Russian horsemen who were cautiously riding towards the Turkish lines. These horsemen were Sergeant Gotsuchakoff and Corporal Shoveloff. They had been visiting the outposts, and, before returning, were making a little private reconnaissance of the enemy's disposition, for Gotsuchakoff and Shoveloff were enthusiasts in their way, and fond of adventure.

The ground at the spot being much broken, and affording facility for concealment, especially to men on foot, Eskiwin and Ali Bobo crept unseen upon a low cliff, and lay down behind a mass of rocks.

The Russians chanced to select the same spot as a point of observation, but, instead of riding to the top of the eminence, where they would have been rather conspicuous, they rode under the cliff and halted just below,—not far distant from the spot where the Turks lay, so that Eskiwin, craning his long neck over the rocks, could look down on the helmets of the Russian cavaliers.

For some minutes the sergeant and corporal conversed in whispers. This was exceedingly tantalising to the friends above! The hiss of their voices could be distinctly heard. Eskiwin's long arm could almost have reached them with a lance. Presently the corporal rode slowly away, became dim in the fog, and finally disappeared, while the sergeant remained immoveable like an equestrian statue.

"This," whispered Ali Bobo solemnly, "is more than I can stand."

Eskiwin whispered in reply that he would have to stand it whether he could or not.

Bobo didn't agree with him (not an unusual condition of mind with friends). He looked round. A huge stone lay at his elbow. It seemed to have been placed there on purpose. He rose very slowly, lifted the stone, held it in a position which is familiar to Scotch Highlanders, and hurled it with tremendous force down on the head of Sergeant Gotsuchakoff.

The sergeant bowed to circumstances. Without even a cry, he tumbled off his horse and laid his helmet in the dust.

The Turks leaped down, seized him in their powerful arms, and carried him away, while the frightened horse bolted. It followed, probably, an animal instinct, and made for the Russian lines.

The corporal chanced to return at that moment. The Turks dropped their burden and lay flat down beside it. Seeing that his friend was gone, and hearing the clatter of his retreating charger, Corporal Shoveloff put spurs to his steed and followed.

The Turks then rose, tied the legs of the sergeant with his own sword-belt, lest he should recover inopportunely, and bore him to a neighbouring thicket which loomed darkly through the fog.

"Fate smiles upon us," whispered Ali Bobo, as the comrades entered the bushes and laid their burden down.

If Bobo had known that he had laid that burden down within ten yards of the spot where Dobri Petroff was preparing, as I have described, to stalk the figure he had discovered in the same thicket, he might have recalled the sentiment in reference to Fate. But Bobo did not know.

Suddenly, however, he discovered the figure that Petroff was stalking. It was leaning against a tree. He pointed it out to Eskiwin, while the scout, interrupted in his plans, sank into darkness and watched the result with much curiosity and some impatience.

Just then the figure roused itself with a heavy sigh, looked sleepily round, and, remarking in an undertone, "It's an 'orrible sitooation," turned itself into a more comfortable position and dropped off again with another sigh.

But Ali Bobo did not allow it to enjoy repose. He glided forward, and, with a spring like that of a cat, laid his hand upon its mouth and threw it violently to the ground. With the aid of Eskiwin he pinned it, and then proceeded to gag it.

All this Dobri Petroff observed with much interest, not unmingled with concern, for he perceived that the new-comers were Turks, and did not like the idea of seeing a man murdered before his eyes. But the thought of his friend Petko Borronow, and what he had at stake, restrained him from action. He was however at once relieved by observing that, while the short Turk kneeled on the prisoner's chest and kept his mouth covered, so as to prevent his crying out, the tall Turk quickly tied his legs and hands. It was thus clear that immediate death was not intended.

The scout's interest, to say nothing of surprise, was increased by what followed. When the short Turk, pointing a revolver at the prisoner's head, removed his hand so as to admit of speech, that prisoner's first utterance was an exclamation of astonishment in tones which were familiar to Petroff's ear. This was followed by exclamations of recognition from the Turks, and the short man seizing one of victim's tied hands shook it warmly.

At that moment the scout's eyes were opened still wider with amazement, for the unfortunate Sergeant Gotsuchakoff—who, as I have said, had been laid down a few yards from him, and whom he had almost forgotten—began to recover consciousness and growled something in an undertone about its being "far too soon to turn out."

Petroff recognised the well-known growl of the sergeant. In an instant he glided to his side, laid his hand on his mouth, and whispered—

"Gotsuchakoff, be still for your life! I am Dobri Petroff. Do you understand?"

He looked close to the sergeant's eyes, and saw that he was understood. At once he removed his hand, and untied the belt which fastened the sergeant's feet.

Gotsuchakoff was too well used to war's alarms to give way to unreasonable curiosity. He instantly perceived that the scout required of him the utmost circumspection for some reason or other, and, in the spirit of a true soldier, awaited orders in total silence, ready for prompt action.

This was well, because there was little time to spare. When Petroff directed the sergeant's attention to the Turks they were busy undoing the bonds of their prisoner.

Without saying another word, the scout glided swiftly forward. He was promptly followed by the sergeant. Next moment both men leaped on the Turks and had them by their throats.

Eskiwin was no match for Gotsuchakoff, who bore him back and held him like a vice. As for Ali Bobo, strong though he was, he felt himself to be a perfect baby in the grasp of the scout. The two men submitted at once, and while Petroff ordered them in a low tone to keep silence, enforcing the order with the touch of a revolver's muzzle, the sergeant quickly bound their arms behind them.

The scout turned to the prisoner, who was sitting on the ground with eyes dilated to the uttermost, and mouth wide open. He sat perfectly speechless.

There was just light enough to make darkness visible. Petroff looked close in to the face of the man whom he had been about to stalk.

"Lancey!" he exclaimed.

"Dobri Peterhuff," gasped the other.

"Why, where *did* you come from?" asked the scout in Turkish, which he was aware Lancey had been attempting to learn.

"Dobri, my friend," replied the other solemnly, in English, "if this is a dream, it is the most houtrageous dream that I've 'ad since I was a babby. But I'm used to 'em now—only I do wish it was morning."

The scout smiled, not because of what was said, which of course he did not understand, but because of the Englishman's expression. But time pressed; too much had already been lost. He therefore contented himself by giving Lancey a friendly slap on the shoulder and turned to the sergeant.

"Gotsuchakoff," said he, "I'm out on special service, and have already been delayed too long. This man," pointing to Lancey, "is an Englishman and a friend—remember that. The others are Turks. You know what to do with them. I cannot help you, but you won't need help."

"Just so," replied Gotsuchakoff, with an intelligent nod, "only lend a hand to tie them together and then be off about your business."

"Lancey," said Ali Bobo, while the operation was being performed, "zat big Bulgar beast he say you's his friend."

"Big he is, a beast he's not, and a friend he was," replied Lancey, with a dazed look.

Further conversation was cut short by the sergeant ordering the trio to move on. He led them towards the Russian lines by a cord passed round Bobo's neck, and carried a revolver in his right hand. Dobri Petroff immediately disappeared in the opposite direction.

At a later hour that night he entered the cottage of young Borronow. Giuana, Petko's sister, reclined on a rude but comfortable couch. She was singularly pretty and innocent-looking, but very delicate and young. Her friends called her Formosa Giuana or Pretty Jane. Petko had been seated beside her, talking about the war, when his friend entered with a quick stealthy motion and laid a hand on his shoulder.

"Dobri!" exclaimed the youth.

"Petko, there is danger at hand. Mischief is in the air. Time is precious. I may not say what it is, but you know me—I am not easily alarmed. You must promise me to quit this village with your sister within one hour."

"But, Dobri, why?—what?—"

"Petko, no questions. More than that, no remarks," interrupted the scout earnestly and firmly. "Another time I will explain. At present I ask you to trust, believe, and obey your friend. If you would save your life and that of Giuana leave this village within an hour. Go where you will, but leave it."

"I will both trust and obey you, Dobri," said Petko, returning the squeeze of his friend's hand, which he had not yet let go.

"I said that time pressed, Petko; God be with you! Farewell."

The scout turned, stooped to kiss Giuana on her pale cheek, and before either could utter another word was gone.

By midnight Dobri Petroff had made his rounds—now as a carter gruffly and clumsily driving a cart and horse of which he had managed to possess himself; anon as a stupid countryman belonging to the village on the height, noisily wanting to know why the Turks had robbed him of the said cart and horse, which he had conveniently tipped over a precipice, and vowing that he would carry his complaint against the army to the Sultan himself; once he was fain to act the part of a drunk man, almost incapable of taking care of himself.

During his perambulations he ran frequent risk of being shot by irascible Bashi-Bazouks or wearied Albanians; was more than once looked on with suspicion, and frequently suffered rough treatment, but he acted his part well. Nothing could draw from him a word or look beyond average intelligence.

No indignity could rouse him to more than the warfare of abuse, and the result was that long before dawn he found himself once more close to the front.

But fortune seemed inclined to fail him here. He was creeping cautiously among a heap of rocks when a sentinel of the advanced line of the Turks discovered and challenged him. Petroff knew well that escape by running would be impossible, for he was only six yards distant. He made therefore no reply, but sank on the ground, keeping his eye, however, sharply on the advancing sentinel. His only cause of anxiety was that the Turk might fire at him, in which case his doom would have been sealed. The Turk, however, preferred to advance and thrust his bayonet into him.

Petroff had calculated on and was prepared for this. He caught the bayonet and checked its progress between his ribs. Another moment and the Turk lay on his back with the stock of his own rifle broken over his skull. The scuffle had attracted the next sentry, who ran to his comrade's assistance. The scout instantly made the best use of his legs. He was as fleet as a mountain deer, but the rifle-ball was fleeter. He felt a sharp pain in his left arm, and almost fell. The alarm was given. Sentries on both sides fired, and another bullet grazed his temple, causing blood to flow freely down his face. Still he ran steadily on, and in a few minutes was safe within the Russian lines.

He was seized, of course, by those who first met him, and, not being known to them, was at once carried before a captain of dragoons, who knew him.

By the captain he was sent to the tent of the General—the younger Skobeleff,—to whom he related the important information which he had obtained at so great risk.

"Thank you, my fine fellow," said the General, when Petroff had finished; "you have done good service—are you badly wounded?"

"No—nothing worth mentioning," replied the scout, but as he spoke a feeling of giddiness oppressed him. He fainted and fell as he left the General's tent, and was carried on a stretcher to the rear.

Before the grey dawn had dissipated the mists of morning, the village on the height was fought for, lost, and won; its dwellings were reduced to ashes, and those of its inhabitants who had escaped massacre were scattered like sheep among the gorges of their native hills; but Petko and Giuana Borronow were safe—at least for the time—with a kinsman, among the higher heights of the Balkan range.

Chapter Eighteen
Treats of one of our Great Ironclads

While these stirring events were taking place among the mountains, I had made arrangements to quit the hospitals at Sistova and proceed with a detachment of Russian troops to the front.

The evening before my departure I received a most unexpected and interesting letter from my friend U. Biquitous, the effects of which were so surprising, and I may add unparalleled, that I cannot forbear quoting it. After a few of those sage reflections in which Biquitous is prone to indulge, he went on to say:—

"You will be surprised to hear that there is some probability of my meeting you shortly, as I have become a special correspondent, like yourself. My paper, however, is an illustrated one, an Irish weekly of some merit, named the *Evergreen Isle*, which will now, it is expected, advance to the front rank of such periodicals. I purpose using the pencil as well as the pen, and, unlike you, and subject to no restrictions of any kind. I have *carte-blanche*, in fact, to draw what I like, write what I please, go where I feel inclined, stay as long as I may, and quit when I must. Veracity is no object. I am told to keep as many servants and as large a retinue as I find convenient, and to spare no expense. For the duties of this situation I am to receive no salary, but am at liberty to pay my own expenses. The honour of the thing is deemed more than sufficient compensation.

"In virtue of this appointment I went recently to see and take notes of Her Majesty's famous ironclad turret-ship, the *Thunderer*. Knowing how much you are interested in the navy of England, I will relate a little of what I saw, premising, how ever, that although strict veracity is not required of me, I am, as you know, a man of principle, and therefore impose it on myself, so that whatever I say in this letter in regard to this splendid man-of-war may be relied on as absolutely true.

"Well, then, the gallant captain of the *Thunderer*, who is said to be one of the best disciplinarians in the service, and to have done many a deed of daring in the course of his adventurous career, received me very kindly. He is every inch a sailor, and as there are full seventy-three inches of him, I may be excused for styling him a splendid specimen. In consequence of my being a friend of a friend of his, the captain invited me to spend several days on board. During my stay I inhabited the captain's 'fighting cabin,'—and this, by the way, reminds me that I was introduced to a young lieutenant on board, named Firebrand, who says he met you not long ago at Portsmouth, and mortally offended your mother by talking to her about the *Thunderer's* crinoline! The 'fighting cabin' is so styled because it may be inhabited in safety while the ship is in action, being within the ship's tremendous armour plating. In times of peace the captain occupies a large handsome cabin on the deck, which, although made of iron capable of resisting winds and waves, and beautifully furnished, is nevertheless liable to be swept bodily into the sea if hit by the giant shot of modern days. A corresponding cabin on the port side of the ship constitutes the ward-room. This also might be blown to atoms, with the officers and all their belongings, if a shell were to drop into it. But the officers also have places of refuge below while in action.

"A large proportion of what meets the eye above the water-line of this ironclad, and looks solid enough, is of this comparatively flimsy build; not meant to resist shot or shell; willing, as it were, to be blown away, if the enemy can manage it, though proof against rifle-bullets. There is a huge central erection, styled the 'flying' or 'hurricane' deck, from which enormous davits project with several boats pendent therefrom. Out of this flying structure rise the great iron mast—with a staircase inside leading to the 'top'—and the two smoke-funnels of the engines. In the heart of it rises 'the fighting tower,' an armoured core, as it were, from which the captain and officers may survey the aspect of affairs while fighting, steer, and, by means of electricity, etcetera, work the monster guns of the ship. If all the flimsy work about the vessel were blown into the sea, her vitality would not be affected, though her aspect would indeed be mightily changed for the worse, but the *Thunderer* in her entirety, with her low-armoured hull, her central fighting-tower, her invulnerable turrets with their two 35-ton and two 38-ton guns, and all her armament and men, would still be there, as able and ready for action as ever.

"Very simply yet very tastefully arranged did the captain's fighting cabin seem to me as I lay down on its narrow but comfortable bed, the first night of my visit, and looked around me. Besides a commodious little chest of drawers, there were on one wall telescopes, swords, and naval caps; on another a compact library. Above my head, stretching diagonally across the bed, was an object which caused me no little surprise and much speculation. In appearance it resembled a giant flute with finger holes that no man of mortal mould could have covered. Not till next morning did I discover that this tube was part of a system of air-distributing pipes, supplied by fanners worked by steam, whereby fresh air is driven to every part of the vessel.

"'So,' said I to myself, turning to the prettily-painted wall at my side, and giving it a slight tap, 'the proverbial two-inch plank between me and death is here increased to somewhere about thirty inches.'

"In this soliloquy I referred to the *Thunderer's* armour-plates, of from ten to twelve inches thick, which are affixed to a timber backing of eighteen inches in two layers. With such a backing of solid comfort between me and 'death,' I felt soothed, and dropped asleep.

"It was Saturday night. On Sunday morning I was awakened by a rushing of water so furious that I fancied the sea must have proved more than a match for the 12-inch armour and 18-inch backing; but a moment or two of attentive reflection relieved me. Your friend Firebrand's voice was audible. I listened. He muttered something, and yawned vociferously, then muttered again— 'Splend—propns—a—yi—a—ou!'

"'Splendid proportions!' he resumed again, after a pause, during which the rush of water became more alarming, sundry gasps and much hard breathing being mingled with it,—'Mag-nificent,' continued Firebrand in the low calm tone of a contemplative connoisseur; 'couldn't have believed it if I hadn't seen it. Quite Herculean!'

"From all this I came gradually to understand that some of the officers were performing their morning ablutions with sponge and towel, while Firebrand was looking languidly over the edge of his hammock, indulging in a critical commentary.

"Just then I was surprised to hear a muffled thunderous bang! It was the big drum, and, next moment, the ship's band announced itself with a single bar, excellently played, of 'God Save the Queen.'

"Every Sunday, I found, was begun by a careful and minute inspection of the crew and ship. After breakfast the captain, followed by all his chief officers, went through every hole and corner of the mighty iron fabric. I followed in his wake. At first the thought did not occur to me, but after all was over it struck me that this act was somewhat appropriate to the day. The great *Thunderer* had, as it were, gone into a condition of introspection.

"It was a species of self-examination on the part of the great war-ship, through the medium of its mind—the captain. Here was the father of a tremendously large family going the rounds on Sunday morning to observe whether his moral precepts and personal example during the week had been attended with appropriate results—to see that his 'boys' were neat and clean, and ready for church, and that they had arranged their rooms before breakfast.

"First of all, the men were mustered (by bugle) on the upper deck,—marines on one side, blue-jackets on the other. Then we walked slowly along the front ranks and down the rear, with critical eyes. I observed a crooked collar; the captain observed it too, and put it straight: I saw an ill-put-on belt; the captain also saw it, pointed and referred to it in an undertone. A hole in a pair of trousers I did not observe, but the captain saw it, and commented on it in a somewhat severer manner. Nothing was passed over. Every brawny, powerful, broad-shouldered blue-jacket there was, in nautical phraseology, overhauled from stem to stern. A comment here, a word of approval there, or a quiet reprimand, was all that passed, but, being uttered to the attentive ears of the responsible officers, this was sufficient. After inspection, the men were dismissed, and the captain with his following descended to the interior of the ship. It would take reams of paper, my dear Jeffry, to refer to all that was said and done. I must give you but a brief outline. We went along the sides of the vessel, where the arms were ranged, and any speck of rust or appearance of careless treatment of the polished and glittering weapons was noted, and the responsible officer called then and there to account. So was it in every department. The *Thunderer* lies low, as I have said; much of her is below water, therefore light is scarce and valuable. During our perambulation we came to some machinery and bulkheads, etcetera, which were dingy in colour. 'Paint them white,' said the captain to the officer of each department; 'I don't point out details, but use as much white paint as you can. It makes the ship look light and cheerful.' Every order given was emphatic yet considerate; given to the officer in whose department the hitch occurred, and retailed by him to subordinates who knew well that they would come to grief if they did not make a note of it. Many of the 'departments' were so well managed that no fault at all could be found, and it was evident that the captain, in such cases, found a pleasure in 'giving honour to whom honour was due.'

"'Some men,' said Firebrand, who chanced to be close to me, and to whom I commented on the advantage of thorough obedience, 'some men, however, carry this quality a little too far. I knew of a man once, named Billy Ewart, who prided himself greatly on the care with which he fulfilled every part of his duty, so that it was impossible for the strictest disciplinarian to find fault with him. He had charge of the main deck. One day the Admiral inspected the ship, and took occasion to praise Billy Ewart for cleaning so well the main deck and everything connected with it. "The only dirty things I see," he said, pointing to a hen-coop, "are the legs of your geese." This was, of course, a joke, but it preyed on Billy's mind, and at next inspection he had the geese whitewashed and their legs and bills blackleaded. Poor Billy had no peace after that; even at the theatres, when he chanced to be observed there by his mates, one would call to another, "I say, Jack, who whitewashed the geese!"'

"As Firebrand concluded, we had completed the inspection of the main deck, and descended to the lower deck, where the men lived and messed, and where a clean and trim blue-jacket—'cook of the mess' for the day—stood at the head of each table. The tables and cans and tins and platters and men were required to be as clean and bright as a new pin. Then on we went to the berth of the warrant-officers, and after that down still lower to the engine-room. There the chief engineer came to the front and became responsible for the mighty cranks and gigantic cylinders and awe-inspiring beams, and complicated mazes of machinery, which raised him, in my mind, to little short of a demigod—for you must know that I, like yourself, am full of admiration and ignorance in regard to engineering forces. Next we went to the lowest depths of all, among the boilers, which appeared to me like an avenue—a positive street, sir—in Pandemonium. It was here that the tremendous explosion occurred in July 1876, when upwards of forty men were killed and many wounded, the captain himself (who was in the engine-room at the time) having narrowly escaped suffocation. Thereafter, the magazines of shot and shell were visited, and, in short, every hole and corner of the ship, and thus in an hour or so it was ascertained that the Nelsonian demand, and England's expectation, had been fulfilled,—'every man' had done 'his duty,' and the great ironclad was pronounced to be in a healthy, Sabbatic state of mind and body.

"In this satisfactory frame we finally went to the fore part of the ship, where we found the crew assembled, and where, standing at the capstan, the captain read the Church of England service, the responses being effectively rendered by the stalwart crew. In regard to this service I will only remark that I observed the introduction of a prayer which was entirely new to me, namely, that for the blessing of God on the ship, its crew, its duties, and its destination, to which I could and did, with all heartiness, respond 'Amen,' because as long as God's blessing rests on the *Thunderer* she will not be sent out to do battle in an unrighteous cause.

"Next morning I had an opportunity of witnessing the big-gun turret drill.

"It was an imposing spectacle, a fine display of the power of mind over matter. Force, might, weight, appeared to have attained their culminating exemplification here, and yet the captain said to me that his 35-ton and 38-ton guns are mere pistols to the things which are being prepared for vessels of our navy yet to come.

"My dear fellow, do you know what a 38-ton gun means? Have you ever seen one? Can you appreciate the fact that its weight is equal to thirty-eight carts of coals? Did you ever see the powder with which it is fed? One grain of it was given to me as a great favour, by the chief gunner's mate—I think that is his correct title, but am not quite sure. He presented it in a cardboard box. I now send you its portrait."

(Facsimile of a grain of powder for the 38-ton guns of the Thunderer—actual size.)

"Here it is, as large as life—really so, without a touch of exaggeration. I have measured it carefully with a tape foot-rule, and I find the dimensions to be five inches and a quarter in circumference.

"It is a solid cube of gunpowder. The cartridge which holds this powder is a pillow, an absolute bolster, of some three feet in length and twelve inches in diameter. It had need be, for the shell which it is meant to propel is the size of a small boy and the weight of an average ox, namely 814 lbs. The length of each 38-ton gun is nineteen feet, and its range about 6000 yards. Just try to imagine an ox being propelled through space, between three and four miles, at a rate which I don't recollect, and which doesn't signify. Try also to remember that each gun costs between 2000 pounds and 3000 pounds, and that, every time a turret lets fly a shot from one of her guns, the expense is 12 pounds, 10 shillings. The 80-ton guns which are to supersede these will, it is said, cost upwards of 10,000 pounds each. This will enable you to form some idea of England's 'greatness.'

"The drill and working of these guns is magnificent. Nearly everything in the fore-turret is worked by steam and hydraulic power, so that comparatively few men are required to move the iron monsters. Let me ask you to imagine the men at their stations. Some are inside the turret, and as guns and turret move in concert the men inside move with them. Those outside the turret stand at its base, and are therefore below the iron deck and protected by the iron sides of the ship. The insiders revolve, aim, and fire the gun; the outsiders load. The first lieutenant, standing at the base of the tower, close to the hole by which it is entered, so that he may be heard by both out and insiders, shouts, 'Close up,' in the voice of a Stentor. At this some men grasp levers, others stand by wheels which let on respectively hydraulic power and steam. The captain of the tower, seated on an elevated position, puts his head through a man-hole in the roof of the turret, which hole is covered with a bullet-proof iron hood, having a narrow opening in front. He surveys the supposed enemy, and his duty is to revolve the tower, take aim, and let go the firing machinery, i.e. pull the trigger. The outsiders stand by the locking bolt, levers, shot-racks, etcetera. Then, in the attitude of ready-for-action, all become motionless attentive statues—a regular *tableau-vivant*.

"Stentor again shouts, 'Cast loose.' To my ignorant eye energetic confusion ensues. The captain of the turret is causing it to revolve this way and that, with its crew and guns, by a mere touch of his finger. Lever and wheel-men do their duty; the guns are run in (or out when required) with the ease of pop-guns, till certain marks on carriages and slides correspond; then they are laid, firing-gear is cleared and made ready, while the outsiders take out the tompion, open the port and scuttle of the gun about to be loaded, bring forward a bolster of powder (or a representative mass of wood), and place a giant shot on a 'trolly,' which is just a little railway-carriage to convey the shot on rails from its rack to the gun. Meanwhile the captain of the turret gives the order, 'Starboard (or port) loading position,' turns the turret until the gun is opposite its 'loading-hole,' and then depresses its muzzle to the same point, jams it against the hole, and the turret is 'locked.'

"'Sponge and load,' is now given—but not by Stentor. The forces at work are too great in some cases to be left to the uncertain human voice. A piece of mechanism, called a 'tell-tale,' communicates with infallible certainty that the monster is quite ready to feed! A hydraulic ramrod thereupon wets his whistle with a sponge, on the end of which is a small reservoir of water. The monster is temperate. This withdrawn, a wad is placed on the end of the ramrod. Three men shove a bolster of powder into the gun's mouth. The huge shot is then hydraulically lifted to the muzzle. No mortal man could move that shot a hair's-breadth in the right direction, but the hydraulic ram is brought to bear, and shoves the delicious *morceau* not *down* but *up* his throat with an ease that would be absurd if it were not tremendous. The tell-tale now intimates to the insiders, 'Gun loaded.' The captain of the turret gives the order, 'Run out.' Hydraulic at work again. In a few seconds the gun muzzle is raised, and projects through its port-hole. When the object and distance are named, the captain of the turret takes aim, and then follows, in more or less rapid succession, 'Elevate,' 'Depress,' 'Extreme elevation,' or the reverse, 'Ready!'— 'Fire!' when the *Thunderer* is shaken to her centre, and twelve pounds ten shillings sterling go groaning uselessly into the deep, or crashing terrifically through the armour-plates of an unfortunate enemy.

"My dear fellow, this gives you but a faint outline of it, but time and paper would fail me if I were to tell in detail of the mode by which all this can be done by the captain of the *Thunderer* himself, by means of speaking-tubes and electricity and a 'director,' so that he can, while standing in the fighting tower, aim, point, and fire, as if with his own hand, guns which he cannot see, and which are forty feet or so distant from him. Would that I could relate to you a tithe of what I have seen!—the day, for instance, when the blue-jackets, to the number of one hundred and fifty, had a field-day on shore, and went through infantry drill—skirmishing and all—as well, to my unpractised eye, as if they had been regular 'boiled lobsters,' to say nothing of their manoeuvres with the Gatling gun. This latter weapon, perhaps you don't know, is simply a bundle of gigantic muskets which load and fire themselves by the mere turning of a handle—a martial barrel-organ, in short, which sends a continuous shower of balls in the face of an advancing or on the back of a retreating foe. The greater involves the less. No one can deny that, and it is my opinion that in the British navy the sailor now includes the soldier. He is, as it were, a bluejacket and a boiled lobster rolled into one tremendous sausage—a sausage so tough that would be uncommonly difficult for any one, in Yankee phrase, to 'chaw him up.'

"Then there is the Whitehead torpedo.

In The Track Of The Troops | 151

"'A thing of beauty,' says the poet, 'is a joy for ever.' The poet who said it was an— no, I won't go that length, but it is clear that he had not seen a Whitehead torpedo. That delicate instrument is indeed a thing of beauty, for it is elegantly formed of polished steel, but when it happens to stick its head into a ship's stern, it is not a 'joy' even for a moment, and it effectually stops, for ever, all consideration of its qualities by those who chance to feel them. It is shaped like a fish, and has a tail. Its motive power is in its tail, which is a screw propeller. It has lungs, consisting of a tank for holding compressed air. It has a stomach, composed of a pair of pneumatic engines which drive it through the water. Its body is fourteen feet long, more or less. Its head contains an explosive charge of 110 pounds of wet gun-cotton, with a dry disc of the same in its heart. It goes off by concussion, and could sink our largest ironclad—there is no doubt whatever about that. Its cost is between four and five hundred pounds sterling. One of the peculiarities of this celebrated torpedo is, that it can be regulated so as to travel at a given depth below water. This is not so much to conceal its course, which is more or less revealed by the air-bubbles of its atmospheric engine, as to cause it to hit the enemy ten or twelve feet below her waterline. What the effect of this new war-monster shall be is at present in the womb of futurity. I hope sincerely that the world may suffer no greater loss from it than its cost.

"By the way, I must not forget to tell you that I have grown at least an inch since I saw you last, in consequence of having been mistaken for the captain of the *Thunderer*! That the mistake was made by a pretty, innocent, sweet, ignorant young girl, with intensely blue eyes, does not abate my vanity one jot. That such a mistake should be made by *anybody* was complimentary. It happened thus:— I was seated alone in the captain's cabin, writing for the *Evergreen Isle*, when a party of ladies and gentlemen passed the door and looked in. They were being shown over the ship. 'That,' said the blue-jacket who conducted them, 'is the captain's cabin.' 'And is that,' whispered blue-eyes, in the sweetest of voices, 'the captain?' My heart stopped! U. Biquitous the captain of the *Thunderer*! I felt indignant when blue-jacket replied, with a contemptuous growl—'No, miss, 'taint.' They passed on, but I could not rest. I rose and followed blue-eyes about the ship like a loving dog, at a respectful distance. I tried to find out her name, but failed—her address, but failed again. Then they left, and she vanished from my sight—for ever.

"But enough of this. Adieu, my dear Jeffry, till we meet.— Yours affectionately, U.B.

"P.S.—I mentioned you to the captain as a friend of mine, and an enthusiastic torpedoist. Be sure you call on him if you should ever find yourself in the neighbourhood of the mighty *Thunderer*."

Chapter Nineteen
Describes a Stirring Fight

It was late when I folded this letter, about the surprising effects of which I have yet to speak.

Having been very much overwrought in the hospitals that day, I flung myself on my bed and fell into a sound sleep, having previously cautioned my assistant, who occupied a couch opposite mine, not to disturb me except in a case of necessity.

It could not have been long afterwards when I was awakened by him violently, and told that a telegram had just arrived summoning me home! I sprang up and read it anxiously. There was no explanation. The telegram was simple but urgent. My mother, my sister, Nicholas, illness, death, disaster of some sort, filled my mind as I huddled on my clothes and made hurried preparations to obey the summons. Of course no inquiries could be made. The telegram was peremptory. I crushed a few things into a portmanteau, and, obtaining permission, left the hospital without a moment's delay.

The distance to the coast was considerable, but I had ample means, and found no difficulties in the way. It is always so in this life—at least in regard to ordinary things—when one possesses unlimited means.

Now I must pause at this point, and beg the reader to bear with me while I relate a few things that may appear at first sight overdrawn. Let judgment be suspended until all has been told.

There was no difficulty whatever, I repeat, in reaching Varna. From thence to Constantinople was merely a matter of a few hours' in an ordinary steamer. My personal acquaintance with several European ambassadors enabled me to pass the lines and travel in the enemy's country without obstruction or delay. My position as occasional war-correspondent of the *Scottish Bawbee* would have procured me interviews with many celebrities, but anxiety prevented my taking advantage of this.

In process of time I arrived at Besika Bay, and here I found the British fleet at anchor. Of course I had been aware of its presence there, and felt some pleasure in contemplating a visit to some of the ships, in several of which I had friends. It was with great surprise that I found the *Thunderer* among the war-ships assembled in the Bay. I had never heard of her having left England, though I had been told that her sister-ship the *Devastation* was at Besika.

Remembering the injunction of my friend Biquitous, I went on board the *Thunderer*, and was hospitably received by the captain. He had only time, however, to shake hands and beg me to make myself at home. There was obviously something of importance about to happen, for great activity prevailed among officers and men. It seemed to my untutored eye as if they were getting up steam and preparing for some sort of expedition. The captain did not invite me to accompany them; nevertheless I went. It was not long before the object of the expedition was revealed. A monster Russian ironclad, it was said, lay somewhere "outside." We were sent to observe her. In the evening we sighted her. There was another Russian war-ship—a frigate—close to her. The ironclad was similar to ourselves: a long low hull—a couple of turrets with a central "flying" structure or "hurricane-deck." We made straight towards her. The bugle sounded and the crew was called to quarters.

"My dear sir," said I to the captain, "has war been declared between England and Russia?"

The captain made no reply. On repeating the question anxiously he merely said—

"Never mind!"

I was surprised, almost hurt, and greatly perplexed, for the captain was noted for politeness and urbanity, but of course I retired at once.

Next moment I saw a puff of smoke burst from the side of the Russian ironclad, and a shot leaped towards us. Its size was such that we could trace it from the muzzle of the gun. Describing, as I thought (for strange is the power of thought), a rather high trajectory, it passed over us and plunged into the sea with a swish that sent hundreds of tons of water like an inverted cascade into the air. A gush of indignation filled my breast. That the warship of a nation with which we were at peace should fire at us without provocation was more than I could endure.

"Are you going to stand *that*, captain?" I asked, with an uncontrollable gush of indignation at the Russian's audacity.

The captain gave one sardonic laugh, and a shrug of his shoulders, but vouchsafed no reply.

Hearing one of the officers give some order about Whitehead torpedoes, I ran to the room where these monsters were kept. I was just in time to see one lifted on to a species of carriage and wheeled to the side of the ship. Here a powerful air-pump was set to work, and the torpedo's lungs were filled almost to the bursting point. Its deadly head—brought from the magazine—was at the same time attached to its body. Another instant and a port was thrown open in the *Thunderer's* side, through which the Whitehead was launched. It went with a sluggish plunge into the sea. While it was in the act of passing out a trigger was touched which set the pneumatic engines agoing. The screw-propelling tail twirled, and the monster, descending ten feet below the surface, sped on its mission. I rushed on deck. The air-bubbles showed me that the engine of destruction had been aimed at the Russian frigate. In a few seconds it had closed with it. I could see that there was terrible consternation on board. Next moment a fountain of foam shot from the deep and partially obscured the frigate. I saw men leaping overboard and spars falling for a few moments, then the frigate lurched heavily to port and went head foremost to the bottom.

I stood gazing in a species of horrified abstraction, from which I was recalled by some of our men running to the side of the vessel. They were about to lower the steam-launch. It was to be sent out as a torpedo-boat, and young Firebrand, whom I now observed for the first time, took command.

Just then a torpedo-boat was seen to quit the side of the Russian. We were ready for her. Our largest Gatling gun had been hoisted to that platform on our mast which is styled the "top."

When within range this weapon commenced firing. It was absolutely horrible. One man turned a handle at the breech, another kept supplying the self-acting cartridge-box. As the handle was turned the cartridges dropped into their places and exploded. Six or nine tubes, I forget which, were thus made to rain bullets without intermission. They fell on the screen of the advancing torpedo-boat like hail, but quite harmlessly. Then I heard a voice within the fore-turret give a command which sounded like "Extreme depression." It was quickly followed by "Fire!" and the *Thunderer* quivered from keel to truck under the mighty explosion. The great 38-ton gun had been splendidly served, for the monster ball hit the boat amidships and crushed the bow under water, at the same instant the stern leaped into the air, and she went down with a dive like a Greenland whale.

Hearty cheers burst from the men in the "top." These were echoed with a muffled sound from the men shut up in the armoured hull below—for it must be remembered that not a soul had been visible all this time on the *Thunderer* except the men in the "top" and those who had been sent to lower the steam-launch.

Apparently rendered savage by this event, the Russians let fly a volley from their four great-guns, but without serious result. They had been admirably pointed, however, for the two outer shots hit our turrets, deeply indented them, and glanced off, while the inner shots went slap through the flying structure as if it had been made of pasteboard, leaving clean-cut holes, which, of course, only made the place more airy.

Night had now fallen. The danger of attack by torpedo-boats having been recognised, both ironclads had let down their crinolines. But the captain of the *Thunderer* had resolved on a—a—what shall I call it?—a "dodge," which would probably deceive the enemy. He had an electric light on board. Every one knows nowadays that this is an intense light, which, being thrown on a given point, illuminates it with a glare equal, almost, to that of day. After dark the captain shot this light from his mast-head straight at the enemy, and in the full glare of it our steam-launch or torpedo-boat was sent out!

I was amazed beyond measure. Forgetting myself for a moment, I exclaimed, "Captain, you are mad!"

As might have been expected, the captain made no reply.

The steam-launch carried two torpedoes, each containing 100 pounds of powder.

"Be careful to sheer off quickly after exploding," said the captain to Firebrand quietly.

Firebrand replied, "Yes, sir," respectfully, but I heard him distinctly add, in a low tone, to himself, "I'll run slap into her and blow her to atoms as well as myself. *Somebody* must fail in every action. It's a forlorn hope at sea, that's all.—Full steam!" he added aloud to the engineer.

As the boat rushed away in the blaze of the electric light, the captain's *ruse* suddenly dawned on my mind. The Russian at once saw the boat, and, with naturally nervous haste, knowing the terrible nature of such boats, made preparations to thwart her. Close in the wake of the boat the *Thunderer* followed with the intent to run the Russian down with her ram, which is a tremendous iron beak projecting, below water, from her bow. The "dodge" was to dazzle the enemy with the electric light, and, while her attention was concentrated on the torpedo-boat, to "ram" her!

"Steady!" said Firebrand, in a deep voice.

Something else was replied by somebody in a deeper voice.

The boat ploughed on its way like a furious hornet.

"Fire!" shouted the Russians.

Instantly, from turret, bulwark, and mast-head leaped livid flames of fire, and the sea was torn up by bullets, while fearful spouts were here and there raised by shots from the heavy guns. Everything was concentrated on the torpedo-boat. It was obvious that the dazzling light at the mast-head of the *Thunderer* had blinded her adversary as to her own movements.

"Let drive!"

I heard the order of the Russian captain as distinctly as if I had been on board his own ship, and was somewhat surprised at its being given in slang English.

The result was a rain of musketry, which rattled on the iron armour of the launch's protecting screen as the sticks rattle on a kettle-drum.

"Ready!" said Firebrand, with suppressed intensity.

As the boat drew near the Russian small shot was tearing up the sea like a wintry storm. The order having been given, the torpedo-spars were lowered, so that each torpedo sank ten feet under water.

"Fire!" yelled Firebrand.

Electricity was applied, both torpedoes exploded, and the launch sheered off gallantly in cataracts of foam.

At the same moment the Russians observed us not ten yards distant, coming stem on at full speed. Her turret guns were concentrated and fired; so were ours. The crash was indescribably hideous, yet it was as nothing compared with that which followed a few seconds later. Our ram, entering the Russian fairly amidships, cut her almost in two. We backed out instantly, intending to repeat the operation. Well was it for us that we did so. We had just backed a few hundred yards astern, and given the order to go ahead full steam, when the Russian's magazine exploded. Our charge had somehow fired it. Instantly there was a crashing roar as if heaven and earth had met in chaotic conflict. The air was darkened with bursting clouds of blackest smoke, in the midst of which beams, guns, pistons, boilers, armour-plates, human limbs and heads were seen hurling about like the débris of a wrecked universe. Much of this came down upon our iron deck. The clatter was appalling. It was a supreme moment! I was standing on the flying structure beside one of the officers. "Glorious!" he muttered, while a pleasant smile played upon his lips. Just then I chanced to look up, and saw one of the Russian fore-turret 85-ton guns falling towards me. It knocked me off the flying structure, and I fell with an agonising yell on the deck below.

"Hallo!" exclaimed a familiar voice, as a man stooped to raise me.

I looked up. It was my hospital-assistant. I had fallen out of bed!

"You seem to have had a night of it, sir—cheering and shouting to such an extent that I thought of awaking you once or twice, but refrained because of your strict orders to the contrary. Not hurt, I hope?"

"So, then," I said, with a sigh of intense relief, as I proceeded to dress, "the whole affair has been— *A Dream* !"

"Ah!" thought I, on passing through the hospital for the last time before quitting it, and gazing sadly on the ghastly rows of sick and wounded, "well were it for this unfortunate world if war and all its horrors were but the phantasmagoria of a similar dream."

Chapter Twenty
Treats of War and some of
its "Glorious" Results

In process of time I reached the front, and chanced to arrive on the field of action at a somewhat critical moment.

Many skirmishes, and some of the more important actions of the war, had been fought by that time—as I already knew too well from the hosts of wounded men who had passed through my hands at Sistova; and now it was my fate to witness another phase of the dreadful "game."

Everywhere as I traversed the land there was evidence of fierce combats and of wanton destruction of property; burning villages, fields of produce trodden in the earth, etcetera. Still further on I encountered long trains of wagons bearing supplies and ammunition to the front. As we advanced these were met by bullock-trains bearing wounded men to the rear. The weather had been bad. The road was almost knee-deep in mud and so cut up by traffic that pools occurred here and there, into which wagons and horses and bullocks stumbled and were got out with the greatest difficulty. The furious lashing of exhausted and struggling cattle was mingled with the curses and cries of brutal drivers, and the heartrending groans of wounded soldiers, who, lying, in many cases with undressed wounds, on the hard, springless, and jolting vehicles, suffered excruciating agony. Many of these, unable to endure their sufferings, died, and thus the living and the dead were in some cases jolted slowly along together. The road on each side was lined with dead animals and men—the latter lying in a state of apparent *rest*, which called forth envious looks from the dying.

But a still sadder spectacle met my eye when, from another road which joined this one, there came a stream of peasantry, old men, women, and children, on foot and in country carts of all kinds, flying from the raging warriors who desolated their villages, and seeking, they knew not where—anywhere—for refuge. Too often they sought in vain. Many of these people had been wounded—even the women and little ones—with bullet, sword, and spear. Some carried a few of their most cherished household articles along with them. Others were only too glad to have got away with life.

Here an old man, who looked as if he had been a soldier long before the warriors of to-day were born was gently compelled by a terror-stricken young woman with a wounded neck to lay his trembling old head on her shoulder as they sat on a little straw in the bottom of a native cart. He had reached that venerable period of life when men can barely totter to their doors to enjoy the sunshine, and when beholders regard them with irresistible feelings of tenderness and reverence. War had taught the old man how to stand erect once more—though it was but a spasmodic effort—and his poor fingers were clasped round the hilt of an old cavalry sabre, from which female hands had failed to unclasp them. There, in another cart, lay an old woman, who had been bed-ridden and utterly helpless for many a year, but war had wrought miracles for her. It had taught her once again to use her shrunken limbs, to tumble out of the bed to which she had been so long accustomed, and where she had been so lovingly nursed, and to crawl in a paroxysm of terror to the door, afraid lest she should be forgotten by her children, and left to the tender mercies of Cossack or Bashi-Bazouk. Needless fear, of course, for these children were only busy outside with a few absolute necessaries, and would sooner have left their own dead and mangled bodies behind than have forgotten "granny"! Elsewhere I saw a young woman, prone on her back in another cart, with the pallor of death on her handsome face, and a tiny little head pressed tenderly to her swelling breast. It was easy to understand that war had taught this young mother to cut short the period of quiet repose which is deemed needful for woman in her circumstances. Still another cart I must mention, for it contained a singular group. A young man, with a powerfully-made frame, which must once have been robust, but was now terribly reduced by the wasting fires of a deadly fever, was held forcibly down by a middle-aged man, whose resemblance to him revealed his fatherhood. Two women helped the man, yet all three were barely able to restrain the youth, who, in the fury of his delirium, gnashed with his teeth, and struggled like a maniac. I knew nothing about them, but it was not difficult to read the history of one who had reached a critical period in a fell disease, who had, perchance, fallen into a long-desired and much-needed slumber that might have turned the scale in his favour, when the hope of parents and the chances of life were scattered suddenly by the ruthless trump of war. War had taught him how to throw off the sweet lethargy that had been stealing over him, and to start once again on that weary road where he had been grappling in imagination with the brain-created fiends who had persecuted him so long, but who in reality were gentle spirits compared with the human devils by whom he and his kindred were surrounded.

On this journey, too, I met many brethren of the medical profession, who, urged by the double motive of acquiring surgical skill and alleviating human woe, were pressing in the same direction. Some had been fortunate enough, like myself, to obtain horses, others, despising difficulties, were pushing forward through the mud on foot. I need scarcely add that some of us turned aside from time to time, as opportunity offered, to succour the unfortunates around us.

At last I reached the front, went to headquarters, presented my credentials, and was permitted to attach myself to one of the regiments. At once I made inquiries as to the whereabouts of Nicholas Naranovitsch, and was so fortunate as to find him. He was in the act of mounting his horse as I reached his quarters.

It is impossible to describe the look of surprise and delight with which he greeted me.

"My dear fellow!" said he, turning at once to his girths and stirrups after the first hearty squeeze, "what breeze of good fortune has blown you here? Any news from home?"

"Yes, all well, and a message—by the way, I had almost forgot it," fumbling in my pocket, "for you."

"Almost forgot it!" echoed Nicholas, looking round with a smile and a glance which was meant for one of withering rebuke.

"Here it is," I exclaimed, handing him a three-cornered note, which had come in my mother's letter. He seized it eagerly and thrust it into the breast-pocket of his coat.

"Now look here, Jeff," he said, having seen to the trappings of his steed, "you know what war is. Great things are at stake. I may not delay even to chat with *you*. But a few words will suffice. Do you know anything about your servant Lancey?"

"Nothing. I would give anything to hear that the poor fellow was alive. Have you—"

"Yes, I have seen him. I chanced this very morning, while galloping across country with an order from the General, to see him among the camp-followers. Why there I know not. To search for him now would be like looking for a needle in a haystack, but I observed that he was in company with our Bulgarian friend the scout Dobri Petroff, who is so well known that he can easily be found, and will probably be able to lead you to him. Now, only one word for myself: don't forget a message to Bella—say—say—bah! You English are such an undemonstrative set that I don't like to put it in words, but—you ought to know what to say, and when you've said it, just add, like a good fellow, that I would have said a great deal more if I had had the saying of it myself. D'you understand?"

"All right," said I, with a laugh. "We English *feel*, although we don't demonstrate much, and can act when occasion requires it with as much energy as Russians I'll say all you could wish, and some things, mayhap, that you couldn't have said yourself.—But where are you going in such haste?"

"To battle, Jeff," he replied, with one of those proud glances of the eyes which must be somewhat akin to the expanded nostrils of the warhorse when he scents the battle from afar. "At least," he added, "to convey orders which will have some bearing on what is about to follow. The Turk is brave. We find that he fights well."

"Ha!" said I quickly, "you find him a plucky fellow, and begin to respect him?"

"Yes, truly, he is a worthy foe," returned Nicholas with animation.

"Just so," I rejoined, unable to repress a feeling of bitterness, "a worthy foe simply because he possesses the courage of the bull-dog; a *worthy* foe, despite the fact that he burns, pillages, violates, murders, destroys, and tortures in cold blood. What if Bella were in one of these Bulgarian villages when given over to the tender mercies of a troop of Bashi-Bazouks?"

Nicholas had his left hand on the reins and resting on the pommel of his saddle as I said this. He turned and looked at me with a face almost white with indignation.

"Jeff, how *can* you suggest? Bashi-Bazouks are devils—"

"Well, then," said I, interrupting, "let us suppose Cossacks, or some other of your own irregulars instead—"

I stopped, for Nicholas had vaulted on his horse, and in another second was flying at full speed over the plain. Perhaps I was hard on him, but after the miseries I witnessed that day I could not help trying to send the truth *home*.

Time pressed now. The regiment to which I was attached had received orders to march. I galloped off in search of it. At first I had thought of making a hurried search for Lancey or the scout, but gave up the idea, well content to have heard that the former was alive.

The Turks at this time were advancing under Mahomet Ali Pasha on the position occupied by the Russians on the Lom river. As I joined my regiment and reported myself, I heard distant cannonading on the left, and observed troops moving off in all directions. We soon got the order to march, and, on going to the top of a small eminence, came in sight of the field of action.

To my unaccustomed eyes the country appeared to be alive with confused masses of moving men, from some of which masses there burst at intervals the rolling smoke of rifle-firing. Of course I knew that there was order and arrangement, but the only order that impressed itself on me was that of the Russian regiment at my side, as the men strode steadily forward, with compressed lips and stern yet eager glances.

The Turkish troops had moved out and taken up a position on the face of a hill under cover of some woods. As battalion after battalion marched away, I, for the first time, became impressed with the multitudes of men who constitute an army, and, at the same time, with the feeling that something like a pitched battle was about to be fought. From the elevated position on which we stood, I could see that numbers of Russian cavalry were prowling about over the plain, as if watching the movements of the enemy. The intention of the Turks soon became evident, for they suddenly swarmed out of the woods and advanced to the attack. A Russian battery on our right instantly opened on them. This was replied to vigorously by a Turkish battery opposite. While these two turned their attention on each other, the troops in the plain below came into action. They swarmed over the numerous undulations, skirmished through the scrub and the fields of corn and maize, attacked a village in a hollow, and charged on various batteries and positions of strength,—sometimes one side, sometimes the other, being successful. The thunder of the great guns increased, the tremendous rattle of small arms became continuous, with now and again exceptionally strong bursts, when whole battalions fired in volleys. The smoke soon became so dense as partly to obscure the vision.

At that moment a Turkish battalion was seen to approach the mound on which we stood, with the evident intention of storming it. At the same time I observed a squadron of Russian cavalry trot smartly round the skirt of a wood on our left and take up a position. They were not fifty yards from the spot where I stood. I could even see the expression of their faces, and I fancied that the figure and countenance of the right-hand man of the troop were familiar to me.

"He's a fine-looking man, sir, is he not?" said a voice at my elbow.

I turned in amazement. It was Dobri Petroff! There was no room for more than a squeeze of the hand at such a moment.

"That is our friend André Vanovitch, sir."

As he spoke I saw the captain of the troop fall from his horse. A stray ball had killed him, and this was the first thing that drew my attention to the fact that bullets were whistling over our own heads now and then.

This happened at the very moment when a staff officer galloped up to the troop with an order. Seeing what had happened, this officer put himself at the head of the troop and gave the command to advance.

I recognised the voice at once as that of Nicholas. They swept past close in front of us at full gallop, and I could see on the face of Nicholas and on that of the stalwart André the same open, gladsome, noble expression, suggestive of high chivalrous sentiment, and a desire to do noble self-sacrificing deeds for fatherland. My own heart bounded within me as I looked at them, and I could not resist bursting into a cheer, which was taken up and prolonged wildly by the troops around.

The squadron came upon the Turks unexpectedly, but they stood like true men. Courage, however, was of no avail. The dragoons were heavy and irresistible. They cut right through the Turks; turned, charged again, and scattered them like chaff. I could perceive, in the midst of the fray, the lithe forms of Nicholas and André laying about them with tremendous impetuosity.

Personal valour is necessary, but it is not omnipotent nowadays. When the squadron returned, reduced almost to a skeleton, the Turks had reformed, were largely reinforced, and came at us again with steady determination. At the same time reinforcements came pouring in on our side, and I soon found that the position we occupied was deemed one of considerable importance.

The Turks came on steadily, and now I learned, for the first time, the power of modern weapons. Our men were armed with breech-loaders, so that no time was lost in loading.

Our commander acted on a principle which is said to be usually adopted by General Skobeleff. He reserved his fire until the Turks were within a hundred yards, and then gave the order to commence. The scene that followed is indescribable. Eight hundred men fell at once before the withering blast of lead. The firing was continuous. No troops on earth could have stood it. The Turks were instantly shattered and repulsed.

When they had retired, and the smoke had partially cleared away, I saw the plain covered with slaughtered men. Some were prone and motionless in death. Some were moving slightly. Others were struggling, as if in a delirium of agony, which it was frightful to witness. A few had life enough to rise, stagger forward several paces, fall and rise again to repeat the process until death ensued.

I stood fascinated.

"God help us!" I exclaimed aloud; "these murdered hundreds represent thousands of bleeding hearts *At Home* , and yet the maniacs continue to kill each other as if human lives were of no account and human souls not worth a thought."

"Pardon me, sir," said a voice at my side, "the maniacs who cause all this are not here, but at the place you mentioned just now—*at home*. These fine fellows are their unhappy tools, who, with untold depths of enthusiasm and kindliness in their nature, and a good deal of devilment too, are compelled, willing or not willing, to fight for what is called 'religion and country'!"

I found that the speaker was the special correspondent of a Scotch newspaper. As brother "specials" we fraternised immediately; but we had scarcely had time to exchange a few rapid queries and replies when our men were ordered to advance to the attack.

Very soon the ambulance corps was busily employed, and I had to devote my entire energies to the wounded who came pouring in.

Oh! it was pitiful to see the hundreds of strong and stalwart youths, who might have been the glory of succeeding generations, brought in with frames shattered beyond recovery, with brave lip compressed to check the rising cry of agony, with eyes glaring in the terrible conflict between lusty manhood and sudden death, or, with nerves utterly unstrung, giving vent to the shrieks of the maniac.

Several surgeons and students among us had extemporised an hospital in the shelter of a cliff.

One of the students, whose mind was in advance of his years and whose spirit seemed roused, came suddenly to me, during a brief interval in our labours.

"Our rulers are fools, or worse," said he, with indignation; "what is the use of diplomacy if it cannot prevent *this*?"

I remonstrated with the youth on the impropriety of his language, but my new friend the "special" broke in with—

"Ah! young man, you have not yet seen enough of life to understand it. A man is a machine which regulates itself, more or less, for its own interests. A household does the same; a town does likewise; so does a state. No doubt a man sometimes fights with himself—so, too, households are addicted to disagreement, and towns are often afflicted with difference of opinion, while a state is not unacquainted with internal commotions, but, in each and all of these cases, reason and common sense prevent the people from degenerating into pure savages. It is reserved for governments alone, when they come into collision with each other, to do that. *Peoples* don't desire war, my good sir, it is government—in other words, the non-combatant gentlemen at the head of the world's affairs—who thirst for blood, backed up, of course, by such of the people as are more or less interested in the breaking out of war. In all ordinary matters humanity is satisfied to submit its cases to courts of law, to umpires, to individual or collective arbitrators. If things don't go right, it is usually understood among Christian men and women that a little touch of forbearance here, of self-sacrifice there, of pocketing of slight affronts elsewhere, will bring things into the best possible condition, and, where these plans won't do,—as in the case of drunkards, maniacs, and villains,—they understand and quietly practise the power of *overwhelming constraint*. If the Turks had been overwhelmingly constrained by Europe during the late Conference at Constantinople, we should have had no war."

I never met with any nation so fond of argument as the Scotch! Surrounded as we were by dead and dying men, the "special" and the student (who was also Scotch) sat down and lighted their pipes to have it out. To do them justice, there was a lull at the time in the arrival of wounded men.

"But," said the student, in that tone which is so well known to the argumentative, "is not overwhelming constraint tyranny?"

"My friend," replied the special, lighting his pipe at the other's cigar, "if a blackguard stole a poor widow's purse, and six policemen took him up, compelled him to restore it, and put him in limbo, would you call that tyranny?"

"Of course not."

"But it would be overwhelming constraint, would it not?"

"Well—ah!—yes—I see—but—"

"Of course there's a *but*. Quite right. That is the word by which it is conveniently stated that the mind is not yet clear. Far be it from me to coerce you. I would, if I could, clear you. Listen, then:—

"Has not the Turk treated his Christian subjects in a way that can only be expressed as diabolical?"

"Unquestionably. Every one admits that: but he promises to govern them better in future."

"If a thief," said the special, "were to promise amendment and restoration of stolen property, would you let him off with the stolen property in his pocket?"

"Certainly not," answered the student.

"Well, then, the Turk has stolen the *liberty* of his Christian subjects—to say nothing of his own subjects—and he only *promises* to give it back. He promised that more than twenty years ago, but has not done it yet. Ought he not to have been overwhelmingly constrained by the European Conference to fulfil his promises? And if he had been thus constrained, would not war have been avoided?"

"But perhaps he would have resisted," said the student.

"No, the Turk is not mad, therefore he would not have resisted united Europe," returned the special; "and, even suppose that he had, his resistance could not have produced such a frightful war as this, for Europe would have crushed him *at once*, with comparatively little bloodshed. As it is, we have left the Muscovite (with good or bad intentions, I know not which) to tackle him alone,—and the result is before you. If the Russian is upright in his intentions we have treated him shabbily, if he is false we have given him a splendid opportunity to carry out his plans. I pronounce no opinion on Russia; the sin of this war lies with Europe; certainly not with England, for, whether she behaved rightly or wrongly, she was not omnipotent at the Conference. Perhaps I should say that the sin lies with the members of that Conference who misrepresented Europe, and allowed a notorious criminal to escape."

"There are various opinions on that subject," said the student.

"There are various opinions on every subject," replied the special, "but that is no reason why men and women should be content to have *no* opinion at all, or a bigoted one—which latter means an opinion founded largely on feeling, and formed before both sides of a question have been considered."

An ambulance-wagon drove up at this moment. The student and I, forgetting the subject of discussion, hastened with our brethren to attend to the wretched beings who were laid shattered, bleeding, and dying on the ground before us, while the special, seeing that we had run short of water, caught up a couple of buckets and ran to a neighbouring spring. It chanced that the ground between our place of shelter and the spring was at that time swept by the fire of contending troops, but in spite of this the special coolly filled his buckets and brought them in—happily without being injured.

The battle raged during the whole of that day all over the plain. Being taken up almost exclusively with our duties, we surgeons had little time to observe the progress of the fight; nevertheless, mindful of my character as a reporter, I took advantage of an occasional moment of relaxation to jot down a few notes.

There was a hill not far from that on which we stood which was held by a Russian regiment. Around it the fight appeared to rage very fiercely. The roar of artillery and the incessant rattle of small arms had by this time gathered in force until it resembled a storm. Hundreds of white puffs all over the field told of death from shots which were too far off to be heard, while the belching of a battery on the hill just mentioned caused the very earth to tremble.

The Turks at this point executed a flank movement, and attempted to take the hill by storm. At the same time one of their batteries appeared on the top of a ridge opposite, and began to play on the hill with terrible precision. To counteract this a Russian battery of three guns was despatched. I saw the horses come galloping in from the rear; one of the guns was limbered up, and off they went like the wind. At that moment a shell from the Turkish battery fell right under the gun, and, exploding, blew it, with the men and horses, into the air. The other guns reached the hill in safety, wheeled into position, and, for a time, checked the Turkish fire. Nevertheless, undeterred by the withering salvos, the Turks came on in powerful columns till they drew near to the hotly contested point.

At the foot of it the Russians had dug trenches and thrown up earth-works the night before. I observed with surprise that, as the attacking columns advanced, the Russian rifle-fire ceased, though the battery continued to cut lanes in the living masses. It occurred to me that our men were reserving fire according to the Skobeleff plan. In this I was right. When the Turks were within a hundred yards of the trenches the defenders fired as one man. The front ranks of the enemy fell like corn before the scythe; those in rear charged with irresistible impetuosity over their dead comrades. But the Russians had anticipated such an event. They had placed mines in the ground, which, when the Turks passed over them, were fired, and hundreds of men were blown into the air. This checked them. For a time they recoiled and were thrown into disorder. At that moment a young officer rallied them and charged again. The trenches were entered and a hand-to-hand conflict ensued. With my field-glass I could see the fierce expressions of the men as they drove their reeking bayonets right through their enemies, and the appalling gasp and glare of eye in those whose mortal career had been thus suddenly brought to a close. Yells of fury, shouts, curses, clubbed rifles, battered skulls, unearthly shrieks, smoke and blood—who can imagine or describe such a scene!

The Russian soldier fights well. His courage is equal to that of the men of other nations, and his weight gives him the advantage over some, but nothing can resist the power of overwhelming numbers.

Sitting on a height, and comfortably watching the battle through telescopes, the Turkish generals quietly move the "men" on the bloody board. Hundreds of Turks have perished. What matter? there are thousands on thousands ready to follow. Turkey must maintain her "integrity." Pashas must wallow in wealth. Millions of peasants must toil to accomplish these ends; if need be, they must die. The need at present is—to die. "Push on more battalions to reinforce them" is the order. No doubt the hundreds who have fallen, and the thousands who must yet fall, will leave hundreds of wives and thousands of children to hopeless mourning; but what of that? they are only *canaille*, cared for by nobody in particular, but God. No doubt the country must suffer for it. We must pay for war. We shall have an enormous national debt—that can't be helped, and other countries have the same,—besides, we can borrow from rich trusting nations, and repudiate our debts; our land shall feel the drain of its best young blood for generations yet to come, but time heals most sores; people will multiply as heretofore; fate is unavoidable, and Allah is great! Moreover, what does it all matter to us so long as our integrity is maintained, our seraglios remain intact, and our coffers are filled? That hillock *must* be taken. It is a priceless hillock. Like other hillocks, no doubt, and not very promising in an agricultural point of view, but still a priceless hillock, which must be carried at any cost, for on our obtaining it depends somehow (we can't say exactly how) the honour of our name, the success of our arms, the weal of the Turkish empire.

And so another order is given; fresh troops are hurled into the trenches, already filled with dead and dying; and the hillock is carried by storm, swept over with fierce cries of "Allah! Allah!" which mingle strangely with Russian curses, and is then left behind and regarded with as much indifference as if it were the most insignificant mass of earth and stone in all Bulgaria!

Flying backwards, the beaten Russians come panting towards the hill on which we stand, and rally, while our men advance, meet and stop the enemy, charge and overthrow them, turn the tide of battle, retake the hillock which has cost so much, and ultimately things remain *in statu quo* when the blessed shades of evening put an end to the frightful scene—leaving nothing whatever accomplished on either side, except the legitimate and ordinary end of most wars, namely—death and destruction!

I had just finished dressing the wounds of a soldier, at the end of this terrible episode, when a touch on my shoulder caused me to look up. It was Dobri Petroff.

"Have you seen your servant Lancey?" he asked quickly.

"No. I had intended to ask if you knew anything about him when the beginning of this carnage drove him and everything else out of my mind. Do you know where he is?"

"I saw him not five minutes since, looking wildly for you."

While Petroff was speaking, Lancey appeared, running towards me, bloodstained, blackened with powder, and with a rifle on his shoulder.

Chapter Twenty One
More of the Results of War

I need not trouble the reader with an account of the meeting with my faithful servant. While we were still engaged in questioning each other, I noticed that the countenance of our friend the scout wore an anxious and almost impatient expression.

"Anything wrong, Dobri?" I inquired.

"God knows!" he replied in a solemn tone, which impressed me much. "A rumour has come that the Circassians or the Bashi-Bazouks—I know not which, but both are fiends and cowards—have been to Venilik, and—"

He stopped abruptly.

"But that village was in the hands of the Russians," I said, at once understanding his anxiety.

"It may be so, but I go to see without delay," he replied, "and have only stopped thus long to know if you will go with me. These brutes kill and wound women and children as well as men. Perhaps your services may—Will you go?"

He spoke so earnestly, and his face looked so deadly pale, that I felt it impossible to refuse him. I was much exhausted by the prolonged labours of the day, but knew that I had reserve strength for an emergency.

"Give me a few minutes," said I,—"just to get leave, you know. I can't go without leave."

The scout nodded. In ten minutes I had returned. Meanwhile, Lancey had prepared my horse and his own. Swallowing a can of water, I vaulted into the saddle. It was very dark, but Petroff knew every foot of the country. For several hours we rode at a smart gallop, and then, as day was breaking, drew near to Venilik. As we approached, I observed that the bold countenance of the scout became almost pinched-looking from anxiety. Presently we observed smoke against the sky, and then saw that the village had undoubtedly been burned. I glanced at Petroff nervously. There was no longer a look of anxiety on his face, but a dark vindictive frown.

He increased his pace to racing speed. As we followed close at his heels, I observed that he drew a knife from his belt, and with that as a spur urged on his jaded steed. At last we reached the outskirts of the village, and dashed through. Blackened beams, ruined houses, dead men and women, met our horrified gaze on every side.

At the well-known turn of the road, where the bypath joined it, Dobri vaulted from his horse, and let the animal go, while he ran towards his dwelling. We also dismounted and followed him. Then a great and terrible shout reached our ears. When we came to the cottage we found the scout standing motionless before his old home, with his hands clasped tightly, and his eyes riveted to the spot with a glare of horror that words cannot describe.

Before him all that had been his home was a heap of blackened ashes, but in the midst of these ashes were seen protruding and charred bones. It did not require more than one glance to show that recognition of the remains was impossible. Everything was reduced to cinders.

As we gazed an appalling cry rang in our ears, and next moment a young woman darted out from behind a piece of the blackened walls with a knife in her hand.

"Hah! are you come back, you devils?" she shrieked, and flew at Dobri, who would certainly have been stabbed, for he paid no attention to her, if I had not caught her wrist, and forced the knife from her grasp. Even then she sprang at him and fastened her fingers in his neck while she cried, "Give me back my child, I say! give me my child, you fiend!"

She stopped and looked earnestly in his face, then, springing back, and standing before him with clenched hands, she screamed—

"Ha, haa! it is you, Dobri! why did you not come to help us? traitor—coward—to leave us at such a time! Did you not hear the shrieks of Marika when they dragged her from your cottage? Did you not see the form of little Dobri quivering on the point of the Circassian's spear? Were you deaf when Ivanka's death-shriek pierced my ears like—. Oh! God forgive me, Dobri, I did not mean to—"

She stopped in the torrent of her wrath, stretched both arms convulsively towards heaven, and, with a piercing cry for "Mercy!" fell dead at our feet.

Still the scout did not move. He stood in the same half-shrinking attitude of intense agony, glaring at the ruin around him.

"Dobri," said I at last, gently touching his arm, and endeavouring to arouse him.

He started like one waking out of a dream, hurled me aside with such violence that I fell heavily to the ground, and rushed from the spot at full speed.

Lancey ran after him, but soon stopped. He might as well have chased a mountain hare. We both, however, followed the track he had pursued, and, catching our horses, passed into the village.

"It's of no use to follow, sir," said Lancey, "we can't tell which way 'e's gone."

I felt that pursuit would indeed be useless, and pulled up with the intention of searching among the ruins of the village for some one who might have escaped the carnage, and could give me information.

The sights that met our eyes everywhere were indeed terrible. But I pass over the sickening details with the simple remark, that no ordinary imagination could conceive the deeds of torture and brutality of which these Turkish irregulars had been guilty. We searched carefully, but for a long time could find no one.

Cattle were straying ownerless about the place, while dogs and pigs were devouring the murdered inhabitants. Thinking it probable that some of the people might have taken refuge in the church, we went to it. Passing from the broad glare of day into the darkened porch, I stumbled over an object on the ground. It was the corpse of a young woman with the head nearly hacked off, the clothes torn, and the body half burnt. But this was as nothing to the scene inside. About two hundred villagers—chiefly women, children, aged, and sick—had sought refuge there, and been slaughtered indiscriminately. We found the dead and dying piled together in suffocating heaps. Little children were crawling about looking for their mothers, wounded mothers were struggling to move the ghastly heaps to find their little ones. Many of these latter were scarce recognisable, owing to the fearful sword-cuts on their heads and faces. I observed in one corner an old man whose thin white hair was draggled with blood. He was struggling in the vain endeavour to release himself from a heap of dead bodies that had either fallen or been thrown upon him.

We hastened to his assistance. After freeing him, I gave him a little brandy from my flask. He seemed very grateful, and, on recovering a little, told us, with many a sigh and pause for breath, that the village had been sacked by Turkish irregular troops, Circassians, who, after carrying off a large number of young girls, returned to the village, and slaughtered all who had not already fled to the woods for refuge.

While the old man was telling the mournful tale I observed a little girl run out from behind a seat where she had probably been secreting herself, and gaze wildly at me. Blood-stained, dishevelled, haggard though she was, I instantly recognised the pretty little face.

"Ivanka!" I exclaimed, holding out my arms.

With a scream of delight she rushed forward and sprang into them. Oh how the dear child grasped me,—twined her thin little arms round me, and strained as if she would crush herself into my bosom, while she buried her face in my neck and gave way to restful moans accompanied by an occasional convulsive sob!

Well did I understand the feelings of her poor heart. For hours past she had been shocked by the incomprehensible deeds of blood and violence around her; had seen, as she afterwards told me, her brother murdered, and her mother chased into the woods and shot by a soldier; had sought refuge in the church with those who were too much taken up with their own terrible griefs to care for her, and, after hours of prolonged agony and terror, coupled with hunger and thirst, had at last found refuge in a kindly welcome embrace.

After a time I tried to disengage her arms, but found this to be impossible without a degree of violence which I could not exert. Overcome by the strain, and probably by long want of rest, the poor child soon fell into a profound slumber.

While I meditated in some perplexity as to how I should act, my attention was aroused by the sudden entrance of a number of men. Their dress and badges at once told me that they formed a section of that noble band of men and women, who, following close on the heels of the "dogs of war," do all that is possible to alleviate the sufferings of hapless victims.—God's work going on side by side with that of the devil! In a few minutes surgeons were tenderly binding up wounds, and ambulance-men were bearing them out of the church from which the dead were also removed for burial.

"Come, Lancey," said I, "our services here are happily no longer required. Let us go."

"Where to, sir?" said Lancey.

"To the nearest spot," I replied after a moment's thought, "where I can lie down and sleep. I am dead beat, Lancey, for want of rest, and really feel unable for anything. If only I can snatch an hour or two, that will suffice. Meanwhile, you will go to the nearest station and find out if the railway has been destroyed."

We hurried out of the dreadful slaughter-house, Ivanka still sound asleep on my shoulder, and soon discovered an outhouse in which was a little straw. Rolling some of this into a bundle for a pillow, I lay down so as not to disturb the sleeping child. Another moment and I too was steeped in that profound slumber which results from thorough physical and mental exhaustion.

Lancey went out, shut the door, fastened it, and left us.

Chapter Twenty Two
The Fall of Plevna

The events which followed the massacre in the Bulgarian village remain in my mind, and ever must remain as a confused dream, for I was smitten that night with a fever, during the course of which—part of it at least—I was either delirious or utterly prostrate.

And who can tell, save those who have passed through a similar condition, the agonies which I endured, and the amazing fancies by which I was assailed at that time! Of course I knew not where I was, and I cared not. My unbridled fancy led me everywhere. Sometimes I was in a bed, sometimes on horseback; now in hospital attending wounded people, most of whom I noticed were women or little children; then on a battle-field, cheering the combatants with all my power, or joining them, but, when I chanced to join them, it was never for the purpose of taking, but of saving life. Often I was visited by good spirits, and also by bad. One of these latter, a little one, made a deep impression on me. His particular mission seemed to lie in his power to present before me, within a flaming frame, pictures of whatever I wished to behold. He was wonderfully tractable at first, and showed me whatever I asked for,—my mother, Bella, Nicholas, and many of my friends,—but by degrees he insisted on showing what I did not wish to see, and among these latter pictures were fearful massacres, and scenes of torture and bloodshed. I have a faint recollection of being carried somewhere in a jolting wagon, of suffering from burning thirst which no one seemed to care to relieve, of frequent abrupt stoppages, while shouts, shrieks, and imprecations filled my ears; but whether these things were realities or fancies, or a mingling of both, I cannot tell, for assuredly the bad spirit never once succeeded in showing me any picture half so terrible as those realities of war which I had already beheld.

One day I felt a peculiar sensation. It seemed to me that my intellectual faculties became more active, while those of my body appeared to sink.

"Come," said I to the demon who had wearied me so much; "come, you troublesome little devil, and show me my man Lancey. I can see better than usual; present him!"

Immediately Lancey stood by my side. He looked wonderfully real, and I noticed that the fiery frame was not round him as it used to be. A moment later, the pretty face of Ivanka also glided into the picture.

"Hallo!" I exclaimed, "I didn't ask you to send *her* here. Why don't you wait for orders—eh?"

At this Lancey gently pushed Ivanka away.

"No, don't do that," I cried hastily; "I didn't mean that; order her back again—do you hear?"

Lancey appeared to beckon, and she returned. She was weeping quietly.

"Why do you weep, dear?" I asked in Russian.

"Oh! you have been *so* ill," she replied, with an anxious look and a sob.

"So, then," I said, looking at Lancey in surprise, "you are not delusions!"

"No, sir, we ain't; but I sometimes fancy that everythink in life is delusions since we comed to this 'orrible land."

I looked hard at Ivanka and Lancey again for some moments, then at the bed on which I lay. Then a listless feeling came over me, and my eyes wandered lazily round the chamber, which was decidedly Eastern in its appearance. Through a window at the farther end I could see a garden. The sun was shining brightly on autumnal foliage, amidst which a tall and singular-looking man walked slowly to and fro. He was clad in flowing robes, with a red fez on his head which was counterbalanced by a huge red beard.

"At all events *he* must be a delusion," said I, pointing with a hitch of my nose to the man in question.

"No, sir, 'e ain't; wery much the rewerse.—But you mustn't speak, sir; the doctor said we was on no account to talk to you."

"But just tell me who he is," I pleaded earnestly; "I can't rest unless I know."

"Well, sir, I s'pose it won't do no 'arm to tell you that 'e's a Pasha—Sanda Pasha by name—a hold and hintimate friend of mine,—the Scotch boy, you know, that I used to tell you about. We are livin' in one of 'is willas. 'E's in disgrace, is Sanda Pasha, just now, an' superseded. The day you was took bad, sir, Russians came into the willage, an' w'en I come back I found 'em swarmin' in the 'ouses an' loop-'oling the walls for defence, but Sanda Pasha came down on 'em with a harmy of Turks an' drove 'em out. 'E's bin a-lickin' of 'em all up an' down the country ever since, but the other Pashas they got jealous of 'im, specially since 'e's not a real Turk born, an' the first

rewerse that come to 'im—as it will come to every one now an' again, sir—
they left 'im in a fix instead of sending 'im reinforcements, so 'e was forced
to retreat, an' the Sultan recalled 'im. It do seem to me that the Turkish
Government don't know good men when they've got 'em; an', what's more,
don't deserve to 'ave 'em. But long before these things 'appened, w'en 'e
found that you was my master an' Ivanka our friend, 'e sent us to the rear
with a strong guard, an' 'ere we are now in one of 'is willas, in what part o'
the land is more than I can tell—near Gallipopolly, or somethink like that,
I believe."

"So, then, we are prisoners?" said I.

"Well, I s'pose we are, sir, or somethink o' the sort, but, bless your 'art,
sir, it's of no manner of consiquence. We are treated like princes and live
like fighting-cocks.—But you mustn't talk, sir, you mustn't indeed, for the
doctor gave strict orders that we was to keep you quiet."

Lancey's communications were of so surprising a nature, so varied and
so suggestive, that my mind was overwhelmed in the mere attempt to recall
what he had said; in another moment I had forgotten all, and dropped into
a deep, dreamless, refreshing slumber.

During the period that I was thus fighting, as it were, with death—in
which fight, through God's blessing, I finally gained the victory—the fight
between the Russians and the Turks had progressed apace; victory leaning
now to the former, now to the latter. Many bloody engagements had taken
place on the plains of Bulgaria and among the Balkan mountains, while
Osman Pasha had carried on for some time that celebrated defence of Plevna
which afterwards carried him to the front rank of the Turkish generals,
and raised him, in the world's estimation, above them all. Everywhere
breech-loading weapons, torpedoes, telegraphs, monster cannon, and novel
appliances of modern warfare, had proved that where hundreds fell in the
days of our fathers, thousands fall in our own—that the bloody game is
immensely more expensive and deadly than it used to be, and that if war
was folly before, it is sheer madness now.

The first great attack had been made on the redoubts in front of Plevna,
and in assaulting one of these poor Dobri Petroff distinguished himself so
highly for desperate, reckless courage, that he drew the special attention of
General Skobeleff, who sent for him, probably to offer him some appointment,
but whatever it might be the scout declined promotion or reward. His object
was to seek what he styled honourable death in the front of battle. Strange
to say, he led a sort of charmed life, and the more he sought death the more
it appeared to avoid him. Somewhat like Skobeleff himself, he stood unhurt,
many a time, when balls were whistling round him like hail, and comrades
were mown down in ranks and heaps around him.

In all armies there are men who act with heroic valour and desperate daring. Some are urged thereto by calm contempt of danger, coupled with a strong sense of duty. It was something like this, probably, that induced Skobeleff to expose himself so recklessly on almost all occasions. It was simply despair, coupled with natural lion-like courage, that influenced the wretched scout.

Nicholas Naranovitsch had also acquired a name among his fellows for that grand sweeping fervour in attack which we are wont to associate with the heroes and demigods of ancient story. But Nicholas's motive was a compound of great physical strength, hot-blooded youth, and a burning desire to win distinction in the path of duty.

One consequence of the scout's return to headquarters was that he frequently met Nicholas, and felt an intense drawing towards him as being one who had shown him sympathy and kindness in that home which was now gone for ever. Deep was the feeling of pity which Nicholas felt when the scout told him, in a few sternly-uttered sentences, what had occurred at Venilik; and when Dobri expressed a desire to attach himself to Nicholas as his servant, the latter was only too glad to agree. Each knew the other well by report, and felt that the connection would be mutually agreeable.

At last one of the greatest events of the war approached. Plevna had been so closely hemmed in by Russian troops, and cut off from supplies, that the garrison was reduced to starvation. In this extremity, as is well known, Osman Pasha resolved on the desperate attempt to cut his way out of the beleaguered position.

Snow had fallen heavily, and the ground was white with it—so were the huts of the Russian soldiers, who, welcoming the snowfall as a familiar reminiscence of home, went about cooking their food and singing joyously. The houses of Plevna, with blue lines of smoke curling above them, were faintly visible through the driving snow. Now and then the sullen boom of a great gun told of the fell work that the forces had assembled there to execute.

"We are ordered to the front to-night, Dobri," said Nicholas, as he entered his tent hurriedly, unbuckled his sword, and sat down to a hasty meal. "Our spies have brought information that Osman means to play his last card. Our field telegraphs have spread the news. We even know the particular point where the attempt to cut through our lines is to be made. The troops are concentrating. I have obtained leave to join the advance columns. Just see that my revolvers are in order, and look to your own. Come after that and feed. Without food a man can do nothing."

The scout made no reply. Ever since the terrible calamity that had befallen him he had been a taciturn semi-maniac, but there was a glitter in his black eye that told of latent fires and deadly purpose within.

During the night another spy came in, reporting that Osman was concentrating his men near the bridge over the Vid, and that he had issued three days' rations to the troops, with a hundred and fifty cartridges and a new pair of sandals to each man. About the same time there came a telegram to the effect that lights were moving about with unwonted activity in Plevna, and something unusual was evidently afoot. Thus the report of the first spy was partly corroborated.

Meanwhile Nicholas and Dobri Petroff, mounting in the dark hours of morning, rode through the snowstorm—which was gradually abating—in the direction of the bridge over the Vid, while Skobeleff himself proceeded towards the Krishina redoubts, which, it was reported, were being abandoned. The report was true; he took possession of these redoubts unopposed, and instantly put them in a state of defence.

Meanwhile Osman, with his brave but worn-out band, made his last sortie from Plevna.

The grey light of a dull wintry morning broke and revealed masses, like darker clouds of the threatening storm, driving across the plain. These were the Ottoman troops—some say 20,000 men—rushing like baited tigers towards the trenches. Suddenly there came the thunderous roar of a hundred heavy guns, followed by the crash and incessant rattle of the rifles. The deciding battle had begun. The mists of early morning mingled with the smoke of fire-arms, so that the movements of men were not visible in many places. In others a few fighting companies were just visible, showing indistinctly through the haze for a minute or two, while sheets of flame played in front of their rifles like trickling lines of electric light. Elsewhere, from the cliffs above the Vid, globes of fire were seen to rend the mists, as cannon played their part in the deadly game, while the fearful cries of maddened and wounded men mingled with the crashing of artillery. Here and there numerous bullock-wagons were seen rolling slowly along, and horses and cattle were galloping wildly about the plain. It was a scene that might have made the flesh of the most callous people creep with pitying horror.

Advancing as far as possible under cover of their bullock-wagons, the Turks began to play their part with vigour, but the Russians opened on them from one of their batteries with shell and shrapnel, whilst the men in the trenches sent a rain of bullets from their Berdan breech-loaders. The terrified oxen, tearing about madly, or falling, soon rendered the wagon-cover useless. Then the Turks forsook it, and, with a wild shout, charged the first line of trenches. These were held by a Siberian regiment. The Turks swept over them like a tornado, poured into the battery, where the artillerymen, who stood to their guns like heroes, were bayoneted almost to a man. Thus the first investing circle was broken, but here Ottoman courage was met by irresistible force, and valour quite equal to its own, and here the tide of battle turned.

Nicholas Naranovitsch, despatched by General Strukoff, galloped towards the scene of action.

"Come, Dobri!" he cried, with blazing eyes that told of excitement almost too strong to be mastered, "there is work for you and me now."

Petroff, mounted and ready, awaiting the orders of his master, sprang out at the summons from a troop of the first brigade of grenadiers, who were at she moment preparing to advance. They dashed forward. An order had been intrusted to Nicholas, but he never delivered it. He was met by advancing hosts of the enemy. He turned aside, intending to execute his mission, if possible, by a détour. In this effort he was caught up, as it were, and carried on by the Russian grenadiers, who flung themselves on the Turks with irresistible fury. In another moment his horse fell under him. Dobri instantly dismounted, but the horse which he meant to offer to his master also fell, and the two were carried onward. The opposing forces met. A hand-to-hand fight ensued—man to man, bayonet to bayonet. The Turks clung to the guns in the captured battery with obstinate bravery. Nicholas and Dobri having both broken their sabres at the first onset, seized the rifles of fallen men and laid about them with a degree of overpowering energy, which, conserved and expended rightly for the good of man, might have made each a noted benefactor of the human race, but which, in this instance, resulted only in the crushing in of a few dozen Turkish skulls!

Gradually the stabbing and smashing of "God's image," on the part of the Russians, began to tell. The Turks gave way, and finally took to flight.

But shortly before this occurred there was a desperate effort made by a handful of Turks to retrieve the fortunes of the day. It was personally led by Sanda Pasha, who, reinstated by the vacillating and contemptible powers at Constantinople, had been sent—too late—to the relief of Plevna.

At the first rush the Pasha fell. He was only wounded, but his followers thought he was killed, and, stung with rage and despair, fought like fiends to avenge him. At that moment the Russian general rode up to a neighbouring eminence and had his attention drawn to this point in the battle.

He ordered up reinforcements. Nicholas and his man now seemed on the point of having their wishes gratified. Poor Petroff's desire to meet an honourable death had every chance of being realised, while the thirst for military distinction in Nicholas had at last a brilliant opportunity of being quenched.

As the fight in this part of that bloody field progressed, it concentrated into a knot around the two heroes. Just then a fresh body of Turkish infantry charged, led by the Nubian, Hamed Pasha, whose horse had been killed under him. Dobri Petroff and Hamed rushed at one another instantly; each seemed at once to recognise the other as a worthy foeman. The great hacked sword whistled for a few minutes round the scout's head so fast that it required his utmost agility to parry cut and thrust with his rifle, but a favourable chance soon offered, and he swung the stock of his piece at his adversary's head with such force as to break the sword short off at the hilt. The Nubian sprang at Dobri like a tiger. They grappled, and these men of herculean mould were so well matched that for a few seconds they stood quivering with mighty but fruitless efforts to bear each other down. It was at this moment that the Russian reinforcements came up, fired a volley, and charged. Dobri and Hamed dropped side by side, pierced with bullets. Nicholas also fell. The raging hosts passed over them, and the Turks were driven over the plain like autumn leaves before the gale.

Immediately after, a battery of horse artillery swept across the hotly-contested ground, the wheels of the heavy ordnance and the hoofs of the half-mad horses crashing over the heads said limbs of all who chanced to lie in their way.

Oh! it is *bitter* to reflect on the grand courage that is mis-displayed in the accursed service of war! Beaten, overwhelmed, crushed, all but annihilated, the poor peasant-soldiers of Turkey, who probably knew nothing whatever about the cause for which they fought, took shelter at last behind the broken wagons under which they had advanced, and then turned at bay. Others made for the deep banks of the Vid, where they re-formed, and instantly began to return the Russian fire.

The sortie was now virtually repulsed. It was about half-past eight. The Turks, evidently apprehensive that the enemy would charge and drive them back into the gorge which led to Plevna, remained on the defensive. The Russians, obviously afraid lest the enemy should attempt another sortie, also remained on the defensive. For four hours they continued in this condition, "during which period the battle raged," it was said, "with the utmost fury," but it is also admitted that very little damage was done to either side, "for both armies were under cover!" In other words, the belligerents remained for four hours in the condition of a couple of angry costermongers, hooting and howling at each other without coming to blows, while shot and shell and powder and lead were being expended for nothing, at a rate which added thousands sterling to the burdens of the peace-loving members of both countries!

"About twelve o'clock," according to an eye-witness, "the firing began to diminish on both sides, as if by mutual agreement."

I have a very thorough appreciation of this idea of "mutual agreement." It is well known among schoolboys. When two of these specimens of the rising generation have been smashing each other's faces, blackening each other's eyes, and bleeding each other's noses for three-quarters of an hour, without having decided a victory, they both feel a strong desire to stop, are ready to "give in," and, on the smallest encouragement from "seconds," will shake hands. Indeed, this well-known and somewhat contemptible state of mind is familiar to a larger growth of boys—happily not in England—called duellists. We deliberately call the state of mind "contemptible," because, if a matter is worth fighting for (physically), it ought to be fought for to the "bitter end." If it is not worth fighting for, there should be no fighting at all!

However, as I have said, the fire began to slacken about mid-day, and then gradually ceased. The silence that succeeded was deeply impressive—also suggestive. Half-an-hour later a white flag was seen waving from the road that ran round the cliffs beyond the bridge.

Plevna had fallen. Osman Pasha and his army had surrendered. In other words—the fate of the Turkish Empire was sealed!

Chapter Twenty Three
Woe to the "Auburn Hair!" After the Battle—Prowling Villains Punished

When the white flag was seen a loud shout went up from the Russian army. Then a party of officers rode forward, and two Turkish horsemen were seen advancing. They stated that Osman himself was coming to treat with the Russians.

The spot on which they stood was covered with the grim relics of battle. The earth had been uptorn by exploding shells. Here lay a horse groaning and struggling in its agony. Close to it lay an ox, silently bleeding to death, his great, round, patient eyes looking mournfully at the scene around him. Close by, was a cart with a dead horse lying in the yoke as he had fallen, and a Turkish soldier, stretched alongside, whose head had been carried away by a cannon shot. Under the wagon was a wounded man, and close to him four others, who, drained of nearly all their life-blood, lay crouched together in helplessness, with the hoods of their ragged grey overcoats drawn down on their faces. These latter gazed at the murky sky in listless indifference, or at what was going on in a sort of weary surprise. Among them was Nicholas Naranovitsch.

Russian surgeons were already moving about the field of battle, doing what they could, but their efforts were trifling compared with the vast necessity.

At last there was a shout of "Osman!" "He comes!"

"We will give him a respectful reception," exclaimed one Russian officer, in what is supposed by some to be the "gallant spirit of true chivalry."

"That we will," cried another; "we must all salute him, and the soldiers must present arms."

"He is a great soldier," exclaimed a third, "and has made a heroic defence."

Even Skobeleff himself seems to have been carried away by the feeling of the moment, if we may credit report, for he is said to have exclaimed—

"He is the greatest general of the age, for he has saved the honour of his country: I will proffer him my hand and tell him so."

"So," thought I, when afterwards meditating on this subject, "the Turks have for centuries proved themselves to be utterly unworthy of self-government; they have shown themselves to be ignorant of the first principles of righteousness,—*meum* and *tuum*; they (or rather their rulers) have violated their engagements and deceived those who trusted them; have of late repudiated their debts, and murdered, robbed, violated, tortured those who differed from them in religious opinions, as is generally admitted,—nevertheless now, because one of their generals has shown somewhat superior ability to the rest, holding in check a powerful enemy, and exhibiting, with his men, a degree of bull-dog courage which, though admirable in itself, all history proves to be a common characteristic of all nations—that 'honour,' which the country never possessed, is supposed to have been 'saved'!"

All honour to the brave, truly, but when I remember the butcheries that are admitted, by friend and foe of the Turk, to have been committed on the Russian wounded by the army of Plevna (and which seem to have been conveniently forgotten at this dramatic incident of the surrender),—when I reflect on the frightful indifference of Osman Pasha to his own wounded, and the equally horrible disregard of the same hapless wounded by the Russians after they entered Plevna,—I cannot but feel that a desperate amount of error is operating here, and that multitudes of mankind, especially innocent, loving, and gentle mankind, to say nothing of tender, enthusiastic, love-blinded womankind, are to some extent deceived by the false ring of that which is not metal, and the falser glitter of a tinsel which is anything but gold.

However, Osman did not come after all. He had been wounded, and the Russian generals were obliged to go to a neighbouring cottage to transact the business of surrender.

As the cavalcade rode away in the direction of the cottage referred to, a Russian surgeon turned aside to aid a wounded man. He was a tall strapping trooper. His head rested on the leg of his horse, which lay dead beside him. He could not have been more than twenty years of age, if so much. He had carefully wrapped his cloak round him. His carbine and sabre were drawn close to his side, as if to protect the weapons which it had always been his pride to keep bright and clean. He was a fresh handsome lad, with courage and loveableness equally stamped upon his young brow. He opened his eyes languidly as the doctor attended to him.

"Come, my fine fellow, keep up your heart," said the doctor tenderly; "you will perhaps—that is to say, the ambulance-wagons will be round immediately, and—"

"Thank you," interrupted the trooper quietly, "God's blessing rest upon you. I know what you mean.—Look, sir."

He tried to take a locket from his neck as he spoke, but could not. The doctor gently assisted him. "See," he said, "take this to Dobri Petroff—the scout. You know him? Every one knows dashing Dobri!"

"I know him. Well?"

"Tell him to give it to her—he knows who—and—and—say it has kept me in—in heaven when sometimes it seemed to me as if I had got into hell."

"From whom?" asked the doctor, anxiously, as the youth's head sank forward, and the terrible pallor of approaching death came on.

"From André—"

Alas! alas for Maria with the auburn hair!

The doctor rose. His services were no longer needed. Mounting his horse, he rode away.

The ground over which he galloped was strewn with weapons. The formal surrender had been made, and each Turk, obeying literally the order to lay down his arms, had deposited his rifle in the mud where he stood.

That night a faint light shone through the murky clouds, and dimly illumined the grim battle-field.

It was deserted by all but the dead and dying, with now and then a passing picket or fatigue-party. As the night advanced, and the cold became piercing, even these seemed to have finally retired from the ghastly scene. Towards morning the moon rose high, and, piercing the clouds, at times lit up the whole battle-field. Ah! there was many a pale countenance turned wistfully on the moon that night, gazing at it until the eyes became fixed in death. There was one countenance, which, deadly white, and gashed by a Turkish sabre, had been ruddy with young life in the morning. It was that of Nicholas Naranovitsch. He lay on his back near his dead horse, and close to a heap of slaughtered men. He was so faint and so shattered by sabre-cuts and bullets as to be utterly unable to move anything but his eyes. Though almost in a state of stupor, he retained sufficient consciousness to observe what went on around him. The night, or rather the early morning, had become very still, but it was not silent, for deep sighs and low moanings, as of men suffering from prolonged and weary pain, struck on his listening ear. Now and then some wretch, unable to bear his misery, would make a desperate effort to rise, only, however, to fall back with a sharp cry or a deep-despairing groan. Here and there a man might be seen creeping a few paces on his hands and knees, and then dropping to rest for a time, after which the creeping was resumed, in the vain hope, no doubt, that some place of shelter or an ambulance might be reached at last. One of these struggling men passed close to Nicholas, and stopped to rest almost at his side. In a few minutes he rose again, and attempted to advance, but instead of doing so writhed in a hideous contortion over on his back, and stretching himself with a convulsive shudder, died with his teeth clenched and his protruding eyeballs glaring at the sky.

Suddenly a low sweet sound broke on Nicholas's ear. It swelled gradually, and was at length recognised as a hymn with which he had been familiar in childhood. Some dying Christian soldier near him had apparently sought relief in singing praise to God. Nicholas wept as he listened. He soon found that there were sympathetic listeners besides himself, for the strains were taken up by one and another, and another, until the hymn appeared to rise from all parts of the battle-field. It was faint, however, and tremulous, for the life-blood was draining rapidly from the hearts of those who raised it. Ere long it altogether ceased.

For some time Nicholas had been aware that a wounded man was slowly gasping out his life quite close to him, but, from the position in which he lay, it was not possible to see more than his red fez. Presently the man made a powerful effort, raised himself on one elbow, and displayed the ghastly black countenance of Hamed Pasha. He looked unsteadily round him for a moment, and then sank backward with a long-drawn sigh.

Close to him, under a heap of slain, Dobri Petroff himself lay. For a long time he was unconscious, and had been nearly crushed to death by the weight of those above him. But the life which had been so strong in his huge body seemed to revive a little, and after a time he succeeded in freeing himself from the load, and raising himself on his hands, but he could not get up on his feet. A wound in the neck, which had partly closed while he was in a recumbent position, now burst out afresh. He looked at the blood with a faint sad smile, and sank down again.

Nicholas recognised him, and tried to speak, but he could neither speak nor move. It seemed to him that every part of his frame had been paralysed except his brain and eyes.

Presently the scout felt for something at his side. His flask was there; putting it to his lips he drank a little and was evidently refreshed, for he raised himself again and began to look about him.

Another moment and Petroff had discovered the Pasha, who lay near him with a look of intense longing in his eyes as he saw the flask and heard the gurgling water. A fierce frown crossed the scout's brow for a moment, but it was instantly chased away by a look of pity. He dragged himself slowly towards the dying Turk, and held the flask to his lips.

With a murmur of thankfulness and a look of gratitude at his late enemy, the Pasha uttered a faint sigh and closed his eyes in the last long sleep of death.

The effort to drag himself even a few paces served to show Petroff how severely he had been wounded. He was in the act of raising the flask to his lips a second time, when Nicholas, by a desperate effort, succeeded in uttering a low groan.

The scout turned quickly, observed his master, and crept to his side.

"Drink, sir," he said, knowing well that water was what Nicholas required most at such a time.

The avidity with which the latter obeyed prevented him observing that the scout was almost sinking. The successive efforts he had made had caused the blood to pour copiously from his wounds.

"You are badly hurt, Dobri, I fear," he said, when the life-giving draught had sent new vigour into his frame, and loosed his tongue.

"Ay," replied the scout, with a faint smile.—"I shall soon be with you now, Marika, and with the little ones and the dear Lord you loved so well and tried so hard to make me follow too. And you succeeded, Marika, though you little th—"

He stopped abruptly, swayed a moment to and fro, then fell heavily forward with his head on the bosom of his friend.

"Take some more water, Dobri," said Nicholas anxiously. "Quick, before you lose consciousness. I have not power to move a limb to help you.—Dobri!"

He called in vain,—the scout had fainted.

Nicholas had not power at first to remove the poor fellow's head from his chest, and he felt as if he should be suffocated. By degrees, however, he managed to roll it slightly to one side, and, at the same time, returning vigour enabled him to raise his right arm. He observed that his hand still grasped a revolver, but for some time he had no power to unclasp it. At last he succeeded, and raising Petroff's flask with difficulty to his lips obtained another draught.

Just at that moment the moon, which had passed behind a dark cloud, shone through an opening, and he saw three men not far off searching among the dead. He was about to call to them, but a thought occurred and he restrained himself.

He was right; the three men, one of whom was habited like a priest, were rifling the dead. He saw them come up to a prostrate form which struggled on being touched. One of the three men instantly drew a knife and stabbed the wounded man. When they had searched the body and taken from it what they required they came towards the spot where Nicholas lay.

A feeling of horror came over him for a moment, but that seemed to give him strength, for he instantly grasped his revolver. Hoping, however that they might pass without observing him, he shut his eyes and lay quite still.

The three murderers drew near, talking in low tones, and seemed about to pass, when one of them stopped.

"Here's a big-looking fellow whose boots will just fit me," he said, stooping and seizing the scout's leg.

"There's an officer behind him," said the villain in the priest's dress; "he will be more worth stripping."

Nicholas pointed his revolver full in the man's face and fired, but his aim was unsteady. He had missed. Again he pulled the trigger, but it had been the last shot. The man sprang upon him. The report, however, had attracted the notice of a picket of Russian soldiers, who, well aware of the deeds of foul villainy that are practised by the followers of an army on battle-fields at night, immediately rushed up and secured the three men.

"They are murderers," exclaimed Nicholas in reply to a question from the sergeant in command.

"Lead them out," said the sergeant promptly.

The men were bound and set up in a row.

"Ready—present!"

A volley rang out in the night air, and three more corpses were added to the death-roll of the day.

It was summary justice, but richly deserved. Thereafter the soldiers made a rough-and-ready stretcher of muskets, on which Nicholas, who had fainted, was carefully laid and borne from the field.

Chapter Twenty Four
Farewell to Sanda Pasha—A Scuffle, and an Unexpected Meeting

Some time after the events narrated in the last chapter I was seated in an apartment of Sanda Pasha's residence in Adrianople, the Turkish city next in importance to Constantinople.

My health had returned, and, although still somewhat weak, I felt sufficiently strong to travel, and had once or twice urged my kind host, who was fast recovering from his wound, to permit me, if possible, to return to the Russian lines. I had had from him, of course, a full account of the fall of Plevna, and I had also learned from another source that Nicholas had been desperately wounded; but the latter information was a mere rumour, which only rendered me the more anxious to get away.

The Pasha's chief secretary, who spoke Russian well, informed me at this time of some of the doings of his countrymen in the city and neighbourhood. I could hardly credit him, but English "correspondents" afterwards confirmed what he said. The daily executions of Bulgarians on the slightest pretexts, without trial, were at that time so numerous that it seemed as if the Turks had determined to solve the question of Bulgarian autonomy by killing or banishing every male in the province. In one instance fifteen Bulgarian children, the youngest of whom was ten years of age, and the eldest fifteen, were condemned to hard labour for life. It was said, but not proved I believe, that these young people had committed murder and contributed to the insurrection. At this time there were over 20,000 refugees in Adrianople, all of whom were women and children whose protectors had either been massacred or forced to join the army.

The secretary evidently rejoiced in the slaying and otherwise getting rid of Bulgarian men, but he seemed to have a slight feeling of commiseration for the helpless refugees, among whom I had myself witnessed the most heart-rending scenes of mental and physical suffering.

Wherever I wandered about the town there were groups of these trembling ones, on whose pallid faces were imprinted looks of maniacal horror or of blank despair. Little wonder! Some of them had beheld the fathers, brothers, lovers, around whom their heart-strings twined, tortured to death before their eyes. Others had seen their babes tossed on spear-points and bayonets, while to all the future must have appeared a fearful prospect of want and of dreary sighing for a touch of those "vanished hands" that had passed from earth for ever.

"Philanthropic societies," said the secretary, "have done great things for Turkey and for Russia too. Had it not been for the timely aid sent out by the charitable people in England and other countries, it is certain that many thousands of these refugees would already have been in their graves."

I did not like the tone or looks of this secretary. He was an oily man, with a touch of sarcasm.

"Doubtless there are many of them," I returned sharply, "who wish that they had fallen with their kindred. But you say truth: the tender-hearted and liberal ones of England and elsewhere have done something to mitigate the horrors of war, and yet there is a party among us who would draw the sword, if they were allowed, and add to the number of these wretched refugees. A pretty spectacle of consistency, truly, is presented by war! If we English were to join the Turks, as of course you wish us to do, and help you to maintain your misrule, to say nothing of the massacres which have been and still are going on around us, we should have to keep our philanthropic societies at work still longer, and thus we should be seen cutting men down with one hand and binding them up with the other,—roaring like fiends as we slaughter sires, and at the same time, with the same voice, softly comforting widows and fatherless children. Oh, sir, if there is a phrase of mockery on the face of this earth, it is the term 'civilised warfare'!"

Before the secretary had time to reply the Pasha entered, accompanied by Lancey.

"Mr Childers," said the Pasha, sitting down on a cushion beside me, "I have managed it at last, though not without difficulty, but when a man wants to help an old school-mate in distress he is not easily put down. You have to thank Lancey for anything I have done for you. There is, it seems, to be an exchange of prisoners soon, and I have managed that you and Lancey shall be among the number. You must be ready to take the road to-morrow."

I thanked the Pasha heartily, but expressed surprise that one in so exalted a position should have found difficulty in the matter.

"Exalted!" he exclaimed, with a look of scorn, "I'm so exalted as to have very narrowly missed having my head cut off. Bah! there is no gratitude in a Turk—at least in a Turkish grandee."

I ventured to suggest that the Pasha was in his own person a flat—or rather sturdy—contradiction of his own words, but he only grinned as he bowed, being too much in earnest to smile.

"Do you forget," he continued, "that I am in disgrace? I have served the Turk faithfully all my life, and now I am shelved at the very time my services might be of use, because the Sultan is swayed by a set of rascals who are jealous of me! And is it not the same with better men than myself? Look at Mehemet Ali, our late commander-in-chief, deposed from office by men who had not the power to judge of his capacities—for what? Did he not say with his own lips, to one of your own correspondents, that although he had embraced the religion of Mohammed they never could forget or forgive the fact that he was not born a Turk, but regarded him as a Giaour in disguise; that his elevation to power excited secret discontent among the Pashas, which I know to be true; that another Pasha thwarted instead of aiding him, while yet another was sent to act the spy on him. Is not this shameful jealousy amongst our leaders, at a time when all should have been united for the common weal, well known to have operated disastrously in other cases? Did not Osman Pasha admit as much, when he complained bitterly, after the fall of Plevna, that he had not been properly supported? Our rank and file are lions in the field—though I cannot allow that they are lambs anywhere else—but as for our— Bah! I have said enough. Besides, to tell you the truth, I am tired of the Turks, and hate them."

Here my servant interrupted the Pasha with a coolness and familiarity that amused me much.

"Sandy," said he, with a disapproving shake of the head, "you oughtn't to go an' speak like that of your hadopted nation."

The Pasha's indignation vanished at once. He turned to Lancey with a curious twinkle in his eye.

"But, my good fellow," he said, "it isn't my hadopted nation. When I came here a poor homeless wanderer the Turks adopted *me*, not I *them*, because they found me useful."

"That," returned Lancey, "should 'ave called hout your gratitood."

"So it did, Lancey. Didn't I serve them faithfully from that day to this, to the best of my power, and didn't I shave my head and wear their garb, and pretend to take to their religion all out of gratitude?"

"Worse and worse," retorted Lancey; "that was houtrageous 'ypocrisy. I'm afraid, Sandy, that you're no better than you used to be w'en you smashed the school-windows an' went about playin' truant on the Scottish 'ills."

"No better indeed," returned the Pasha, with a sudden touch of sadness; "that is true, but how to become better is the difficulty. Islamism fills a land with injustice, robbery, and violence; while, in order that such things may be put right, the same land is desolated, covered with blood, and filled with lamentation, in the name of Christianity."

Here I could not refrain from reminding the Pasha that the professors of religion did not always act in accordance with their profession, and that the principles of the "Prince of Peace," when carried out, even with average sincerity, had an invariable tendency to encourage peace and good-will among men, which was more than could be said of the doctrines of Mohammed.

"It may be so," said the Pasha, with a sigh.

"Meanwhile, to return to our point, you will find everything ready for your journey at an early hour to-morrow."

"But what of little Ivanka Petroff?" I asked. "She must go with us."

The Pasha seemed a little perplexed. "I had not thought of that," he said; "she will be well-cared for here."

"I cannot go without her," said I firmly.

"No more can I," said Lancey.

"Well, that shall also be arranged," returned the Pasha, as he left us.

"Never saw nothink like 'im," observed Lancey; "'e sticks at nothink, believes nothink, cares for nothink, an' can do hanythink."

"*You* are showing want of gratitude now, Lancey, for it is plain that he cares a good deal for you."

Lancey admitted that he might, perhaps, have been a little harsh in expressing himself, and then went off to prepare for the journey.

"We are going back again to your own country, Ivanka," said I, gently stroking the child's head, as we sat together in the same room, some hours later.

Ivanka raised her large eyes to mine.

"There is no *home* now," she said, in a mournful voice.

"But we shall find father there, perhaps."

The child dropped her eyes, and shook her head, but made no further remark. I saw that tears were trickling down her cheeks, and, feeling uncertain as to how far she realised her forlorn condition, refrained from further speech, and drew her little head upon my breast, while I sought to comfort her with hopes of soon meeting her father.

Snow lay on the ground when we bade farewell to our kind host. "Good-bye, Sanda Pasha; I shall hope to see you in England one of these days," said I at parting.

"Farewell, Sandy," said my man, grasping the Pasha's hand warmly, and speaking in a deeply impressive tone; "take the advice of a wery old friend, who 'as your welfare at 'art, an' leave off your evil ways, w'ich it's not possible for you to do w'ile you've got fifty wives, more or less, shaves your 'ead like a Turk, and hacts the part of a 'ypocrite. Come back to your own land, my friend, w'ich is the only one I knows on worth livin' in, an' dress yourself like a Christian."

The Pasha laughed, returned the squeeze heartily, and said that it was highly probable he would act upon that advice ere another year had passed away.

Half an hour later we were driving over the white plains, on which the sun shone with dazzling light.

I felt unusual exhilaration as we rattled along in the fresh frosty air, and crossed the fields, which, with the silvered trees and bushes, contrasted so pleasantly with the clear blue sky. I began to feel as if the horrible scenes I had lately witnessed were but the effects of a disordered imagination, which had passed away with fever and bodily weakness.

Ivanka also appeared to revive under those genial influences with which God surrounds His creatures, for she prattled a little now and then about things which attracted her attention on the road; but she never referred to the past. Lancey, too, was inspirited to such an extent that he tackled the Turkish driver in his own tongue, and caused the eyes of that taciturn individual occasionally to twinkle, and his moustache to curl upwards.

That night we slept at a small road-side inn. Next day we joined a group of travellers, and thus onward we went until we reached the region where the war raged. Here we were placed under escort, and, with some others, were exchanged and set free.

Immediately I hired a conveyance and proceeded to the Russian rear, where I obtained a horse, and, leaving Ivanka in charge of Lancey at an inn, hastened to headquarters to make inquiries about Nicholas and Petroff.

On the way, however, I halted to telegraph to the *Scottish Bawbee*, and to write a brief account of my recent experiences among the Turks.

I was in the midst of a powerful article—powerful, of course, because of the subject—on one of the war-episodes, when I heard a foot on the staircase. I had placed my revolver on the table, for I was seated in a room in a deserted village. One wall of the room had been shattered by a shell, while most of the furniture was more or less broken by the same missile, and I knew well that those sneak-marauders who infest the rear of an army were in the habit of prowling about such places.

Suddenly I heard a loud shout on the staircase, followed by the clashing of swords. I leaped up, seized the revolver, and ran out. One man stood on the stair defending himself against two Circassians. I knew the scoundrels instantly by their dress, and not less easily did I recognise a countryman in the grey tweed shooting coat, glengarry cap, and knickerbockers of the other. At the moment of my appearance the Englishman, who was obviously a dexterous swordsman, had inflicted a telling wound on one of his adversaries. I fired at the other, who, leaping nearly his own height into the air, fell with a crash down the staircase. He sprang up, however, instantly, and both men bolted out at the front door and fled.

The Englishman turned to thank me for my timely aid, but, instead of speaking, looked at me with amused surprise.

"Can it be?" I exclaimed; "not possible! *you*, Biquitous?"

"I told you we should probably meet," he replied, sheathing his sword, "but I was not prophetic enough to foretell the exact circumstances of the meeting."

"Come along, my dear fellow," said I, seizing his arm and dragging him up-stairs; "how glad I am! what an unexpected—oh! never mind the look of the room, it's pretty tight in most places, and I've stuffed my overcoat into the shell-hole."

"Don't apologise for your quarters, Jeff," returned my friend, laying his sword and revolver on the table; "the house is a palace compared with some places I've inhabited of late. The last, for instance, was so filthy that I believe, on my conscience, an irish pig, with an average allowance of self-respect, would have declined to occupy it.—Here it is, you'll find it somewhere near the middle."

He handed me a small sketch-book, and, while I turned over the leaves, busied himself in filling a short meerschaum.

"Why, how busy you must have been!" said I, turning over the well-filled book with interest.

"Slightly so," he replied. "Some of these will look pretty well, I flatter myself, in the *Evergreen Isle*, if they are well engraved; but that is the difficulty. No matter how carefully we correspondents execute our sketches, some of these engravers—I won't say all of them—make an awful mess of 'em.

"Yes, you may well laugh at that one. It was taken under fire, and I can tell you that a sketch made under fire is apt to turn out defective in drawing. That highly effective and happy accidental touch in the immediate foreground I claim no credit for. It was made by a bullet which first knocked the pencil out of my hand and then terminated the career of my best horse; while that sunny gleam in the middle distance was caused by a piece of yellow clay being driven across it by the splinter of a shell. On the whole, I think the sketch will hardly do for the *Evergreen*, though it is worth keeping as a reminiscence."

My friend and I now sat down in front of a comfortable fire, fed with logs from the roof of a neighbouring hut, but we had not chatted long before he asked me the object of my visit to headquarters.

"To inquire about my friend Nicholas Karanovitsch," I said.

From the sudden disappearance of the look of careless pleasantry from my friend's face, and the grave earnest tone in which he spoke, I saw that he had bad news to tell.

"Have you not heard—" he said, and paused.

"Not dead?" I exclaimed.

"No, not dead, but desperately wounded." He went on in a low rapid voice to relate all the circumstances of the case, with which the reader is already acquainted, first touching on the chief points, to relieve my feelings.

Nicholas was not dead, but so badly wounded that there was no chance of his ever again attaining to the semblance of his old self. The doctors, however, had pronounced him at last out of danger. His sound constitution and great strength had enabled him to survive injuries which would have carried off most men in a few days or hours. His whole frame had been shattered; his handsome face dreadfully disfigured, his left hand carried away, and his right foot so grievously crushed by a gun-carriage passing over it that they had been obliged to amputate the leg below the knee. For a long time he had lain balancing between life and death, and when he recovered sufficiently to be moved had been taken by rail to Switzerland. He had given strict orders that no one should be allowed to write to his friends in England, but had asked very anxiously after me.

Biquitous gave me a great many more particulars, but this was the gist of his sad news. He also told me of the fall of Dobri Petroff.

"Nicholas had fainted, as I told you," he said, "just before the picket by which he had been rescued lifted him from the ground, and he was greatly distressed, on recovering, to find that his faithful follower had been left behind. Although he believed him to be dead, he immediately expressed an earnest wish that men should be sent to look for and recover the body. They promised that this should be done, but he never learned whether or not they had been successful."

"And you don't know the name of the place in Switzerland to which Nicholas has been sent?" I asked.

"Not sure, but I think it was Montreux, on the Lake of Geneva."

After all this sad news I found it impossible to enjoy the society of my eccentric friend, and much though I liked him, resolved to leave the place at once and make arrangements to quit the country.

I therefore bade him farewell, and hastened back to the inn where I had left Ivanka and Lancey.

The grief of the dear child, on hearing that her father had fallen on the battle-field, was for a time uncontrollable. When it had abated, I said:—

"There is no one here to love you now, my little darling, but God still loves you, and, you see, has sent me and Lancey to take care of you.—Come, we will return to Venilik."

I did not dare at this time to raise hopes, which might soon be dashed to pieces, in the heart of the poor forlorn child, and therefore did not say all that was in my mind; but my object in returning to Venilik was to make inquiry after her mother. My own hopes were not strong, but I did not feel satisfied that we had obtained sufficient proof that Marika had been killed.

Our search and inquiries, however, were vain. Venilik was almost deserted. No one could tell anything about the Petroff family that we did not already know. It was certainly known that many persons—men and women—had fled to the neighbouring woods, and that some had escaped, but it was generally believed that Marika had been burnt in her own cottage. No doubt, however, was entertained as to the fate of her little boy; for there were several people who had seen him thrust through and held aloft on the point of a Circassian spear. When I told of Dobri Petroff having fallen by the side of Nicholas, several of the villagers said they had heard of that from other sources.

As nothing further could be done, I resolved to adopt Ivanka, and take her away with me.

My preparations were soon made, a conveyance was obtained, and before many days were over I found myself flying by road and rail far from the land where war still raged, where the fair face of nature had been so terribly disfigured by human wrath—so fearfully oppressed with human woe.

Chapter Twenty Five
Describes a Wreck, and the Triumph of Love

A Swiss châlet on a woody knoll, high up on the grand slopes that bathe their feet in the beautiful Lake of Geneva.

It is evening—a bright winter evening—with a golden glory in the sky which reminds one powerfully of summer, and suggests the advent of spring.

In the neighbouring town of Montreux there are busy people engaged in the labours of the day. There are also idlers endeavouring to "kill" the little span of time that has been given them, in which to do their quota of duty on the earth. So, also, there are riotous young people who are actively fulfilling their duty by going off to skate, or slide down the snow-clad hills, after the severer duties connected with book and slate have been accomplished. These young rioters are aided and abetted by sundry persons of maturer years, who, having already finished the more important labours of the day of life, renew their own youth, and encourage the youngsters by joining them.

Besides these there are a few cripples who have been sent into the world with deficient or defective limbs—doubtless for wise and merciful ends. Merciful I say advisedly, for, "shall not the Judge of all the earth do right?" These look on and rejoice, perchance, in the joy of the juveniles.

Among them, however, are some cripples of a very different stamp. The Creator sent these into the world with broad shoulders, deep chests, good looks, gladsome spirits, manly frames, and vigorous wills. War has sent them here—still in young manhood—with the deep chests pierced by bullets or gashed by sabres, with the manly frames reduced to skeletons, the gladsome spirits gone, the ruddy cheeks hollow and wan, and the vigorous wills—subdued *at last*.

A few of these young cripples move slowly about with the aid of stick or crutch, trying to regain, in the genial mountain air, some of the old fire which has sunk so low—so very low. Others, seated in wheel-chairs, doubled up like old, old men, are pushed about from point to point by stalwart mountaineers, while beside them walk sisters, mothers, or, perchance, young wives, whose cheery smiles and lightsome voices, as they point out and refer to the surrounding objects of nature, cannot quite conceal the feelings of profound and bitter sorrow with which they think of the glorious manhood that has been lost, or the tender, pitiful, heart-breaking solicitude with which they cherish the poor shadow that remains.

In a large airy apartment of the châlet on the woody knoll, there is one who occupies a still lower level than those to whom we have just referred— who cannot yet use the crutch or sit in the wheelchair, and on whose ear the sounds of glee that enter by the open window fall with little effect.

He reclines at full length on a bed. He has lain thus, with little effort to move, and much pain when such effort was made, for many weary weeks. Only one side of his face is visible, and that is scarred and torn with wounds, some of which are not yet healed. The other side is covered with bandages.

I am seated by his side, Ivanka is sitting opposite, near to the invalid's feet, listening intently, if I may be allowed to say so, with her large black eyes, to a conversation which she cannot understand.

"You must not take so gloomy a view of your case, Nicholas. The doctors say you will recover, and, my good fellow, you have no idea what can be done by surgery in the way of putting a man together again after a break-down. Bella would be grieved beyond measure if I were to write as you wish."

I spoke cheerily, more because I felt it to be a duty to do so, than because I had much hope.

The invalid paused for a few minutes as if to recover strength. Then he said—

"Jeff, I insist on your doing what I wish. It is unkind of you to drag me into a dispute when I am so weak. Tell the dear girl that I give her up—I release her from our engagement. It is likely that I shall die at any rate, which will settle the question, but if I do recover—why, just think, my dear fellow, I put it to you, what sort of husband should I make, with my ribs all smashed, my right leg cut off, my left hand destroyed, an eye gone, and my whole visage cut to pieces. No, Jeff—"

He paused; the light vein of humour which he had tried to assume passed off, and there was a twitching about the muscles of his mouth as he resumed—

"No, Bella must never see me again."

Ivanka looked from the invalid's face to mine with eyes so earnest, piercing, and inquiring, that I felt grieved she did not understand us.

"I'm sorry, Nicholas, very sorry," said I, "but Bella has already been written to, and will certainly be here in a day or two. I could not know your state of mind on my first arrival, and, acting as I fancied for the best, I wrote to her."

Nicholas moved uneasily, and I observed a deep flush on his face, but he did not speak.

That evening Ivanka put her arms round my neck, told me she loved Nicholas because of his kindness to her father, and besought me earnestly to tell her what had passed between us.

A good deal amused, I told her as much as I thought she could understand.

"Oh! I should so like to see Bella," she said.

"So you shall, dear, when she comes."

"Does she speak Russian?"

"Yes. She has been several times in Russia, and understands the language well."

As I had predicted, Bella arrived a few days after receiving my letter. My mother accompanied her.

"Oh, Jeff, this is dreadful!" said my poor mother, as she untied her bonnet-strings, and sat down on the sofa beside Bella, who could not for some time utter a word.

"What child is that?" added my mother quickly, observing Ivanka.

"It is the daughter of Dobri Petroff.—Let me introduce you, Ivanka, to my mother, and to my sister Bella—you know Bella?"

I had of course written to them a good deal about the poor child, and Bella had already formed an attachment to her in imagination. She started up on hearing Ivanka's name, and held out both hands. The child ran to her as naturally as the needle turns to the pole.

While my mother and I were talking in a low tone about Nicholas, I could not avoid hearing parts of a conversation between my sister and Ivanka that surprised me much.

"Yes, oh! yes, I am quite sure of it. Your brother told me that he said he would never, never, never be so wicked as to let you come and see him, although he loved you so much that he—"

"Hush, my dear child, not so loud."

Bella's whisper died away, and Ivanka resumed—

"*Yes*, he said there was almost nothing of him left. He was joking, you know, when he said that, but it is not so much of a joke after all, for I saw—"

"Oh! hush, dear, hush; tell me what he said, and speak lower."

Ivanka spoke so low that I heard no more, but what had reached my ear was sufficient to let me know how the current ran, and I was not sorry that poor Bella's mind should be prepared for the terrible reality in this way.

The battle of love was fought and won that day at Nicholas's bedside, and, as usual, woman was victorious.

I shall not weary the reader with all that was said. The concluding sentences will suffice.

"No, Nicholas," said Bella, holding the right hand of the wounded soldier, while my mother looked on with tearful, and Ivanka with eager, eyes, "no, I will not be discarded. You must not presume, on the strength of your being weak, to talk nonsense. I hold you, sir, to your engagement, unless, indeed, you admit yourself to be a faithless man, and wish to cast me off. But you must not dispute with me in your present condition. I shall exercise the right of a wife by ordering you to hold your tongue unless you drop the subject. The doctor says you must not be allowed to talk or excite yourself, and the doctor's orders, you know, must be obeyed."

"Even if he should order a shattered man to renounce all thoughts of marriage?" asked Nicholas.

"If he were to do that," retorted Bella, with a smile, "I should consider your case a serious one, and require a consultation with at least two other doctors before agreeing to submit to his orders. Now, the question is settled, so we will say no more about it. Meanwhile you need careful nursing, and mother and I are here to attend upon you."

Thus with gentle raillery she led the poor fellow to entertain a faint hope that recovery might be possible, and that the future might not be so appallingly black as it had seemed before. Still the hope was extremely faint at first, for no one knew so well as himself what a wreck he was, and how impossible it would be for him, under the most favourable circumstances, ever again to stand up and look like his former self. Poor Bella had to force her pleasantry and her lightsome tones, for she also had fears that he might still succumb, but, being convinced that a cheerful, hopeful state of mind was the best of all medicines, she set herself to administer it in strong doses.

The result was that Nicholas began to recover rapidly. Time passed, and by slow degrees he migrated from his bed to the sofa. Then a few of his garments were put on, and he tried to stand on his remaining leg. The doctor, who assisted me in moving and dressing the poor invalid, comforted him with the assurance that the stump of the other would, in course of time, be well enough to have a cork foot and ankle attached to it.

"And do you know," he added, with a smile, "they make these things so well now that one can scarcely tell a false foot from a real one,—with joint and moveable instep, and toes that work with springs, so that people can walk with them quite creditably—indeed they can; I do not jest, I assure you."

"Nothing, however, can replace the left hand or the lost eye," returned Nicholas, with a faint attempt at a smile.

"There, my dear sir," returned the doctor, with animation, "you are quite wrong. The eye, indeed, can never be restored, though it will partially close, and become so familiar to you and your friends that it will almost cease to be noticed or remembered; but we shall have a stump made for the lower arm, with a socket to which you will be able to fix a fork or a spoon, or—"

"Why, doctor," interrupted Nicholas, "what a spoon *you* must be to—"

"Come," returned the doctor heartily, "that'll do. My services won't be required here much longer I see, for I invariably find that when a patient begins to make bad jokes, there is nothing far wrong with him."

One morning, when we had dressed our invalid, and laid him on the sofa, he and I chanced to be left alone.

"Come here, Jeff," he said, "assist me to the glass—I want to have a look at myself."

It was the first time he had expressed such a desire, and I hesitated for a moment, not feeling sure of the effect that the sight might have on him. Then I went to him, and only remarking in a quiet tone, "You'll improve, you know, in the course of time," I led him to the looking-glass.

He turned slightly pale, and a look of blank surprise flitted across his face, but he recovered instantly, and stood for a few seconds surveying himself with a sad expression.

Well might he look sad, for the figure that met his gaze stooped like that of an aged man; the head was shorn of its luxuriant curls; the terrible sabre-cut across the cheek, from the temple to the chin, which had destroyed the eye, had left a livid wound, a single glance at which told that it would always remain as a ghastly blemish; and there were other injuries of a slighter nature on various parts of the face, which marred his visage dreadfully.

"Yes, Jeff," he said, turning away slowly, with a sigh, and limping back to his couch, "there's room for improvement. I thought myself not a bad-looking fellow once. It's no great matter to have that fancy taken out of me, perhaps, but I grieve for Bella, and I really do think that you must persuade her to give up all idea of—"

"Now, Nic," said I, "don't talk nonsense."

"But I don't talk nonsense," he exclaimed, flushing with sudden energy, "I mean what I say. Do you suppose I can calmly allow that dear girl to sacrifice herself to a mere wreck, that cannot hope to be long a cumberer of the ground?"

"And do you suppose," I retorted, with vehemence, "that I can calmly allow my sister to be made a widow for life?—a widow, I say, for she is already married to you in spirit, and nothing will ever induce her to untie the knot. You don't know Bella—ah! you needn't smile,—you don't indeed. She is the most perversely obstinate girl I ever met with. Last night, when I mentioned to her that you had been speaking of yourself as a mere wreck, she said in a low, easy-going, meek tone, 'Jeff, I mean to cling to that wreck as long as it will float, and devote my life to repairing it.' Now, when Bella says anything in a low, easy-going, and especially in a meek tone, it is utterly useless to oppose her: she has made up her mind, drawn her sword and flung away the scabbard, double-shotted all her guns, charged every torpedo in the ship, and, finally, nailed her colours to the mast."

"Then," said Nicholas, with a laugh, "I suppose I must give in."

"Yes, my boy, you had better. If you don't, just think what will be the consequences. First of all, you will die sooner than there is any occasion for; then Bella will pine, mope, get into bad health, and gradually fade away. That will break down my mother, whose susceptible spirit could not withstand the shock. Of course, after that my own health would give way, and the hopes of a dear little—well, that is to say, ruination and widespread misery would be the result of your unnatural and useless obstinacy."

"To save you all from that," said Nicholas, "*of course* I must give in."

And Nicholas did give in, and the result was not half so disastrous as he had feared.

Chapter Twenty Six
Some More of War's Consequences

Let us turn once more to the Balkan Mountains. Snow covers alike the valley and the hill. It is the depth of that inhospitable season when combative men were wont, in former days, to retire into winter quarters, repose on their "laurels," and rest a while until the benign influences of spring should enable them to recommence the "glorious" work of slaying one another.

But modern warriors, like modern weapons, are more terrible now than they used to be. They scout inglorious repose—at least the great statesmen who send them out to battle scout it for them. While these men of super-Spartan mould sit at home in comfortable conclave over mild cigar and bubbling hookah, quibbling over words, the modern warrior is ordered to prolong the conflict; and thus it comes to pass that Muscovite and Moslem pour out their blood like water, and change the colour of the Balkan snows.

In a shepherd's hut, far up the heights, which the smoke of battle could not reach, and where the din of deadly strife came almost softly, like the muttering of distant thunder, a young woman sat on the edge of a couch gazing wistfully at the beautiful countenance of a dead girl. The watcher was so very pale, wan, and haggard, that, but for her attitude and the motion of her great dark eyes, she also might have been mistaken for one of the dead. It was Marika, who escaped with only a slight flesh-wound in the arm from the soldier who had pursued her into the woods near her burning home.

A young man sat beside her also gazing in silence at the marble countenance.

"No, Petko, no," said Marika, looking at the youth mournfully, "I cannot stay here. As long as the sister of my preserver lived it was my duty to remain, but now that the bullet has finished its work, I must go. It is impossible to rest."

"But, Marika," urged Petko Borronow, taking his friend's hand, "you know it is useless to continue your search. The man who told me said he had it from the lips of Captain Naranovitsch himself that dear Dobri died at Plevna with his head resting on the captain's breast, and—"

The youth could not continue.

"Yes, yes," returned Marika, with a look and tone of despair, "I know that Dobri is dead; I saw my darling boy slain before my eyes, and heard Ivanka's dying scream; no wonder that my brain has reeled so long. But I am strong now. I feel as if the Lord were calling on me to go forth and work for Himself since I have no one else to care for. Had Giuana lived I would have stayed to nurse her, but—"

"Oh that the fatal ball had found my heart instead of hers!" cried the youth, clasping his hands and gazing at the tranquil countenance on the bed.

"Better as it is," said Marika in a low voice. "If you had been killed she would have fallen into the hands of the Bashi-Bazouks, and that would have been worse—far worse. The Lord does all things well. He gave, and He has taken away—oh let us try to say, Blessed be His name!"

She paused for a few minutes and then continued—

"Yes, Petko, I must go. There is plenty of work in these days for a Christian woman to do. Surely I should go mad if I were to remain idle. You have work here, I have none, therefore I must go. Nurses are wanted in the ambulance corps of our—our—deliverers."

There was no sarcasm in poor Marika's heart or tone, but the slight hesitation in her speech was in itself sarcasm enough. With the aid of her friend Petko, the poor bereaved, heart-stricken woman succeeded in making her way to Russian headquarters, where her sad tale, and the memory of her heroic husband, at once obtained for her employment as a nurse in the large hospital where I had already spent a portion of my time—namely, that of Sistova.

Here, although horrified and almost overwhelmed, at first, at the sight of so much and so terrible suffering, she gradually attained to a more resigned and tranquil frame of mind. Her sympathetic tenderness of heart conduced much to this, for she learned in some degree to forget her own sorrows in the contemplation of those of others. She found a measure of sad comfort, too, while thus ministering to the wants of worn, shattered, and dying young men, in the thought that they had fought like lions on the battle-field, as Dobri had fought, and had lain bleeding, crushed, and helpless there, as Dobri had lain.

Some weeks after her arrival there was a slight change made in the arrangements of the hospital. The particular room in which she served was selected as being more airy and suited for those of the patients who, from their enfeebled condition, required unusual care and nursing.

The evening after the change was effected, Marika, being on what may be called the night-shift, was required to assist the surgeons of the ward on their rounds. They came to a bed on which lay a man who seemed in the last stage of exhaustion.

"No bones broken," said one surgeon in a low tone to another, to whom he was explaining the cases, "but blood almost entirely drained out of him. Very doubtful his recovery. Will require the most careful nursing."

Marika stood behind the surgeons. On hearing what they said she drew nearer and looked sadly at the man.

He was gaunt, cadaverous, and careworn, as if from long and severe suffering, yet, living skeleton though he was, it was obvious that his frame had been huge and powerful.

Marika's first sad glance changed into a stare of wild surprise, then the building rang with a cry of joy so loud, so jubilant, that even those whose blood had almost ceased to flow were roused by it.

She sprang forward and leaped into the man's outstretched arms.

Ay, it was Dobri Petroff himself—or rather his attenuated shadow,— with apparently nothing but skin and sinew left to hold his bones together, and not a symptom of blood in his whole body. The little blood left, however, rushed to his face, and he found sufficient energy to exclaim "Thank the Lord!" ere his senses left him.

It is said that joy never kills. Certainly it failed to do so on this occasion. Dobri soon recovered consciousness, and then, little by little, with many a pause for breath, and in tones that were woefully unlike to those of the bold, lion-like scout of former days, he told how he had fainted and fallen on the breast of his master, how he had lain all night on the battle-field among the dead and dying, how he had been stripped and left for dead by the ruffian followers of the camp, and how at last he had been found and rescued by one of the ambulance-wagons of the Red Cross.

When Marika told him of the death of their two children he was not so much overwhelmed as she had anticipated.

"I'm not so sure that you are right, Marika," he said, after a long sad pause. "That our darling boy is now in heaven I doubt not, for you saw him killed. But you did not see Ivanka killed, and what you call her death-shriek may not have been her last. We must not be too ready to believe the worst. If I had not believed you and them to have been all murdered together, I would not have sought death so recklessly. I will not give up hope in that God who has brought *you* back, and saved *me* from death. I *think* that darling Ivanka is still alive."

Marika was only too glad to grasp at and hold on to the hope thus held out—feeble though the ground was on which it rested, and it need scarcely be said that she went about her hospital duties after that with a lightness and joy of heart which she had not felt for many a day.

Dobri Petroff's recovery was now no longer doubtful. Day by day his strength returned, until at last he was dismissed cured.

But it must not be supposed that Dobri was "himself again." He stood as erect, indeed, and became as sturdy in appearance as he used to be, but there was many a deep-seated injury in his powerful frame which damaged its lithe and graceful motions, and robbed it of its youthful spring.

Returning to the village of Venilik at the conclusion of the armistice, the childless couple proceeded to rebuild their ruined home.

The news of the bold blacksmith's recovery, and return with his wife to the old desolated home, reached me at a very interesting period of our family history—my sister Bella's wedding day.

It came through my eccentric friend U. Biquitous, who, after going through the Russo-Turkish war as correspondent of the *Evergreen Isle*, had proceeded in the same capacity to Greece. After detailing a good many of his adventures, and referring me to the pages of the *EI* for the remainder of his opinions on things in general, he went on, "By the way, in passing through Bulgaria lately, I fell in with your friend Dobri Petroff, the celebrated scout of the Balkan army. He and his pretty wife send their love, and all sorts of kind messages which I totally forget. Dobri said he supposed you would think he was dead, but he isn't, and I can assure you looks as if he didn't mean to die for some time to come. They are both very low, however, about the loss of their children, though they still cling fondly to the belief that their little girl Ivanka has not been killed."

Here, then, was a piece of news for my mother and family!—for we had regularly adopted Ivanka, and the dear child was to act that very day as one of Bella's bridesmaids.

I immediately told my mother, but resolved to say nothing to Ivanka, Nicholas, or Bella, till the ceremony was over.

It was inexpressibly sad to see Nicholas Naranovitsch that day, for, despite the fact that by means of a cork foot he could walk slowly to the church without the aid of a crutch, his empty sleeve, marred visage, and slightly stooping gait, but poorly represented the handsome young soldier of former days.

But my sister saw none of the blemishes—only the beauties—of the man.

"You've only got quarter of a husband, Bella," he said with a sad smile when the ceremony was over.

"You were unnecessarily large before," retorted Bella. "You could stand reducing; besides, you are doubled to-day, which makes you equal to two quarters, and as the wife is proverbially the better half, that brings you up nearly to three quarters, so don't talk any more nonsense, sir. With good nursing I shall manage, perhaps, to make a whole of you once more."

"So be it," said Nicholas, kissing her. When they had left us, my mother called me—

"Jeff," she said, with a look of decision in her meek face which I have not often observed there, "I have made up my mind that you must go back to Turkey."

"Indeed!"

"Yes, Jeff. You had no right, my dear boy, to bring that child away from her home in such a hurry."

"But," said I remonstratively, "her home at the time I carried her off was destroyed—indeed, most of the village was a smoking ruin, and liable at any moment to be replundered by the irregular troops of both sides, while Ivanka's parents were reported dead—what could I do?"

"I don't know what you could do in those circumstances, but I know what you can do now, and that is, pack your portmanteau and prepare to take Ivanka to Venilik. The child must be at once restored to her parents. I cannot bear to think of their remaining in ignorance of her being alive. Very likely Nicholas and Bella will be persuaded to extend their honeymoon to two, or even three, months, and join you in a tour through the south of Europe, after which you will all come home strong and well to spend the winter with me."

"Agreed, mother; your programme shall be carried out to the letter, if I can manage it."

"When," asked my mother, "did your friend say he passed through that village?"

I opened his letter to ascertain, when my eye fell on a postscript which had escaped me on the first perusal. It ran thus—

> "P.S. I see no reason why I should not ask you to wish me joy. I'm going to be married, my boy, to Blue-eyes! I could not forget her. I had no hope whatever of discovering her. I had settled in my mind to live and die an old bachelor, when I suddenly met her. It was in Piccadilly, when I was home, some months ago, in reference to an increase of my nominal salary from the *EI* (which by the way came to nothing—its original figure). I entered a 'bus and ran my head against that of a lady who was coming out. I looked up to apologise, and was struck dumb. It was Blue-eyes! I assisted her to alight, and stammered, I know not what, something like— 'A thousand pardons—surely we have met—excuse me—a mistake—*Thunderer*—captain, great guns, torpedoes, and blazes—' in the midst of which she smiled, bowed, and moved on. I moved after her. I traced her (reverentially) to a house. It was that of a personal friend! I visited that friend, I became particularly intimate with that friend, I positively bored that friend until he detested me. At last I met her at the house of that friend and—but why go on? I am now 'captain' of the Blue-eyes, and would not exchange places with any officer in the Royal Navy; we are to be married on my return, if I'm not shot, assassinated, or hanged in the meantime. U.B."

"Ah, Jeff," said my mother, "how I wish that you would—"

She stopped.

"I know what you're going to say," I returned, with a smile; "and there *is* a charming little—"

"Well, Jeff, why don't you go on?"

"Well, I don't see why I should not tell you, mother, that there *is* a charming little woman—the very best woman in the world—who has expressed herself willing to—you understand?"

"Yes, I understand."

Reader, I would gladly make a confidant of yourself in this matter, and tell you all about this charming little woman, if it were not for the fact that she is standing at my elbow at this very minute, causing me to make blots, and telling me not to write nonsense!

Before dismissing U. Biquitous, I may as well introduce here the last meeting I had with him. It was a considerable time after the war was over—after the "Congress" had closed its labours, and my friend had settled—if such a term could be applied to one who never settled—near London. Nicholas and I were sitting in a bower at the end of our garden, conversing on the war which had been happily brought to a close. Bella and my mother were seated opposite to us, the latter knitting a piece of worsted-work, the size of whose stitches and needles was suited to the weakness of her eyes, and the former busy with a pencil sketch of the superb view of undulating woodland which stretched away for miles in front of our house.

"No doubt it is as you state, Jeff," said Nicholas, in reply to my last remark; "war is a miserable method of settling a dispute, quite unworthy of civilised, to say nothing of Christian, men; but, then, how are we to get along without it? It's of no use saying that an evil must be put down—put a stop to—until you are able to show *how* it is to be stopped."

"That does not follow," said I, quickly; "it may be quite possible for me to see, point out, and condemn an evil although I cannot suggest a remedy and my earnest remonstrances regarding it may be useful in the way of helping to raise a general outcry of condemnation, which may have the effect of turning more capable minds than my own to the devising of a remedy. Sea-sickness is a horrible malady; I perceive it, I know it to be so. I loudly draw attention to the fact; I won't be silenced. Hundreds, thousands, of other miserables take heart and join me. We can't stand it! we shan't! is the general cry. The attention of an able engineer is attracted by the noise we make, and the *Calais-Douvre* steamboat springs into being, a vessel which is supposed to render sea-sickness an impossibility. Whether it accomplishes this end or not is beside the question. The point is, that, by the vigorous use of our tongues and pens in condemnation of an admitted evil, we have drawn forth a vigorous *attempt* to get the better of it."

"But you don't expect to do away with war altogether?" said Nicholas.

"Certainly not; I am not mad, I am only hopeful. As long as sin reigns in this world we shall have more or less of war, and I don't expect universal peace until the Prince of Peace reigns. Nevertheless, it is my duty to 'seek peace,' and in every way to promote it."

"Come, now, let us have this matter out," said Nicholas, lighting a cigar.

"You are as fond of argument as a Scotsman, Nic," murmured Bella, putting a powerful touch in the foreground of her sketch.

"Suppose, now," continued Nicholas, "that you had the power to influence nations, what would you suggest instead of war?"

"Arbitration," said I, promptly; "I would have the nations of Europe to band together and agree *never* to fight but *always* to appeal to reason, in the settlement of disputes. I would have them reduce standing armies to the condition of peace establishments—that is, just enough to garrison our strongholds, and be ready to back up our police in keeping ruffians in order. This small army would form a nucleus round which the young men of the nation would rally in the event of *unavoidable* war."

"Ha!" exclaimed Nicholas, with a smile of sarcasm, "you would then have us all disarm, beat our swords into reaping-hooks, and melt our bayonets and cannon into pots and pans. A charming idea! Now, suppose there was one of the nations—say Russia or Turkey—that declined to join this peaceful alliance, and, when she saw England in her disarmed condition, took it into her head to pay off old scores, and sent ironclads and thousands of well-trained and well-appointed troops to invade you, what would you do?"

"Defend myself," said I.

"What! with your peace-nucleus, surrounded by your rabble of untrained young men?"

"Nicholas," said my mother, in a mild voice, pausing in her work, "you may be as fond of argument as a Scotsman, but you are not quite as fair. You have put into Jeff's mouth sentiments which he did not express, and made assumptions which his words do not warrant. He made no reference to swords, reaping-hooks, bayonets, cannon, pots or pans, and did not recommend that the young men of nations should remain untrained."

"Bravo! mother; thank you," said I, as the dear old creature dropped her mild eyes once more on her work; "you have done me nothing but justice. There is one point, however, on which I and those who are opposed to me coincide exactly; it is this, that the best way to maintain peace is to make yourself thoroughly capable and ready for war."

"With your peculiar views, that would be rather difficult, I should fancy," said Nicholas, with a puzzled look.

"You fancy so, because you misunderstand my views," said I; "besides, I have not yet fully explained them—but here comes one who will explain them better than I can do myself."

As I spoke a man was seen to approach, with a smart free-and-easy air.

"It is my friend U. Biquitous," said I, rising and hastening to meet him.

"Ah, Jeff, my boy, glad I've found you all together," cried my friend, wringing my hand and raising his hat to the ladies. "Just come over to say good-bye. I'm engaged again on the *Evergreen Isle*—same salary and privileges as before—freer scope, if possible, than ever."

"And where are you going to, Mr Biquitous?" asked my mother.

"To Cyprus, madam,—the land of the—of the—the something or other; not got coached up yet, but you shall have it all *in extenso* ere long in the *Evergreen*, with sketches of the scenery and natives. I'll order a copy to be sent you."

"Very kind, thank you," said my mother; "you are fond of travelling, I think?"

"Fond of it!" exclaimed my friend; "yes, but that feebly expresses my sentiments,—I *revel* in travelling, I am mad about it. To roam over the world, by land and sea, gathering information, recording it, collating it, extending it, condensing it, and publishing it, for the benefit of the readers of the *Evergreen Isle*, is my chief terrestrial joy."

"Why, Mr Biquitous," said Bella, looking up from her drawing, with a slight elevation of the eyebrows, "I thought you were a married man."

"Ah! Mrs Naranovitsch, I understand your reproofs; but *that*, madam, I call a celestial joy. Looking into my wife's blue eyes is what I call stargazing, and that is a celestial, not a terrestrial, occupation. Next to making the stars twinkle, I take pleasure in travelling—flying through space,—

"Crashing on the railroads,
    Skimming on the seas,
Bounding on the mountain-tops,
    Battling with the breeze.
Roaming through the forest,
    Scampering on the plain,
Never stopping, always going,
    Round and round again."

"How very beautiful,—so poetical!" said Bella.

"So suggestively peaceful," murmured Nicholas.

"Your own composition?" asked my mother.

"A mere *morceau*," replied my friend, modestly, "tossed off to fill up a gap in the *Evergreen*."

"You should write poetry," said I.

"Think so? Well, I've had some notion at times, of trying my hand at an ode, or an epic, but, man, I find too many difficulties in the way. As to 'feet,' now, I can't manage feet in poetry. If it were inches or yards, one might get along, but feet are neither one thing nor another. Then, rhyme bothers me. I've often to run over every letter in the alphabet to get hold of a rhyme— click, thick, pick, rick, chick, brick—that sort of thing, you know. Sentiment, too, is very troublesome. Either I put too much or too little sentiment into my verses; sometimes they are all sentiment together; not unfrequently they have none at all; or the sentiment is false, which spoils them, you know. Yes, much though I should like to be a poet, I must content myself with prose. Just fancy, now, my attempting a poem on Cyprus! What rhymes with Cyprus? Fyprus, gyprus, highprus, kyprus, lyprus, tryprus, and so on to the end. It's all the same; nothing will do. No doubt Hook would have managed it; Theodore could do anything in that way, but *I* can't."

"Most unfortunate! But for these difficulties you might have been a second Milton. You leave your wife behind, I suppose," said Bella, completing her sketch and shutting the book.

"What!" exclaimed my volatile friend, becoming suddenly grave, "leave Blue-eyes behind me! leave the mitigator of my woes, the doubler of my joys, the light of my life behind me! No, Mrs Naranovitsch, Blue-eyes is necessary to my existence; she inspires my pen and corrects my spelling; she lifts my soul, when required, above the petty cares of life, and enables me to take flights of genius, which, without her, were impossible, and you know that flights of genius are required, occasionally, of the correspondent of a weekly—at least of an Irish weekly. Yes, Blue-eyes goes with me. We shall levant together."

"Are bad puns allowed in the *Evergreen*?" I asked.

"Not unless excessively bad," returned my friend; "they won't tolerate anything lukewarm."

"Well, now, Biquitous," said I, "sit down and give Nicholas, who is hard to convince, your opinion as to the mode in which this and other countries ought to prepare for self-defence."

"In earnest, do you mean?"

"In earnest," said I.

"Well, then," said my friend, "if I were in power I would make every man in Great Britain a trained soldier."

"Humph!" said Nicholas, "that has been tried by other nations without giving satisfaction."

"But," continued U. Biquitous, impressively, "I would do so without taking a single man away from his home, or interfering with his duties as a civilian. I would have all the males of the land trained to arms in boyhood—during school-days—at that period of life when boys are best fitted to receive such instruction, when they would 'go in' for military drill, as they now go in for foot-ball, cricket, or gymnastics—at that period when they have a good deal of leisure time, when they would regard the thing more as play than work—when their memories are strong and powerfully retentive, and when the principles and practice of military drill would be as thoroughly implanted in them as the power to swim or skate, so that, once acquired, they'd never quite lose it. I speak from experience, for I learned to skate and swim when a boy, and I feel that nothing—no amount of disuse— can ever rob me of these attainments. Still further, in early manhood I joined the great volunteer movement, and, though I have now been out of the force for many years, I know that I could 'fall in' and behave tolerably well at a moment's notice, while a week's drill would brush me up into as good a soldier as I ever was or am likely to be. Remember, I speak only of rank and file, and the power to carry arms and use them intelligently. I would compel boys to undergo this training, but would make it easy, on doctor's certificate, or otherwise, for anxious parents to get off the duty, feeling assured that the fraction of trained men thus lost to the nation would be quite insignificant. Afterwards, a few days of drill each year would keep men well up to the mark; and even in regard to this brushing-up drill I would make things very easy, and would readily accept every reasonable excuse for absence, in the firm belief that the willing men would be amply sufficient to maintain our 'reserve force.' As to the volunteers, I would encourage them as heretofore, and give them more honour and privileges than they possess at present. Thus would an army be ever ready to spring into being at a day's notice, and be *thoroughly* capable of defending hearths and homes in a few weeks.

"For our colonies and our authority at home, I would have a very small, *well-paid*, and thoroughly efficient standing army, which would form a perfect model in military matters, and a splendid skeleton on which the muscle and sinew of the land might wind itself if invasion threatened. For the rest, I would keep my bayonets and artillery in serviceable condition, and my 'powder dry.' If all Europe acted thus, she would be not less ready for war than she is now, and would have all her vigorous men turned into producers instead of consumers, to the immense advantage of the States' coffers, to the great comfort of the women and children, to the lessening of crime and poverty, and to the general well-being of the world at large."

"My dear sir," said Nicholas, with a laugh, "you were born before your time."

"It may be so," returned the other, lightly, "nevertheless I will live in the hope of seeing the interests of peace more intelligently advanced than they have been of late; and if the system which I suggest is not found to be the best, I will rejoice to hear of a better, and will do my best to advocate it in the *Evergreen Isle*. But now I must go; Blue-eyes and Cyprus await me. Farewell."

U. Biquitous shook hands heartily, and walked rapidly away down the avenue, where he was eventually hidden from our view by a bush of laurel.

To return from this digression.

It is not difficult in these days to "put a girdle round the world." Ivanka and I soon reached the village of Venilik.

It was a sad spectacle of ruin and desolation, but we found Dobri Petroff and Marika in the old home, which had been partially rebuilt. The blacksmith's anvil was ringing as merrily as ever when we approached, and his blows appeared to fall as heavily as in days gone by, but I noticed, when he looked up, that his countenance was lined and very sad, while his raven locks were prematurely tinged with grey.

Shall I describe the meeting of Ivanka with her parents? I think not. The imagination is more correct and powerful than the pen in such cases. New life seemed from that moment to be infused into the much-tried pair. Marika had never lost her trust in God through all her woes, and even in her darkest hours had refused to murmur. She had kissed the rod that smote her, and now she praised Him with a strong and joyful heart.

Alas! there were many others in that village, and thousands of others throughout that blood-soaked land, who had no such gleam of sunshine sent into the dark recesses of their woe-worn hearts—poor innocent souls these, who had lost their joy, their possessions, their hope, their all in this life, because of the mad, unreasonable superstition that it is necessary for men at times to arrange their differences by war!

War! what is it? A monster which periodically crushes the energies, desolates the homes, swallows thousands of the young lives, and sweeps away millions of the money of mankind. It bids Christianity stand aside for a time. It legalises wholesale murder and robbery. It affords a safe opportunity to villainy to work its diabolic will, so that some of the fairest scenes of earth are converted into human shambles. It destroys the labour of busy generations, past and present, and saddles heavy national debt on those that are yet unborn. It has been estimated that the national debts of Europe now amount to nearly 3000 millions sterling, more than three-fourths of which have been required for war and warlike preparations, and that about 600 millions are annually taken from the capital and industry of nations for the expense of past, and the preparation for future wars. War tramples gallantry in the dust, leaves women at the mercy of a brutal soldiery, slaughters old men, and tosses babes on bayonet-points. All this it does, and a great deal more, in the way of mischief; what does it accomplish in the way of good? What has mankind gained by the wars of Napoleon the First, which cost, it is said, two million of lives, to say nothing of the maimed-for-life and the bereaved? Will the gain or the loss of Alsace and Lorraine mitigate or increase in any appreciable degree the woe of French and Prussian widows? Will the revenues of these provinces pay for the loss consequent on the stagnation of trade and industry? What has been gained by the Crimean war, which cost us thousands of lives and millions in money? Nothing whatever! The treaties which were to secure what had been gained have been violated, and the empire for which we fought has been finally crushed.

When waged in self-defence war is a sad, a horrible necessity. When entered into with a view to national aggrandisement, or for an *idea*, it is the greatest of crimes. The man who creeps into your house at night, and cuts your throat while you are asleep in bed, is a sneaking monster, but the man who sits "at home at ease," safe from the tremendous "dogs" which he is about to let loose, and, with diplomatic pen, signs away the peace of society and the lives of multitudes without serious cause, is a callous monster. Of the two the sneak is the less objectionable, because less destructive.

During this visit to Venilik, I spent some time in renewing my inquiries as to the fate of my yacht's crew, but without success, and I was forced to the sad conclusion that they must either have been drowned or captured, and, it may be, killed after reaching the land. Long afterwards, however, I heard it rumoured that Mr Whitlaw had escaped and returned to his native country. There is, therefore, some reason to hope that that sturdy and true-hearted American still lives to relate, among his other stirring narratives, an account of that memorable night when he was torpedoed on the Danube.

Before finally bidding adieu to the Petroff family, I had many a talk with Dobri on the subject of war as we wandered sadly about the ruined village. The signs of the fearful hurricane by which it had been swept were still fresh upon it, and when I looked on the burnt homesteads, the trampled crops, and neglected fields, the crowds of new-made graves, the curs that quarrelled over unburied human bones, the blood-stained walls and door-posts, the wan, almost bloodless, faces of the few who had escaped the wrath of man, and reflected that all this had been brought about by a "Christian" nation, fighting in the interests of the Prince of Peace, I could not help the fervent utterance of the prayer: "O God, scatter thou the people that delight in war!"